This Fire Inside

This Fire Inside

JORDAN NASSER

Also by Jordan Nasser
Home is a Fire
The Fire Went Wild

To all the people I could have kissed.

1

SCHOOL'S OUT AND SO ARE WE

"Luke?" My ass was sticking straight up in the air. "Luke, where are you? I need you."

I called out for him again, but no such luck. The sound was probably muffled by the fact that I was stretched to full extension, back arched, bottom half vulnerable, my arms reaching in vain for that last dusty cardboard box under the bed. *This would make a great chalk line at the scene of a homicide*, I thought.

"What are you up to *now*, Derek?" I heard Luke's voice above me, through the mattress. Was my boyfriend irritated? I turned my head towards the direction of the sound as best as I could, my cheek resting on the cool hardwood floor. I spotted his running shoes, as well as the many boxes and quilts and various pieces of sports equipment

I had already dragged out from every seemingly endless dark corner of his bedroom.

"What's in this box?" I called out, ignoring the tone in his voice. My fingertips were just barely grazing the last item I hadn't been able to excavate.

"Babe, you're under the bed. I have no idea what you're talking about." He sighed.

"It's cardboard. And heavy. I can't back up, but I've got my hands on it. Pull me out?"

He reached down and grabbed me by the ankles, sliding me and the box out from under the bed in one swift move, my favorite t-shirt collecting fluffy grey dust bunnies along the way. Ahhh, sunlight!

"Babe, what are you doing? I go out for a quick run and I come back to find my place deconstructed." He saw my face and caught himself, just a little too late. "Sorry. *Our* place. Our place, of course. You know what I mean." He was flustered.

Yes, I knew what he meant. I decided to let it slide, rather than make a fuss though. Our transition from enemies to frenemies to live-in boyfriends had been the talk of the town. We had endured enough battles, so I wasn't going to start a new one over one poorly chosen word. Besides, after what we had been through my skin was pretty thick. I shook the dust from the front of my t-shirt, and then gave my boyfriend a quick peck on the cheek. He was sweaty from his run and his skin smelled naturally of campfire wood and pine. It drove me crazy, in a good way of course.

"Sorry," I said. "I get kind of focused on one thing, you know? I'm a greyhound, remember? I was trying to find my Louis Vuitton duffel. I can't show up in New York City with some cheap canvas gym bag with a Parkville High School Commodores logo. Anyway, sorry for the mess. I'll put everything back, I promise. But really, have you seen the Vuitton?"

"You mean the *faux* Vuitton?" he teased.

"Seriously?" I cocked my head. "How do you even know that? You're a jock, remember?"

"I *do* pay attention, unlike you," he said, placing a finger on my chest and letting it linger, then explore. That felt nice. "You gave that to Barry, remember?" he said, giving me a final sturdy tap with his forefinger.

"Crap! Yes. I totally forgot. I need to ask him if I can borrow it." I could feel my brow furrowing excessively.

"Babe, what is going on? Why are you so freaked out about this trip? I can feel how tense you are." His hands explored my shoulders and for a split second I forgot about the knots in my stomach. He was right. Leaving *this* home and going back to my *other* home, even temporarily, was giving me nightmares. I loved New York, truly. I still did. But I had left her and not looked back. How would she treat me now that we were finished? Would I be just another tourist? The city was part of my past and I was a bit nervous to step through that door again.

"I don't know," I lied, unconvincingly. "I just want everything to go smoothly for you. It's your first trip to the city and I just want it all to be perfect."

"Hey, it's gonna be great," he reassured me. "I happen to be dating this really cute tour guide and he's promised me the trip of a lifetime." He leaned over to kiss me and the stress in my shoulders released as I instantly melted into his strong arms. He was right. Together we could meet any challenge. We'd already proven that.

"But," he said softly as he released me from his lips, "I don't think we'll be needing my old trophies for the trip."

"Trophies?"

"The box." He looked down as his foot tapped the dusty cardboard container at our feet. "It's full of trophies. Not so useful in New York, unless you think we need them for self-defense."

"Funny guy," I said. I bent down and popped open the box. It was indeed full of his high school laurels, predominantly gold and shiny, with a few silver and bronze. He wasn't 100% perfect after all. Just mostly. "Wow." I glanced up at him. "Someone was an overachiever."

"Hey, quit complaining," he said. "I worked hard for those, but you're the one who took home the best prize of them all."

I smiled. What he said might sound conceited to some, but he was right. He was definitely the best prize in town, and the love of my life.

■ ■ ■

School was out and so were we. Literally. Somehow my super-closeted football coach boyfriend had decided to take the leap and publicly declare his love for me, his fellow Parkville High School staff member. The reaction from the community was swift, and decidedly unfriendly. Even worse, his sister Lana, along with his former high school sweetheart Amber and her son Jett, had been at the forefront of an intense reactionary campaign against us. Thankfully our other family members and friends rallied to our defense, but it took a few backroom deals and surprise revelations to tie up all the loose ends. Ultimately we were able to keep our jobs, but was that what we really wanted? I was pretty sure I didn't, after the way we had been treated.

Luke and had I talked to each other about leaving the school, and we decided to look for other options. My Uncle Barry's friend, Lloyd Barton, had let it slip that he was considering selling his catering company, Lloyd's. He was tired of the hard work and he wanted to spend his twilight years playing around, like his pals in the Bears' Club. He asked Uncle Barry if he wanted to buy the whole thing as a turnkey business, but Barry was enjoying his own retirement, so he passed. Lloyd then suggested that Luke and I might like to try our hands at something new. It was an easy decision for me to quit teaching, but it was harder for Luke to walk away from coaching. Instead of saying yes or no right away, we decided to splurge on a summer trip to New York to clear our minds and get back to the question at hand when we returned. We went ahead and set up a meeting with Lloyd in two weeks. It wouldn't hurt to get all the details before we said no, right?

Luke's place…I mean, *our* place…was located near the university campus. A hidden gem in a sea of run-down Victorians, it had somehow escaped the wrecking ball that had turned so many colorful dollhouses into concrete parking structures and mini marts. It was home for now, and we were both working hard to make it a place that felt just as comfortable to me as it did to him.

To a Southerner, home is everything. When I came back to Parkville from my decade-long adventure in New York, I moved back in with my mom, Audrey, and her brother, my Uncle Barry. When my long-lost dad, Johnny, reappeared and swept her off her feet again, she moved in with him, and we all hoped their relationship would last this time. My uncle didn't react well at first, but now that Mom has fully settled in at *Casa de Johnny*, Barry has taken the opportunity to turn Mom's old place into the gay bachelor palace of his dreams. Did I mention that he finally came out after 60?

I pulled my old junker into Barry's driveway and took a look at the chaos. Lovingly nicknamed Willie Nelson thanks to the "Honk if you love Willie Nelson" sticker Mom had placed on its bumper years ago, my car was the least out of place thing here. The men from the local construction crew milled about with Styrofoam coffee cups in hand, walking between well-ordered stacks of lumber and bricks. There was even a small bulldozer parked in the yard. *Barry, this isn't a teardown. What are you doing?*

I stepped out of the car and walked up the small, wobbling wooden gangplank that led into the house, using my hands to part the thick sheets of plastic in front of me. My friend Tommy, clipboard in hand, gave me a quick nod as he directed a small group of men. I'm glad he was here to act as the foreman of this circus and to keep Barry on track. They were definitely in the mid-demolition phase.

"Barry?" I called out. "Where are you?"

"Over here, Dolly!" he answered. I was rarely "Derek" to my Uncle Barry. He preferred "Dolly" or "nephew" or even "kid." I took this as a sign of love; especially coming from a man who called himself "Beret" while he was lip-syncing show tunes in sparkly drag gowns at the Bears' Club downtown.

"Watch your step, kid. They're taking this wall down today." He walked over and gave me a hug, and then hand-ed me a plastic construction helmet to wear. His headgear was bedazzled of course, but this simple yellow plastic one would just have to do for me. "This house has never *seen* so much action. Just wait till we're done! *Ha!* Come on. Let's take a walk out to the front. It's pretty safe out there."

We stepped gingerly over a few two-by-fours and walked out onto the front porch. He pulled the glass door tight to silence the noise from inside, and the screen door shut itself, squeaking softly along the way.

"I thought you were just putting in a hot tub?" I said, staring amazed at the chaos.

"Oh, you know me, Dolly. Diamonds and sequins on feathers. Once I started I couldn't stop. When your mom moved out I realized that I finally had the chance to make something of my own. I feel invigorated. The bitch is back!"

I had to laugh. Barry's coming out wasn't a major surprise, but he was embracing it with full gusto after he had seen Luke and me survive the town pitchforks. His generation may have led the way historically, but now he had some catching up to do, and he was tackling it with all the glitter he could find.

"So," he started, excitedly, "first I was just going to put in a hot tub, but then I sat down with Tommy, and things just kind of escalated. We're taking down the dining room wall and making more of an open plan layout here on the first floor. The kitchen will flow into the living room and eating area. Better for entertaining, you know? This happy gal plans on throwing a few parties! Then Tommy suggested opening up the room a bit more by putting in a double sliding glass door to the terrace. Great idea, right?! The hot tub will go over to the left on an extended deck. We're putting in a line of tall shrubs to create a little privacy hedge, if you catch my drift. We'll have a fire pit, grilling station, the whole enchilada. I'm *so* excited!"

"Do you have the money for this?" I asked.

"Well, your Aunt Janey and I always were good with our finances. We saved up a healthy nest egg for our retirement. After she passed, I had enough saved for two, and well, now there's just me. I'm pretty sure she'd like me to have some fun." He didn't speak with an air of sadness. It was honest, and he was right. Janey would be pleased with the new Barry.

"It sounds great and I can't wait to see it," I said, reassuring him. "Listen, I came over to ask a favor. Is it all right if I borrow that designer duffel bag I brought you from Chinatown? Luke just has gym bags and they won't let me back into New York City with one of those. I'm afraid they may even have velvet ropes at the airport now."

"Even if they did they'd still let you in, kid. You've got that look on your face that says *step aside. I know what I'm doing.* You always have. And I have *no* idea where you got that," he said, winking. "Come on. The duffel is in my old room."

We made our way back through the maze of plastic tarps and sheetrock and up the stairs into Barry's former bedroom. He dramatically flung open the double doors to his closet while I removed my construction hat and sat on his bed, watching the show. This was a free ticket, and no matter how many times I had seen it, I loved it, every time.

"Now, let's see," he said, pushing his way through a sea of sequined gowns, "I just used that bag the other day. Oh, yes! Here we go." He opened the faux leather duffel, emptied it of a few brassieres and a pair of shiny red patent heels, and then handed it over. "Good as new! And I expect that back, by the way. Actually, I could use a new tote bag, too, if you happen to see one." He grinned.

"No problem," I said, smiling. "If I can still find my sources. I've heard Chinatown isn't the same since I left. I'm afraid a lot of New York won't be the same."

"Do your best, nephew. No worries. Oh, you're gonna have a blast," he assured me. He sat next to me on the bed and carefully placed his sparkly helmet beside him. "And Luke will love it. Help him come out of his shell, a bit. I think you'll be surprised."

I hadn't even thought of that. Luke had spent his whole life here in Parkville. He was the local football hero turned coach, with a secret that he couldn't share, until I showed up and turned his head. He had a lot of amazing qualities, but I like to think that I brought out his *best* side.

"Yeah, that's true. Luke's knowledge of gay bars includes Bottom's Up, and that's it. We haven't even trekked down to Atlanta for a weekend. He's barely been exposed to anything."

"Well, watch out for him, then," he counseled me. "That country hunk of yours is bound to attract some attention, wanted or not."

"Oh, we'll be fine," I assured him. "I'm taking him to some of my favorite old haunts. If they're still there, that is. It seems each consecutive mayor of New York decides to 'revitalize' more and more of the seedier parts of town that I loved so much. CBGB is now a designer clothing store and Mars Bar is a bank. Punk is dead, long live punk." I flipped my middle finger into the air in a mock salute and stuck out my tongue.

"Who are you trying to kid, kid? You were never punk. *Spunky*, sure, but punk?"

"Hey, gimme a break! I saw some things," I said, defensively. "Maybe I didn't *do* as much as I wanted to, but I definitely observed."

"That'll make a great headstone."

"Well, at least I left Parkville for a few years." I knew he was just teasing me, but sometimes I did feel a bit defeated, considering I eventually left the city of my dreams to return to the scene of my fumbling youth. "I'm so happy I lived in New York. I needed that time away, you know?"

"Of course you did, Dolly. And I'm proud of you. I wish I'd had the courage to move up there for a few years. My situation was a bit different of course, with Janey." He grew quiet for a moment as he collected his thoughts, and I could feel his emotions shift. "I'm really glad you stopped by today, actually. Now that I've granted you a favor, your fairy god-uncle needs to ask one of his own. You up for it?"

"Sure," I said, cautiously. You never knew what to expect with Barry.

"I made a few solo trips of my own up to New York back in the '80s, you know. I had a buddy there I used to visit. Just a friend, nothing more, so don't give me those eyes. But we did have some crazy nights together. He did drag, of course. I guess you could say he was my inspiration." He paused, and then launched directly to his request. "I was wondering if you could look him up for me? We lost touch years ago. We were friends before e-mail and cell phones and all that social media hoopla that you're into. Back then, we actually met people. In person. And if you said you'd be there, well you actually showed up. Crazy, I know. Anyway, it was one of those interminably hot summer months. Janey and Mabel were going to spend a week in Florida so I decided to take a bus up to New

York for a few days, on my own. Some *me* time, you know? It took forever. I think we stopped in every podunk town along the way. When the bus pulled into Port Authority I could just feel the electricity in the air. It was early in the morning but the city was just buzzing with life. I got my bearings and walked down a few blocks and over a few avenues and checked myself right into the Hotel Chelsea. I had seen Lance Loud on that *American Family* documentary on PBS and I was kind of hoping I would run into him, if you want to know the truth. I never did, though. Can you imagine?! Ha! I could have had a totally different life."

He shifted his body on the bed and used the palms of his hands to smooth his trousers. Uncle Barry had lived through some amazing times. My respect for him grew every day of every year, and definitely with every new story.

"I spent the day exploring the town, and then came home to clean up for my nighttime adventures. I was alone in the city, after all. Far from home, with no prying eyes from Parkville. I was free to be me and to have some fun, with Janey's approval, of course. AIDS was ravaging New York City at the time, but I was informed enough to make smart decisions. At least, the best decisions I could with the limited information that we had then. Those were scary times. Anyway, I had freshened up and I was just stepping out of my room at the Chelsea to go dancing when I bumped into Charlie in the hallway. He smiled. I smiled. And, well, *you* know how it goes, Dolly. We theatre folk just seem to find one another. He asked if I was alone and I said yes, and before I knew it, we were running down the stairs to catch a cab to the Village. He took me *everywhere*. Places I'd never seen and things I could never have imagined even existed. Midtown, downtown, discos, the bathhouses! It was a different scene then. Trust me. We stayed out until five in the morning, only coming home to nap for a few hours and then we went out and started all over again. You know how it goes. Charlie performed in drag on the weekends so I tagged along to see his shows. He had real star power. Such a following! Young boys just threw themselves at him. *Ha!* His female illusion was just tops. The *best*. He had gowns and sparkles and heels. And the wigs! *Oh!* His room at the Chelsea was just chock-full of fantasy. He was really living his life to the fullest. Charlie took advantage of everything that city had to offer, and he loved every minute of it. Even better, kid, he was *out*. Out and proud, *out*. I have to admit, I was so jealous of him, and I couldn't help but wish that I could do the same. But some things just weren't meant be, at least not in the same timeline. My moment came later, of course. Hell, I didn't even come out officially until this year. But here's the thing. That queen showed me what I *could* be. *Who* I could be. He was my goal and my inspiration…and then I lost him. I just know he went on to do great things. I do." He turned to look at me, very seriously. "So you think you can find him for me, Dolly? I can't even imagine the exciting life he is leading now, after all these years. I just need to know what he has done with his amazing gifts."

"Absolutely, Uncle Barry. I'd be honored. Charlie, right?" I made a mental note. "Do you have any other info on him? His last name? He can't still be living at the Chelsea?"

"Oh, sorry, nephew. I don't know why I did that. Old habits. I met him as Barry, not Beret, so my pronouns are all messed up. I don't think you can find *him*. But you'll definitely find *her*. He never went by Charlie. She was *fabulous*, after all. I'm sure you'll be able to find her. Just go to the best clubs and ask around for me? There must be someone who knows the amazing *Chinois Zarée*."

■ ■ ■

I made my way back through the construction maze and tossed the borrowed duffel bag onto the passenger seat beside me. Chinois Zarée? Where do they come up with these names? Funny, though. I didn't ever remember hearing that one before, so we must have frequented different bars and clubs. I was more of an East Village guy. Maybe she was popular in Hell's Kitchen or Chelsea? Well, she shouldn't be too hard to find. How many Asian drag queens around my uncle's age can there be in New York?

My sneezing fit started just as I placed the key into the ignition. Damn. I hoped I wasn't getting a cold? We were leaving for our trip in just under a week and I didn't want to be sick. I'm a terrible patient and I didn't want to put Luke through that, just yet. To tell you the truth, all this talk of AIDS had me wigged out. I knew I was fine, but I hadn't been tested for HIV or any other STDs since I came back to Parkville just under a year ago. I'd be willing to bet that Luke had never been tested at all. It was time for me to reconfirm my negative status and for us to share that uncomfortable anticipation of waiting for our results, together.

Now that he was out, my boyfriend needed to experience *everything*. Even the not-so-fun stuff.

2

HOMESICK

I couldn't believe how wonderful this hot tub felt.

The bubble jets were on full speed and I was relaxing in the warm water, cocktail glass in hand. But this wasn't a chill kind of night, this was a party! Uncle Barry had a playlist of Top 40 hits blaring. The whole place was wired for sound with fancy built-in speakers. Wasn't this music a little young for him, though? He was easy to spot, running from guest to guest, making sure everyone was impressed with his renovations. I couldn't believe he was brave enough to wear that outfit, but somehow he was pulling it off. Well, *she*. My uncle was in full Carmen Miranda mode: bright yellow one-piece swimsuit with a tropical-themed wraparound skirt, giant hoop earrings, and an enormous turban of plastic fruit balanced precariously on her head. Beret had style, that's for sure.

As for her guests? I couldn't place half of them. Where did all these gays come from? Parkville was a far cry from Atlanta. Surely she didn't hire them? They ranged in age from far too young to old enough to know better, with a larger percentage fresh out of college. The younger ones were definitely not afraid to show off their...*assets*, while the older ones were craning their necks and ogling so much that they were about to cause some serious self-inflicted physical damage. The chiropractors of Parkville would surely have their appointment books filled for weeks.

This roiling water was getting hotter by the minute. Too hot, actually. I could feel myself starting to sweat, so I pulled myself up to the edge and just left my legs dangling in the bubbles. The couple to my right needed a room, not a hot tub, so I decided to step out and look for Luke. I grabbed a towel and made my way through one of the brand new sliding glass doors into the living room. There were men everywhere and the only women in sight weren't really women. Where was he?

"Great party, isn't it?" a voice said to my left. I turned my head to see Mayor Bellman, but instead of the standard grey suit I was used to I was shocked to see he was in full drag as his alter ego, Belle, in a floor length red and white floral jumpsuit and a red straw hat with an enormous brim that threatened to take out everyone and everything in its path. She reached out to place a strong, reassuring hand on my back.

"Listen, I've been meaning to speak to you since all that mess we had at the end of the school year," she started.

"Now, I know you understand my particular predicament, what with your uncle being a member of the Bears' Club and all, but I just wanted to say how sorry I am that it went that far. Y'all know I think you boys are just fine educators, but I have this damn constituency I have to worry about now. You know how it goes. Two faces and all that. Let's just let bygones be bygones. Waddya say?" She held out her hand, fingernails lacquered in bright red with a charm bracelet of plastic yellow pineapples dangling from her wrist. Was I supposed to shake it or kiss it? I smiled and numbly clasped it to mine.

"All in the past, Mayor Bellman," I said. Or was I supposed to refer to her as Belle right now? That felt strange, since we didn't really acknowledge her transformation to begin with. I'd never actually met the mayor as Belle. One more thing to add to my "Parkville's Strangest Moments" list. I had to get out of this situation, and quick. "Now, if you'll excuse me, I just need to find Luke. I haven't seen him in a while."

"You know, I was thinking," she said, ignoring my comment about my boyfriend, "Beret does a wonderful act at the club of course, but she and I have a little competitive rivalry going on. Not sure if you knew that. She's fond of big show numbers and I tend to stick to standards and torch songs. Say, you lived in New York City, right? Did you ever hit up any of those famous jazz clubs in the Village?"

"Uh, yeah, of course," I answered, still not quite comfortable. "I know the East Village a lot better, but the West

Village has some amazing old venues. I was thinking of introducing Luke to a few, in fact. We're taking a trip up there next week." I started to feel very hot. Was I nervous talking to Belle? I wiped my hand across my forehead and I could feel the sweat start to drip down the small of my back, as well. I felt out of breath, actually, like someone was sitting on my chest. Was I having an anxiety attack? I really wanted to get away. I just needed to find a few polite words to excuse myself from this conversation.

"Oh, that's fantastic," she continued. "Reason I ask is, I was looking for a new number for the club, and well, I know you're a theatre guy, of course. I thought it would be a kick if you and I did a little something together. We could surprise Beret. Wouldn't that be a hoot?"

No. No, I can't say that it would. Beret would probably kick my ass. But I couldn't admit that.

"Um, well, sure. Maybe we could talk about that another time?" Why was I lying? "Sorry, I really need to try and find Luke."

"Oh, there's no rush," she said, looking past me. "I see him right over there. He looks like he's having a great time, if you ask me."

I turned my head, and sure enough, there was Luke with his back to me. He wasn't wearing a shirt, but I would have recognized those broad shoulders anywhere. His longboard shorts fit him perfectly, his firm butt leaning against the island in the kitchen. He had his strong arms dancing up in the air and he was moving seductively to the beat of the music, grinding his hips and rolling his stomach. He started to move his arms down and quickly pulled the guy in front of him towards his bare chest, roughly. They crashed together, and Luke started kissing him, passionately. My heart started pounding. What the hell was going on?

Belle smiled and looked at me, took another quick sip from her cocktail, and then started singing the first verse to *Stormy Weather*. Was she taunting me? Did she expect me to join in for a duet? I wanted to cry. I wanted to scream. The sweat was pouring from my body and I could feel my throat tightening up, but I couldn't find my voice.

Luke turned to see me staring at him, my eyes wide open with betrayal. It was obvious that his actions were killing me. I was crushed and I wanted to die, truly. That's when the man in his arms flashed me a wicked grin of his own.

"What's your problem, Derek?" Luke's new friend sneered. "Don't you know that open relationships are the thing, now?"

I dropped my drink and the glass shattered on the floor, the shiny fragments of glass traveling to every corner of the room. It must have spilled all over me, because it felt like everything I was wearing was suddenly wet. I searched for my voice, but it was still hard to find the right muscles to activate it. I was ready to kill. My heart started racing double time. How did he even get here? Luke had my ex-boyfriend from New York in his arms, and they were both laughing and loving every minute of it.

"*David!*" I screamed.

That's when I woke up.

■ ■ ■

"David?" I mumbled. My mouth was so dry it felt like cotton balls.

"Babe, it's Luke. Everything's okay. You were dreaming."

"Luke? I... but," I couldn't really breathe. I was sitting up in our bed, my entire body covered in sweat.

"It's okay. You're going to be all right." He reached over to the nightstand, turned on the lamp and handed me a glass of water. "Here, take a sip."

I took the glass and held it gingerly in my hands. It felt so heavy. It was just a dream. A bad dream. But it felt so real. Luke came back from the bathroom with a cool washcloth and started wiping the sweat from my brow and chest.

"Looks like your fever broke. That means you're getting better. You'll be good as new soon enough, babe."

I took a big gulp of water. I needed it, but my mind was still a jumble. "I feel like shit," I said. "I'm so sorry." The tears started streaming down my face. I couldn't help it. "When I'm sick I'm the world's worst baby."

"*Hey, hey, hey.* It's okay. Nothing to be sorry about." He put his arm around my shoulder and kissed my forehead. "I promise, a few more hours of sleep and you'll feel so much better."

"What time is it?"

"It's early. Just after four. Let's get you into a quick shower and then let you sleep some more."

"Luke, I didn't mean…when I called for David, I…" He looked down. He was hurt, I could tell. "It wasn't about David. I didn't *want* him. I wanted you. But you were…"

"Hey, stop. My mother always taught me that you never tell a dream before breakfast unless you want it to come true. C'mon. Let's get you in the shower."

I wanted to explain, but right now I couldn't make sense of it all. Anything I said would just make it worse. How could I tell him that I saw him kissing my ex? I couldn't really process it. I needed to just let it go, right?

"Right. Shower. Yes," I said, letting him have his way, because his mind was thinking clearly and mine obviously was not. "I just need a shower and some sleep. Thanks for taking care of me, babe."

I reached over with the intention to kiss him, but he got out of the bed, reached for my hands and helped me walk towards the bathroom before I even had the chance.

■ ■ ■

Luke was right of course. After a few more hours of sleep I felt so much better. Physically, at least. Mentally I was scatterbrained, and emotionally I was exhausted. Being sick was bad enough, but that nightmare set me on edge, and calling out my ex-boyfriend's name in bed made for a tense moment that I would have rather forgotten. Maybe I should just let this go, rather than overanalyze, as I normally did? I spent the next few days taking it easy at home, and I was better in no time.

We had some errands to run before our trip and that kept us occupied during the week. As I had suspected, Luke had never been tested for any sexually transmitted diseases, ever. He just never felt that he was at risk. Humans may make decisions based on race or gender or lifestyle, but these diseases do not, and it was time to educate my boyfriend a bit.

The walk-in health clinic was located near the university campus, and they set time aside a few days a week for free testing. It was important to try and get the word out to these sexually active college kids. STDs do not discriminate. Everyone was at risk, whether they were straight, gay, bi, white, black, Asian, male or female. Back when I first started getting checked it was a scarier process. After they drew a vial of blood you had to wait a few days before the results were available, in person or by phone. My mind always went to the darkest places then. Now they have quick HIV tests that can deliver results in minutes, painlessly. We were in and out in less time than it takes to play a few rounds of our favorite games on our phones. Luke was hesitant to go and a little nervous, of course, but he knew it was important for both of us. I told him that not knowing your status was worse than any shame or anxiety of being tested.

"I'm glad that's over," he said, as we headed back out to the parking lot with our results in hand. The results were negative, both of us.

"Yeah, I know the feeling," I said. "I always dread going, but I know it's the right thing to do. From now on, you and I are coming here together, every six months. I plan on living a long, healthy life with you."

"I never saw a negative as something positive before, but now I get it," he said. "I definitely feel relieved. You're on your way to meet the girls, right?"

"Yep, lunch with Bammy and Kit at the Tater Tot. You wanna join?"

"Can't. I'm catching up with Lana at the country club. If I'm lucky I'll escape without any fresh wounds."

I was happy they were working their way towards each other again. Luke and Lana had been so close growing up, but all this upheaval about our relationship had pulled them apart, unfortunately.

"Oh, just don't mention me too much and you'll be fine."

"Not much chance of that," he said, then headed towards his Jeep. "Don't drink too much, okay babe? You're just getting over that cold, remember?"

"But what about the medicinal powers of alcohol?!" I said, smiling.

He *must* love me, I thought. Look at the way I've turned his life upside down.

■ ■ ■

When we weren't getting our drink on at the Firelight, we were eating our weight in fried food and falafel sandwiches at the Tater Tot. Bammy and Kit were seated on the sunny outdoor terrace when I arrived and they had already ordered a round of Monster Mimosas for the three of us.

"Did you girls get me a present?" I said as I approached. "Really, I'm not sure I can accept. It's not even noon, yet."

"Oh, please," said Bammy, not getting up. "Since when have you ever turned down a cocktail?"

"Exactly," Kit chimed in. "Besides, baby, what has champagne ever done to you but bring you happiness? How could you reject that?"

"Ah, the words of a sage. You are indeed a wise one, Kit Lange." I reached for the glass and took a healthy sip. "But maybe we should order another round of these before the bar gets too busy?"

"Seriously, Derek?" said Bammy, smiling. "We're not amateurs. Already done."

The waitress came by to offer us three menus, but we stopped her before they even left her hand. She should have known better by now. We'd been there so many times; they should probably start naming dishes after us. We placed our lunch order and our second round of drinks came out just as we started our catch-up session.

"I *love* that you are taking Luke to New York!" said Kit. "*Tell. Us. Everything!* What's the plan?"

"Well, we're staying with my friend Reggie," I said.

"Oh, I remember him!" said Bammy, a furtive smile forming. "Give him a hug for me?"

"Just a hug?" I teased. Kit gave me some side eye, but I forged ahead. "Sure thing. He's moved since the last time you came up to visit me. He has this amazing apartment on the Upper West Side, now. It's a one bedroom, but it's on the top floor. Sixth floor, actually, with no elevator. Yeah, it's a workout. If you're out of milk you have to *really* want it to hike up and down six flights of stairs in the morning."

"What if there's nothing left to drink?" asked Bammy. She clutched her pearls in mock despair.

"Oh, the liquor store delivers. Easy," I said, understanding her fear.

"Wow," said Kit, eyes wide. "New York really *does* have everything. I can't believe I never visited you when you lived up there. I'm kicking myself now, of course, but in a way, I'm kinda glad I never went."

"Why's that?" I asked, smiling because I already knew the answer. Kit and I were so much alike.

"Oh, baby, you know me. I'm all about the addictive personality stuff. Can you imagine me in New York City? One second off the bus and I would have never come back. You would have lost me. *Gone. For. Good.* Right down the rabbit hole." She smiled and reached for her mimosa, pleased that she knew herself so well. "Besides, maybe I wouldn't have met Shawn?"

"I get that," I said. "That's pretty much what happened to me. It was like that moment in *The Wizard of Oz*, when Dorothy steps out of the black and white movie and into brilliant Technicolor. I just couldn't imagine wanting to be anywhere else."

Bammy started to cough loudly, then comically, with great force. "Excuse me. I seem to have a huge cliché stuck in my throat. I'm sure it will pass."

"Oh, please," I said, throwing her some shade. "You're just jealous. You never got the appeal."

"No, Derek, not really," she said, placing her now empty glass on the table. "You were so happy there. So alive. You saw the magic in everything, and I just saw garbage, homeless people and rats. And the smell? Oh, my god. There's not enough perfume in the world. New York needs one giant air freshener on every corner. And that subway? I just felt like a mouse in an endless, stifling maze, like I was some kind of participant in this huge science experiment."

"Do you remember what Reggie called you?" I asked. "He said you were a 'red coat girl in a black coat world.' He couldn't get over how fresh and happy and Southern you were. Meanwhile, he and I were decked out head to toe in shades of grey and black. And you kept talking to everyone, everywhere we went."

"Well, why wouldn't I?" she asked. "Isn't it nice to say hello to people and ask about their day? I will never lose my Southern sensibilities, regardless of the gloom and doom around me, that's for sure."

"I just wish you could have seen the city through my eyes," I said, dreamily. "I just saw signs of life everywhere. The people, the architecture, the energy."

"I'm with you," said Kit, jumping back in. "I'm ready to go for a long walk in Andy Warhol's old haunts. Take me with you, please! I'm sure I can fit in your suitcase!"

"Maybe next time," I said, laughing. "Speaking of suitcases, Tommy tells me you may have a move planned for the future. Exciting!"

"What'd I miss?" asked Bammy. She shifted forward in her chair.

"Oh, it's not a big deal," said Kit, casting her eyes downward, but clearly pleased. "Shawn and I have been living together for a while now, but we just decided we're tired of paying rent, so we're looking for a place to buy."

"I love that!" said Bammy. She was all for cohabitation and happy relationships, especially since she started dating Luke's half-brother, Michael. She no longer felt like the odd woman out when we started discussing our significant others.

"The art gallery has been doing really well since Meredith and I started representing Johnny Ray here in the Southeast," Kit continued. "He has quite a following. We're super lucky to have him."

"You're welcome," I said, though I really had nothing to do with my dad's recent reappearance. But I was glad Kit and Meredith were able to benefit from selling his sculptures. "Mom seems to be pretty happy, as well."

"Well, he *is* in pretty good shape for a man his age. You'd better hope that's genetic," said Bammy, glancing my way.

"When the topic of my sex life comes up I *know* that means your second mimosa finally kicked in," I said, kidding my bestie. "But I agree. No more drinks for me today, ladies. That was just enough bubbly to kick whatever's left of my little cold in the ass. Let's hope it did the trick. Luke and I are leaving for New York in two days and I have to start my packing list."

"Are you bringing the Vuitton?" squealed Kit, eyes aflutter.

"Oh, Kit, you and I are truly connected," I said laughing. "More important than the bag though, can I get some quick advice on something else from y'all?"

"Anything," she said.

"Do you think eight pairs of shoes is too many for a one week trip?"

3

THE CONCRETE JUNGLE

"Derek, you've walked back into the house three times. Get a move on, babe. We need to go!"

Luke was standing with one hand on the wide-open front door, trying to coax me through. His car was already loaded with our bags and I was making "one last check" to make sure the stove was off, the back door was locked, and the toilet wasn't running. My travel anxiety was in full bloom, but more than that, I was nervous, excited and scared, all at once.

"I set the timers to turn the living room lights on and off while we're gone so no one will think to break in," I said, as he grabbed my hand and pulled me towards the car.

"That would be a great idea, babe, if the whole town didn't already know we're taking a trip up to New York," he said, closing the door as I stepped into the Jeep.

Damn you, Parkville, and your small town ways. At least I tried?

"Oh! Did you put the newspaper on hold?" I asked. "Because we don't want those piling up on the doorstep. And did you lock the front door? I once left my apartment in New York unlocked by accident for a whole week when I was on vacation."

"Yes, babe. Please, calm down," he said, taking my hand again. "What is wrong with you? You've been acting funny this whole week."

I didn't want to tell him about my nightmare. I just didn't want to talk about it. He was right, though. I was acting strange, but I needed to get over it, and fast.

"I have a one-eyed headache, which means it's either stress or a tumor."

"Did you Google that?" he teased.

"Shut up. I just get a little panicky before I travel. I always have," I explained, removing my left hand from my eye. "It's kind of like the night before a test in school. I was always super nervous and couldn't sleep, but once the exams were handed out and I picked up my pencil, I breezed right through it. I'm the same way with flying. I just need to get to the airport, get through security, board the plane and sit down. Once we take off, I'll be fine."

"Hey, I got you," he reassured me, still holding my hand. "Besides, this is your town we're going to. I want to see the city you fell in love with."

I did, too. But I hoped she still wanted to see me. New York can be a fickle bitch.

■ ■ ■

We pulled into long-term parking at the airport and Luke grabbed his small, wheeled carry-on from the back seat. My shiny silver beast of a suitcase was in the back, and Luke lifted it out and placed it on the ground. I had my own small carry-on, as well as the bag I borrowed from Uncle Barry. Luke packed light, obviously. And me? Well, I brought clothes for every possible occasion. And shoes. Lots and lots of shoes.

"Are we running behind?" I asked as he locked the doors with a tap of his keychain. "Sorry if I made us late."

"All good. We're super early, as a matter of fact," he said. "I may have fibbed a little about the time to get your ass in gear."

"Wow. That was a good move. Where'd you learn to be so manipulative?" I teased.

"Trust me. You're a great teacher," he said, smirking. He nodded towards my overstuffed suitcase. "I'll take the big one."

"You know I love it when you say that."

He pulled me in and gave me a rock star kiss, right there in the parking lot. My knees went weak, and I sucked in a bit of air when he finally released me.

"Better?" he asked. This guy knew exactly what he was doing.

"Um, yeah," I said, smiling like a shy schoolboy with a secret crush.

"Good. Now let's go." That's my man. All business.

We had already checked in online, and our boarding passes were mobile, so all we had to do was drop off our luggage. It was a self-service line, of course. I remarked that everything at the airport was do-it-yourself, now. We printed out the tags, attached them to the bags and sent them off down the conveyor belt. No one even spoke to us. I wasn't really looking forward to the day when we would have to fly the planes ourselves, too. They had better have breathalyzers for my crew.

"Are Red and Rosa coming to see us off?" I asked.

Flying was still special to my family, and coming to the airport for a big send-off was kind of a tradition in our house. We had invited Luke's family, too.

"Yep, they should be here soon, if they're not here already."

We rounded the corner right before the lone security checkpoint, and sure enough, we saw everyone waiting for us in the bar. We used to do the big good-bye at the gate, but since only ticket holders can go that far now, we amended our traditions. Being able to have a few extra drinks was just a pleasant bonus that worked out in our favor.

"There they are!" Uncle Barry called from a table upfront by the door. "Hurry up, boys. You only have time for two cocktails before the flight, now. We've already ordered for you. Have a seat!"

This felt really odd. It was like having drinks with my Scooby Gang at the Firelight, but one generation removed. Barry was seated at the head of the table, with Red and Rosa to his right. My parents were seated across from them, to his left. Luke and I pulled up two chairs and joined them on the free end. The tabletop was already littered with empty glasses, the ice cubes clinging to the last spirited remains of whatever house vodka they served up at this fine airport establishment. I doubted that Red was pleased with the bourbon selections available, but the smile on his face proved that he was indeed enjoying the company. He really lit up around my Uncle Barry, and I wondered if I was the only one to notice that?

"Hi there, sweetie," my mom spoke up. "We decided to come a little early and catch up with Red and Rosa. We don't see them nearly as much as we ought to."

"Well, you and Johnny are welcome by the house any time, Audrey. Rosa and I would be so pleased," said Red. "We do not get out to socialize very much, any more. It seems our days and nights of wild parties are in the past, to be remembered fondly."

"*Fondling?*" spurted Barry. "I need to go to your parties more often, old friend. It's been a while since this gal's seen any action."

"*Fondly*, you old glamour girl!" said Red, who clearly had more of a sense of humor than I had originally imagined. Exactly how many drinks had they imbibed before we arrived?!

"That's 'Glama Gal,' Red," said Barry, correcting Luke's dad. "Why, I haven't heard that in ages." My mom looked at me with a sly look. Now that Barry was out, he was "spilling the tea" more and more. I'm sure there were lots of things she knew that they had never discussed openly.

"Do tell?" I asked. Was this another secret between Red and Barry?

"We'll save that for another day, nephew," said Barry, coolly realizing the need to shift gears. He shot Red a quick glance and they both regained their composure. "Now, tell us all about New York. What do you have planned?"

"Yes, we're so excited for you!" said Rosa, settling herself into Red's arm, firmly claiming her space. Don't worry Rosa. Barry was in your man's past, and I'm pretty sure that's where he'll remain. No need to lose any sleep over that one.

"Derek is going to show me all his favorite places," said Luke. "I really want to see the city through his eyes."

"We'll do as much as we can in a week," I said, jumping in. "I want him to see the Lower East Side, the East Village, the West Village, Union Square."

"I hope you have some time for a few galleries?" asked Johnny. "I checked online and there are some pretty great exhibits going on right now. And the Museum of Modern Art, of course."

"We'll try," I said. "We want to get some culture in, but we have a pretty busy schedule."

"Oh, stop telling us stories to make us feel good," said Barry. "We know it's all bars and restaurants and shopping. Just have fun, take pics and do *everything* I would do and more!"

The hour passed quickly, with plenty of laughs. Soon, it was time for us to board, so we made our way towards security, with lots of kisses and hugs before we joined the line.

"Don't forget, Dolly," Barry whispered in my ear as we parted. "Chinois Zarée."

"You got it," I assured him.

■ ■ ■

I was settled comfortably in my seat, my head leaning against the cold window of the airplane. The drinks had helped to calm me, and as I had explained to Luke before, the moment the flight took off, all my anxieties flew away with the clouds. No more one-eyed headache. This was going to be a fantastic trip, and I was so looking forward to jumping back into everything New York City had to offer.

"Would you care for something to drink, sir?" The flight attendant roused me from my reverie. I looked up to see a dark haired Ken doll smiling his robotic smile.

"Vodka soda, please," I said, perking up.

"I'll just have a beer, thank you," said Luke.

The steward pulled a plastic cup from his stack and popped a few cubes of ice into it, and then handed me a mini bottle of vodka and a can of soda water. He opened Luke's beer and placed it on his tray table, reached down with his foot to unlock his carriage and began to push away to the next row of passengers. "Enjoy your beer, cowboy."

Cowboy? I looked at Luke with furrowed eyebrows and he began to turn scarlet. "What was that?" I asked, knowing full well what the answer would be. *Well, Luke, let's see how you handle this one*, I thought.

"Babe, I..." He reached up and wiped the tiny beads of sweat from his forehead.

"Let me guess, *Cowboy*," I said, helping him out. "The Huntr app?"

He gulped, clearly unsure of what to do next.

"Luke, it's okay. I understand." I didn't want to torture him. "We both have a past that made us who we are today. We wouldn't be human if we didn't have needs to be met. I just hope I'm all you need, now."

"I'm really sorry about that," he started, his voice not quite finding its place in his throat.

"There's nothing to be sorry about." I meant it. "I know I'm not the first guy you slept with. I'm just the last. And the *best*."

He smiled and then reached over to kiss me. I mixed my vodka and soda and turned my eyes towards the Earth below us. I'm kind of glad that happened, to be honest, because we were about to enter my old playground, and I had no idea how many of my former "friends" from Huntr would appear. How many would be *too* many?

■ ■ ■

I had ordered a black town car in advance so we wouldn't have to deal with the trains and buses and taxi lines that stretched for miles around concrete pillars. Plus I was too impatient to wait for a car to show up. I wanted to get into the city as quickly and painlessly as possible, so I was quite happy to pay a man to stand there with a sign with my name on it.

"Say good-bye to grass, Luke! We're in the concrete jungle." He was holding my hand outside of baggage pick-up, staring up at the many on-ramps and off-ramps that surrounded us. Black limousines and yellow cabs honked at each other in a rhythmic code while tourists pushed lug-gage-filled trolleys towards the bus lines. Our driver took our suitcases and placed them in the trunk as we found our seats in the back.

"Upper West Side, please," I said to him.

"Yes, sir. I have the address right here," he said. "You mind if I keep the music on?"

"As long as you get us there in one piece, you can listen to anything you want."

We snaked our way slowly through the underground maze and made our way towards the highway. Luke's eyes were wide open, his mouth in a permanent state of awe. I don't think he had ever seen anything like this before. For a guy who came from a wealthy background, he sure hadn't traveled much. I was reminded of that old, fake mil-itary slogan. "Join the Army, travel the world, meet inter-esting people. And kill them." I was hoping to avoid that last part on this trip.

Forty minutes later the car pulled up to Reggie's building, and we opened the door while the driver removed our bags, deposited them on the curb, and sped off to pick up his next fare. I couldn't believe I was about to see my old friend again. I had only been gone a year, but my hasty exit seemed like a lifetime ago.

Reginald "Reggie" Rex III was my Tommy here in New York City. We met forever ago at a house party that neither one of us could really remember. The only thing we recalled was that we ended up being better friends with each other than with the host. Reggie was a Southern guy, like me, and we bonded over stories of cornbread and warm social graces, but that's pretty much where the similarities ended. Whereas I came to New York to find work as an actor, and hopefully a boyfriend, Reggie chased a dream of music and women, and he definitely caught both. Tall, black, and as handsome as a model, he could charm anyone with his smile and personality. He first tried to break into the music scene as DJ Black Pharaoh, specializing in '90s R&B music, but his tastes in music broadened, his mixing skills improved and his following grew. He eventually settled on a new name that was less polarizing. "DJ Rex, King of the Groove" now had a slew of regular gigs across the city, as well as numerous private events that kept him busy at least six nights a week.

We both lived in illegal sublets on the Upper East Side when we first met. When his superintendent found out he wasn't on the lease, Reggie got kicked out and moved in with his girlfriend, a beautiful Japanese girl with a mouth like a sailor. She was small in stature, but she scared the hell out of me, in a good way. She looked so delicate, but you just knew she could kick your ass. They lived in Brooklyn before Brooklyn was cool, until she eventually kicked him out as well. (Too bad. I liked her.) He then bounced his way around town, couch surfing and subletting for a few more years, but as his reputation as a DJ grew, so did his savings. He finally found a place of his own here on the Upper West Side.

Reggie lived in a pre-war building that had seen better days, but it was worth it when you saw his apartment, perched on the very top floor. His unit used to belong to the superintendent's second (as in, other) girlfriend, and this guy had done everything he could to keep her happy, including installing an illegal spiral staircase that went straight through the living room ceiling onto the roof, where he had constructed a 200 square foot greenhouse just for her. She was a friend of Reggie's from the club scene, and when she decided to break up with the super for good, she handed Reggie the keys and told her ex to take care of the paperwork. He'd do anything to try and win her back, and Reggie benefited from that. With his name on the lease, DJ Rex finally had his own home in the city.

We climbed the cement steps to the building and punched in the code on the buzzer. One uncomfortably long minute later he answered with a "Yo."

"Reggie? We're here, man!"

"Come on up," he said with a groggy voice.

The door buzzed and we entered the old lobby, lit with fluorescent lights. Hauling the suitcases up six flights of stairs took a bit of work and a few moments of rest on the landings, but we finally made it up.

"That just gets more and more fun every time," I panted, as Reggie opened the door.

"Welcome! Man, it's great to see you guys. Come on in. You must be Luke," he said, reaching over for a handshake and a half-hug, in the Southern style.

"Thank you so much for putting us up, Reggie," said my boyfriend. "We really appreciate it."

"Oh, it's nothing, man," he said. "I'm practically never here, anyway. I'm out most nights and then sleeping it off during the day. Let's bring your stuff up to the greenhouse."

Reggie's apartment was a railroad style, with the kitchen leading into the living room, leading into the bedroom. We took our bags towards the spiral staircase and climbed up one last set of stairs, finally arriving inside the huge glass and iron cube that sat on the roof. Reggie had long ago transformed the gardening space into an extra room, complete with a fold-out couch, widescreen TV, gaming system and amazing views of the city. It was kind of a see-through man cave. The only problem was the temperature. In winter it was colder than a witch's tit in a brass bra, and in summer it was hotter than a thousand hells. But it was free, so we weren't complaining. We tossed our stuff in the corner and settled down on the sofa to catch up.

"It's been forever, man," said Reggie. "How was your trip?"

"Great," I answered. "A few drinks with Mom and Barry before we took off, of course. And Bammy says hello, by the way."

"The red coat girl! Yeah, I remember her." He smiled. I sure hoped he did, considering how much they made out on her last trip up here. I was pretty sure she would have stayed in New York just for Reggie, if she hadn't hated the city so much.

"Oh, man, did you tell Luke about that night?"

"Which one?" I laughed.

He leaned back on the couch, smiling. "Yeah, I guess you're right. We did some crazy stuff. I was thinking of that time you and Bammy and I almost got arrested, though. Remember that?"

"Oh, this I've got to hear," said Luke, enjoying every minute. "Bammy? Arrested?"

"We didn't get arrested," I said, trying to save face. "Just almost. Seriously, Reggie? This is how you wanna start? All right. Well," I gave in and turned to Luke, "it was one of those weekends that Bammy was up here visiting. I was living in this sublet on the Upper East Side at the time, and the three of us decided to go out for a drink before dinner. None of us really had much money back then, but somehow we always had enough for drinks, right? One cocktail turned into several, and before you know it, we drank our dinner at the bar. A few cheap chicken wings and mozzarella sticks didn't do much to sober us up, and the bartender thought he was going to score with Bammy, so he kept pouring these ridiculously strong cocktails. Since we're all from the South, we started talking about hot summer nights and how to cool down, and that led to the topic of skinny-dipping, of course. Next thing I know, we're asking the bartender for the closest public pool. But it was like two o'clock in the morning. He told us we were crazy, but we paid our tab and headed over to York Avenue anyway. There's this huge recreational pool there, and it was dimly lit by a few streetlights, but definitely closed and definitely not accessible, unless we climbed this massive iron fence with spikes on top. Before I knew it, Reggie had shimmied up and landed on his feet on the other side. It took all of my drunken effort, but I helped Bammy up, and then climbed over, too. We stripped off our clothes and jumped right in! Our splashing lasted, what, about three minutes, Reggie?" He nodded, enjoying this.

"What happened?" asked Luke. "Cops?"

"You got it," I answered. "Cars, flashing lights and plenty of men in blue. You would have thought it was a jewel heist. We were so drunk that we were too stupid to be scared, though. One of the cops flashed a light in my eyes from the other side of the fence and I pulled myself up and out of the water. I quickly remembered I was na-ked, so I turned my back and threw my jeans on, without grabbing anything else. There was no use in running. No place to go, anyway. I stood there dripping wet and decided to put on my best Southern charm, along with the worst accent this side of Mayberry. 'Yes, officer, sir?' I said, drawling out the words for full effect. Somehow he fell for my act and suggested I 'get my ass outta there now.' Reggie and I climbed back over the fence in no time, but we had totally forgotten about Bammy. She couldn't do it herself. 'You just gonna leave her there, bub?' the officer asked me. 'No, sir.' I hightailed it back over, but she was so completely out of energy that she could barely climb. In the end, I had to hoist her up on my shoulders and practically throw her over. One of those spikes on top of the fence pierced her in the ass, and she let out this bloodcurdling scream before she tumbled to the other side. I almost peed my pants, I was laughing so hard. I climbed over to join her and Reggie, and the police officers pretty much let us have it. They just wanted to scare us, and they would have done a damn good job of it if we hadn't been so wasted. We just stared at them and politely nodded a lot, holding our shirts in our hands. Bammy was still in her bra, her arms covering her chest. Finally, they just told us to take off. She still has that scar on her butt, you know."

"Oh, yes she does," said Reggie, with a twinkle in his eye. "At least she did the last time I saw her."

"Well, you won't be seeing that scar again anytime soon," I said. "Bammy's dating Luke's brother, Michael, now.

"All good, all good," said Reggie, and then clapped his hands and stood up. "All right guys, sorry to hug and run, but I've got some errands to take care of before my gig. There are two sets of keys for you on the kitchen counter. You've got my number if you need anything. Pencil me in for brunch on Sunday though?"

"You got it, Reggie," I said. "And thanks again."

He made his way down the spiral staircase, leaving Luke and me alone to watch the sun as it began to set over the city.

"He's a great guy," he said, pulling me in close on the couch. "And this is a crazy beautiful space. I've never seen anything like it."

I was so happy to be sharing this with my boyfriend. "How's it feel to be so loved?" I asked.

"I don't know. You tell me?" He leaned over and gave me a soft kiss.

"Just you wait, Coach," I said, beaming. "New York has everything. How about we get cleaned up and go grab a bite to eat? I'm craving sushi. Or tacos. Or Vietnamese."

"Let's do it." He stood up to take another look at the view, breathed it in, and then turned to look at me. "By the way, what were you and Barry whispering about as we left the airport? I meant to ask you earlier, but it slipped my mind."

"Oh, nothing major. He just wants me to look up an old friend of his."

"Cool." He paused. "I'd like to do the same, if you don't mind," he said, his face not betraying anything.

"Really? You know someone up here?" I asked, cocking my head. "Not another Huntr guy, like our flight attendant?" I teased.

"No, nothing like that," he said. "Someone else."

"Who?" I asked.

"Fletcher Powell."

4

A FINE BROMANCE

Fletcher Powell. Now, there's a name I never thought I'd hear again.

When I was an awkward fourteen-year-old freshman at Parkville High School, Luke Walcott was the kid in my class who everyone wanted to be, or in my case, just plain wanted. Fletcher Powell was the star senior quarterback, and for everything young Luke embodied, Fletch casually added an -er, with little or no effort. He was taller, blonder, bigger, better, faster, stronger, and even though it doesn't seem possible by the way I have described Luke, he was even hotter. Barbie would have ditched Ken (and her panties) in a nanosecond for Fletch. He had a megawatt smile, won every athletic award, and had every girl in the school chasing after him. Even some of the teachers had crushes on him, if one was to believe the rumors. Parents routinely compared their kids to Fletch and wished they could trade in their own for a similar model. He had never worked too hard at anything. He rarely completed his assignments, but he was so easygoing and charming that the staff adored him, nonetheless. He was the golden boy of Parkville High, our version of the sun god Apollo, and anyone who walked in his path was bathed in glowing light. When it came time for him to graduate and leave us for expected greatness, he could have chosen anyone to be his successor. And he chose Luke Walcott.

Every now and then a senior takes an underclassman under his wing. It's not uncommon, but the universe scored a double whammy when Fletch Powell met Luke Walcott. Together, no one else stood a chance. Fletch took the proper steps to ensure that Luke wasn't just a benchwarmer on the football team his freshman year. They worked out together before and after practice to make sure that Luke was worthy of succeeding him as the top Parkville High Commodore. And when he encouraged him to date our classmate Amber and to cement their status as the high school's hottest new couple, their social status grew and the party invitations just started rolling in. Friday nights would find them cruising up and down Commodore Way in Fletch's 1965 custom-detailed Big Orange Mustang convertible. He had one goal and one goal only. Fletch was going to play football for the University of Tennessee Volunteers.

When he graduated from Parkville High, our golden boy Fletch had offers from every single school in the Southeastern Conference, as well as a few of the Ivy Leagues, but he had his heart set on UT and they didn't let him down. Very few freshmen players get a chance to come off the bench, let alone start as a quarterback, but Fletch Powell wasn't just any player. He was a Heisman trophy winner in the making. He threw perfect passes that landed every time in his first four games of the season, bringing UT a much needed boost from the previous not-so-illustrious year. The booster money started rolling in and the team was riding high on its success.

Fletch's life couldn't get any better.

That is, until it all came crashing down. When that bright, beautiful Mustang hit that telephone pole, it folded up like a crumpled orange flyer discarded after game day. He'd been drinking, of course, and he was lucky to walk away from that twisted hunk of shiny amber with nothing but a broken leg and a wrecked career. The police didn't press any charges. No one wanted to damage the golden boy any further than he had already hurt himself. There wasn't even another car involved. Fletch later said that he didn't remember a thing and he wanted to put it all in the past. He went through an exhaustive physical rehabilitation program, but at the end of it, his football career was over. It wasn't a big surprise, but it was a huge loss to the program and to his fans.

He took a semester off school to fully recover, but he didn't feel sorry for himself. He'd had his chance, and he blew it. He knew it was nothing more than that. After his recovery he had an opportunity to create a new Fletcher Powell. It wasn't that he was a bad student in high school; he had just never applied himself. So now he set about to reinvent his life. Four years later he graduated with a business degree in hand, and Fletch was quickly scooped up by one of the big pharmaceutical companies. The former football star used his charm and personality to become a star sales representative in the Southeast. But his days of football glory were still too close and too fresh on his psyche, so he packed his bags and headed far away, cutting ties with the community that loved him because it continually reminded him of his "what ifs."

I hadn't thought of Fletcher Powell in years. But apparently Luke had, and he knew exactly where he was. Right here in New York City.

"So, you're still friends with Fletch Powell?" I asked, confused. We were still sitting on the couch in Reggie's greenhouse. We'd barely been in the city for an hour, and things were already getting weird. *If Uncle Barry shows up in his yellow Carmen Miranda get-up, I'm outta here*, I thought to myself.

"Why wouldn't I be? He was one of my best friends."

"Well, yeah, I get that…but…" My voice trailed off.

"But what?" he said, just a tad defensively. "What's so strange?"

"Nothing, it's just. I mean," I was stumbling badly. My own outdated prejudices were getting in the way of reason. Of course Luke could still be in touch with Fletch. Being gay didn't have to be the end of their friendship. "Sorry.

Maybe I just thought he was more close-minded than that. I shouldn't assume those things. I didn't know him like you did... like you do. I guess that's stupid of me."

"Derek," he answered. "You're better than that. And no, you didn't know Fletch like I did, but since you and I are together maybe you should try to get to know him now? If *he's* cool with it, shouldn't you be?"

"So you told him about us?" Why did that surprise me so much?

"Of course I did. You're part of my life. You're my boy-friend." He said it so freely now that it still shocked me. It was just a matter of fact. His initial coming out was hard, but once those doors flew open, he ran for a touchdown and made it all look so easy. In a way, I was resentful of how effortless it all seemed to him, but I knew I shouldn't be. *Everybody's journey is different*, I repeated internally.

"You're pretty amazing, you know that?" I said. I felt slightly ashamed of myself, but proud of him.

"So you keep telling me." His face softened. "It's a good thing I'm not afraid of compliments, otherwise I'd have a complex."

"So, when was the last time you saw him?" I asked, fishing. "Do you guys talk often, or what?"

"Fletch and I have a history. He's the one who hooked me up with Amber in high school remember? But I don't hold that against him. And you know we were in the same fraternity at UT, right? We spent a lot of time together." He hesitated. "Wait, are you jealous?" He was teasing me, but I knew there was an air of seriousness to his question.

"No," I said with too much force, but I didn't even convince myself. I wasn't jealous of Fletch. I was just surprised, and a little uneasy to tell you the truth. I'd never spoken to him in high school, of course. He was way too far above me in the social hierarchy. Sometimes it was still hard for me to wrap my brain around the idea that Luke and I were even together. But Fletch was just a whole different level, altogether.

"I'm not jealous," I continued. "I just think it's cool that I'm still finding out things about you, that's all. I was pretty sure I was the best stalker ever, but now you're making me question my skills." I hoped he accepted that answer. I didn't want to admit that people like Fletch still made me feel nervous. Some old high school habits are hard to break.

"Well, I have to keep you on your toes, babe," he said, smiling. "Otherwise it gets boring, and we can't have that, can we? Now, waddya say we go out and get that food you were talking about? I need a recharge. I'm just gonna give Fletch a call, first. Maybe we can meet him out for a drink later, or something?"

"Yeah, sure. Great idea," I said, trying to sound as positive as possible. I had nothing to be afraid of, anyway. *Dreams come true, but nightmares don't, right?* I thought.

■ ■ ■

We rode the subway down to Union Square Park and had dinner at this amazing Asian fusion place that served

Brazilian and Japanese small dishes. I was happy to see they still had flash-fried salt and pepper baby crabs on the menu, and the look on Luke's face was priceless when I told him that you're supposed to eat them shells and all. We ordered enough tapas and sushi to fill the table, and after a few beers and two vodka and sodas we hailed a taxi and headed over to the Meatpacking District to meet Fletch.

When I first moved to New York, that part of town was still an actual meatpacking district. Stepping off the curb and over a stream of blood was not only commonplace, it was expected, as was the smell. I vividly remembered my friends and I traipsing through the red-hued, glistening streets, artfully lit by moonlight, and being enchanted by the morbid beauty. Eventually the sounds of rats foraging through the trash bins filled with discarded animal parts would disturb our reverie, and we would flee for our favorite random dirty dive bars, hidden behind unmarked black doors covered in obscure band stickers and hasty graffiti. It all felt unsafe and scary, but it was our secret place, and we loved it because no one else knew about it. It was ours, and ours alone.

The only restaurant in the area was Florent, and it was the best place in the world to catch up on the real late night culture of drag queens and club kids. The wee hours of the morning were rush hour, and you could find yourself sharing an after-party table with a famous author, artist, or long-lost musician. My favorite waitress was transsexual, before I even really understood any of that, and I liked to sit in her section if I could. I always ordered a veggie burger with bacon and she'd looked down at me from her order pad and say, "You're twisted," and then smirk and walk away. She got me. It was definitely a far cry from Parkville.

Then, seemingly overnight, it was all gone. The butcher shops were replaced by art galleries, designer clothing stores popped up, and Florent himself was priced out of his space by greedy landlords looking to cash in on the latest neighborhood craze. The only blood on the streets came from the fraternity boy fistfights as they argued on the sidewalks, trying desperately to get past the velvet ropes of the city's hottest new clubs.

Fletcher Powell lived several stories above what passed for nightlife these days in a modern addition constructed on the rooftop of a hundred-year-old brownstone on Washington Street, just a few blocks from the new, bustling Meatpacking District. It was ostentatious and horrible, but amazing and stunning at the same time. His wife, Brandee, later informed us that their apartment had been featured in the world's leading home decor and industrial design magazines. I must have missed that between teaching high school theatre classes and hitting up the Tater Tot. Life in Parkville had its own version of exciting.

The yellow cab dropped us off and we were buzzed in. We walked towards the private elevator in the back of the hallway and took the express trip to the penthouse. I looked over at Luke and he was eager with anticipation, practically salivating like Pavlov's dog, waiting for the bell to ring. I looked up at the camera peering down at us, transmitting the image of our faces to the apartment above. I imagined that Fletch was watching us right now. I started to sweat. Then the doors opened.

"*Lukey*! There's my number one! Get your pretty little ass in here, boy!" We spotted our first view of the top floor as Fletch bellowed, his big arms outstretched like a proud daddy. Lukey?

My boyfriend practically threw himself into Fletch's open arms. I'm pretty sure he would have jumped into them if he had been able to. As it was, he almost knocked Fletch over; the collision of their muscled chests causing a slight sonic boom that I was afraid would shatter the glass and concrete walls of the architectural oddity surrounding us. I looked over at his wife, Brandee, and she was smiling her cheerleader smile. A beautiful redhead with ample curves, she was every inch a real woman, not a stick thin model whose reality had been airbrushed away. There was a secret hidden behind those eyes, though, and I definitely wanted to find out more. But first and foremost, her husband commanded the attention in the room.

Fletch was even more handsome than I remembered, the blond prince in every fairy tale you ever read. Think Robert Redford meets Chris Hemsworth. The deep laugh lines around his eyes added a degree of gravitas that he had lacked in his younger years. Dressed in a tight white designer t-shirt with a very deep v-neck to show off his bulging pecs and biceps, he was truly a stunner. His sandy blond hair flopped over his forehead and I had to resist the urge to reach over and sweep it to the side, à la Barbra

Streisand in *The Way We Were*. He was magnetic, and I couldn't take my eyes off him. Neither could Luke.

"Derek, you better get on over here too, boy," said Fletch, his deep, commanding voice snapping me out of my reverie. "If my Lukey's sweet on you, you must be one helluva guy." I stepped towards him gingerly, knowing I had no say in the matter, and he reached out to pull me in for a three-way hug with Luke. I felt heavy with all that combined muscle on top of me.

"Aren't y'all so cute?" said Brandee, gleefully. "Oh! Let me grab my phone. I wanna take a pic. Y'all don't move, okay?"

I heard her step out of the foyer, but Fletch really took her words to heart. He wasn't moving, at all. If anything, he was holding us tighter, one arm around Luke and the other around me, his fingers firmly wrapped around my ribs. I could feel someone else's heart pounding more than mine. But whose?

"Y'all ready to have some fun tonight?" he said to us, his low voice practically growling out the words. *What kind of fun did he have in mind?* I wondered.

"Done!" said Brandee, as she snapped the picture, cell phone in hand. "Now that's going on Instagram, right now! Y'all are on Instagram, right? You should follow me. I post all sorts of fun stuff. I can show y'all."

"Brandee's a blogger," said Fletch, somewhat dismissively. He loosened his grip around my torso, but held on to the both of us. I felt a little helpless in King Kong's arms. Luke was still looking at his idol as if he'd completely forgotten I was there. "She's great at taking pictures. Watch out, though. Your bare asses will be on the internet before you know it. Trust me. I know from experience." He laughed heartily.

"Oh, Fletch! You love the attention," said his wife. "I don't know why you're acting like you don't like it. Now let's get inside and get you boys some drinks."

We turned to follow Brandee, and Fletch's left hand slid down to the small of my back, firmly guiding me into the living room. "Nice glutes," he said. I turned to spy his right hand land solidly on my boyfriend's butt cheek. "You been doing those Bulgarian squats, like I taught you? Good boy!" He gave Luke's ass an extra squeeze, for good measure.

"Yes, sir," said Luke, at full attention, almost rapturous.

"We need to get a workout in while you're here," said Fletch. "Sex isn't the only thing that'll keep us in shape, am I right boys?" He winked. Now it was my turn to get my ass squeezed. I laughed, nervously. What the hell was going on here?

Compared to my old studio apartment in midtown, Fletch and Brandee's place had its own zip code. A full kitchen stood to our left, and the room opened out to a massive rooftop terrace. Everywhere you looked there were spectacular views of the city. It was the perfect apartment for voyeurs and exhibitionists alike. A giant chandelier of mirrored globes lit up the room, and I looked around to admire the entertainment space on this floor. Brandee explained that the bedrooms were located one level below in the brownstone, for privacy. As if they were even concerned about that.

"Fletch said you boys already had dinner. I made a pitcher of Cosmos, and we have a whole fridge full of beer. What can I get for ya?" asked Brandee.

"Luke's a beer guy, like me," answered Fletch, taking charge. "Get him one of those imported ones, will ya baby?"

I looked up, unsure if I was allowed to speak for myself or wait for Fletch to lead the way. Brandee smiled at me, waiting on my answer. Obviously she had enough experience to know how this was going to play out.

"I'd love a vodka and soda, actually," I said, as Fletch walked Luke out to the terrace, his arm never leaving my boyfriend's shoulder. I knew better than to be jealous. Or, at least, not to show it.

"Those two," said Brandee, reaching for a cocktail glass and filling it with ice. "I can't tell you how many times I chased after Fletch at UT just to find him hanging out with Luke over at the frat house. I swear, they spent more nights together than we did. Half the time I called they'd be up in Luke's room watching some movie. It's great seeing them together, again, though. They're so gay for each other. I swear."

"What?" I sputtered.

"Oh, *shoo,*" she said, handing me my vodka. "Sorry. All this politically correct stuff. I need to watch my mouth and mind my manners, as my mama'd say. I just meant *gay* like...not *real* gay. Like *sweet* on each other. Like boys get, you know?"

"Right," I said, slowly. "*Like boys get.* Yeah."

"I mean," she continued, "we are *so* cool with y'all being *real* gay. We've been up here in New York for a few years now, after all. This ain't the South! If it's out there, we've seen it. Y'all know what I mean?" She laughed and tossed back the remainder of her Cosmo, then swiftly refilled it from the pitcher. Her hand reached down to an engraved silver box on the bar and she opened it, nonchalantly retrieving two pills from within and deftly popping them into her mouth. Practice makes perfect.

"Oh, I do," I said, slowly taking all of this in. "I've definitely seen some things you wouldn't believe." Like right here, right now, as I continued my conversation with an apparently self-medicated wife who was looking the other way while her man was off "being a boy" with my man.

"So, you and Fletch dated in college?" I asked.

"We met our freshman year at UT. I'm a Florida girl. Daddy was a Gator. He wasn't too happy about me going to UT, let alone dating a Tennessee Volunteer. 'At least it ain't 'Bama!' he said. We always laughed about that one. Anyway," she took another sip, "Fletch and I dated, and then broke up after his accident. He was just so moody, you know? He ended up getting involved with his rehab nurse. She's the one that turned him onto pharmaceuticals. Being a rep, I mean. He even invited me to the wedding. His family thought it was gracious, but I saw things real different. He asked me to dance with him at his wedding reception, and I whispered in his ear, 'It should have been me,' and don't ya know it? Just two years later he was divorced and running back to my arms, where he belongs. We hightailed it up here and left that whole mess behind us. What's in the past is in the past, right? That's what they say, anyway. So here we are. All this." She waved her arms around the room. "Fletch is pretty busy with work, but like I said, I'm *super* happy with my life," she added, trying to convince herself. You keep on repeating that, Brandee. Maybe it will come true. "I need to show you my blog. I really do. You need to follow me. I think you'd really love it. I just have so many friends, so many wonderful people. I can just *feel* all that love, you know what I mean? Like, all those admirers who just want to watch me, see my every move, live their lives through mine. I'm so *happy* I can help them all out, share my life with them, give them a glimpse of all this, you know?"

She waved her free hand around the room again, the other one still gripping her cocktail, which was almost gone in record time. Even Uncle Barry would be impressed with how much she could get down her throat in such a short time. She definitely had a gift.

"Maybe we should check on the guys?" I offered, not feeling the urge to play therapist. I couldn't add Brandee to the list of fragile souls in my life who needed a sympathetic ear. I already had my hands full back in Parkville.

"Oh, I'm sure they're doing fine," she said, her speech beginning to slur. "Knowing Fletch, they're probably in the hot tub by now. I'm feeling kinda woozy, you know? I'm just gonna lay down in here for a minute, if you don't mind. Y'all have fun without me. He always does."

"Sure thing," I said, as she glided across the room and lay face down on a white leather sofa. I followed her, grabbed a cashmere throw to cover her body and placed an emergency glass of water on the coffee table beside her. She was out before I even finished tucking in the corners. I stepped out onto the terrace to take a look at the incredible view.

"Do you shave 'em, now?" I heard Fletch ask. The voice came from the corner of the roof, behind a latticework privacy fence. I followed the sound to find the "boys" perched on the edge of the hot tub, naked as the day they were born.

"Yeah, Derek likes it, so I started a few months ago," said Luke, beer bottle in hand.

"Hell, if I did everything Brandee asked me to do I'd have no time in the day," said Fletch. He stepped out of the tub and bent over to get a fresh beer from the mini-fridge, giving me a new insight to his...personality? To tell you the truth, though, Brandee was right. Nothing shocked me, anymore. Even the site of Fletch and Luke comparing their balls.

"Hey there, buddy!" said Fletch, spotting me. He walked over and put his arm around me. His wet, naked body pressed up against mine, and all I could think was *this guy has no filter.*

"Glad you decided to join us!" He winked at me, again.

"What's going on here?" I asked, making a point to not look down.

"Aw, hell, your boyfriend's just showing me his shiny new balls," he said with a grin as he ran his fingers through his damp hair, and they both laughed. Fletch handed me a beer, then hopped up over the edge and back into the tub.

"So, you getting naked, or what?" he asked.

5

THE HOZE

The rest of the night played out like my hottest man-on-man football player fantasy, but without any of the action, as if the director was a religious conservative who believed that men just needed to embrace the urge to hug it out, naked, and "all the gay will just go away."

After they finished their very informative and lengthy discussion about their balls, Luke and Fletch went on to compare everything else. It was a science experiment, and they were both subject and researcher. They measured their biceps, their quads, their…well, you get the idea. Way more than I needed to see, actually. It wasn't long before I truly got a grip on what was happening in front of me. I had little reason to be jealous or angry, after all. Sure, here I was sharing a naked hot tub with my boyfriend's ex, but Fletch wasn't *really* Luke's ex. In their minds they were back in college and just hanging with each other's best bud. They had never been in a homo*sexual* relationship. They were in a homo*social* one. Fletch wasn't gay at all. He just preferred the company of men.

I recalled a study in which a group of researchers noted that we tend to value our same gender friendships more than our cross gender friendships. For some people this can lead to a fully realized relationship that includes everything except sex. It's a social, rather than a sexual preference. But put two incredibly handsome guys like Luke Walcott and Fletcher Powell together in the same room (or frat house or locker room or hot tub), and sparks were bound to fly, regardless of their sexual preferences. I was willing to bet that they had crossed swords at least once in their lives, I just wasn't sure I wanted to ask about the details.

It was well after four in the morning by the time the frat buddies stopped telling stories and we all decided we needed to get some rest. Luke and Fletch went through every beer in the place, so they were pretty wasted. I was sober enough to get my boyfriend back into his clothes and we all headed towards the elevator. We passed Brandee on the way out, still sleeping it off on the couch. As long as she was "happy," right? There was one last wet, naked hug from Fletch and we were finally off.

I poured Luke into a cab and he slumped down next to me in the back seat as we sped back uptown to Reggie's place. That six floor walk-up nearly did us in. We were powering through our second glass of water in the kitchen when Reggie walked in, fresh from one of his club gigs.

"Why are y'all up so early?" he half whispered, closing the door behind him. I just glared at him, by way of responding. "Oh, snap! You haven't slept, yet. *Ha!*"

Luke rubbed his hands over his eyes and croaked out a greeting. "Good morning, Reggie. And good night. Thanks again for the bed. I'll see you upstairs, babe." He turned and gave me a half-hearted kiss on the cheek and stumbled towards the spiral staircase in the living room.

Reggie leaned back on the counter and had a good laugh. "You trying to kill him on his first day?" he asked.

"Trust me, I had very little to do with it," I said. "He's doing fine on his own. We just need to sleep it off a bit and then we're up and at 'em, again."

"All good. All good. Listen, I don't have a gig on Thursday night. How about we meet up for dinner?"

"You're on," I answered.

"Are y'all up to anything fun tonight?"

"I was thinking that Luke should get a taste of the real gay New York. Drinks, go-go boys. That whole thing."

"His first New York gay bar?" said Reggie, smiling. "Look out, Chelsea, here comes Luke."

"That's what she said." I made the gesture of "dropping the mic" and Reggie just shook his head and grinned. We had a big day ahead of us, but first I needed to join my guy and get some rest.

■ ■ ■

A few hours of sleep (and a couple of highly sugared sports drinks later) and we were as energized as we were going to get. We headed down the block to the subway station and took the train downtown to do some shopping. We hit Union Square, Broadway and SoHo. In Chinatown I was lucky to stumble upon a hidden storefront that housed a pretty decent array of designer knock-offs. New faux leather tote bag for Barry? Check!

We picked up new running shoes and a few clothes, but overall Luke was just happy to experience what he called "the real New York," through my eyes. He was in full tourist mode, his wide eyes staring up at every building, noting every foreign language he heard and dragging me into every corner deli and tourist shop to find the perfect postcards to send to his dad and Rosa. He wanted to eat a street pretzel, visit the Statue of Liberty and go to the top of the Empire State Building. There was Radio City Music Hall, Rockefeller Center, the World Trade Center Memorial and Central Park. It was impossible to accomplish everything in one day, but we did our best and hoped to see the rest during the coming week. We definitely should have planned a longer trip.

After a long afternoon of sightseeing and shopping we carried our loot up the six flights of stairs and deposited our bags on the floor of Reggie's living room. Exhausted, Luke plopped down on the couch and put his feet up on the coffee table. He held his hands out, gesturing for me to come join him and cuddle.

"In a second, babe," I said. "I just need to wash my hands."

"The first thing you do when you walk in the door is wash your hands. Did you know that?"

"I'm always washing my hands. It's a New York thing. We touch subways and taxis and homeless people."

"You touched a homeless person? I must have missed that."

"Sure," I said. "Everyone needs love."

"I like being touched." He smiled at me, tired but *oh*, so handsome.

"You *are* touched," I laughed. "Come on. Let's go take a disco nap."

"This town is exhausting," he said, taking my hand and getting up slower than usual.

"Just you wait, Coach. Just you wait."

■ ■ ■

Most of my favorite dive bars closed after I left the city. Since I wasn't one for flashing lights and disco balls, I preferred the grunge of the East Village. But this trip was for Luke, so I wanted to make an exception and show him an extra special good time. I used to be a regular at a dive bar that had recently been purchased by the boyfriend of a very well known news anchor. It used to be a fairly run-down mess, full of slumming NYU students, cheap drinks, and dirty bathroom stalls with no doors. But with the influx of the celebrity boyfriend's cash, I heard that miracles had happened.

The location was a turn-of-the-century fire station that had somehow escaped the eyes of the voracious developers this town was famous for, and had remained in the hands of a couple who wanted to see it returned to its former glory. A two-story structure, it originally housed sleeping quarters upstairs and a garage and office on the ground floor. Of course it had a fireman's pole that was left on site, centered on the back wall. What a perfect spot for a go-go boy you say? The new owners had the same idea and they paid a pretty penny, but they could afford it. They promised to renovate the space and turn it into the best gay bar on this side of town, and they did not disappoint.

The Hoze was *the* place to be, for gays, straights and in-betweens. Catering to the heteroflexible crowd was becoming much less of a marketing risk, and the Hoze promised to explore the needs of its clientele better, harder, and deeper than anyone else.

The line to get in was enormous, but we had access to a secret weapon. The black car dropped us off near the door and Luke and I walked up to the front near the velvet rope. There was one queue on the left for the bridge and tunnel crowd, and another on the right for the regulars. We stood in the center and I nodded my head to get the attention of the walking clipboard.

"We're guests of Reggie Rex," I said, confidently. It paid to be friends with one of the cities hottest DJs. Reggie's name was gold. One glance at the list confirmed our status and the rope was lifted. I held Luke's hand as we entered to the sounds of a pulsing beat and surveyed the space to get our bearings.

Most of the upper floor had been removed, leaving a balcony of sorts that overlooked the large dance floor, already full of grinding bodies of both sexes. A stage was added to the fireman's pole in the back, which was currently being treated to an aerial performance by a very nubile go-go boy, the likes of which I had never seen. *Tammy should come up here to learn a few tricks for Chesty Cheese*, I thought. To the left there was a series of curtains, backlit in a way so that we could see the shadows of the extremely muscular men and very voluptuous ladies who were writhing behind them to the beat of the music, some alone, some coupled, and some engaged in very interesting threesomes. There was a small bar upstairs for those who preferred watching from above, but the main bar was here on the ground floor, to the right.

"Wow," said Luke, clearly impressed.

"This isn't even the half-time show," I said. "Come on. Let's get a drink."

I pulled his hand and we pushed our way through the writhing crowd to the main bar. The hunky male bartenders were all shirtless and had on nothing but sparkly gold underwear that left very little to the imagination. On their heads they wore glittery gold, strap-on unicorn horns. Gilt letters were hand stenciled on their impressive abs, with an arrow pointing suggestively downwards and a hashtag that read #TasteTheGold.

"*Taste The Gold?*" I said, looking at the bartender. "What the hell is that?"

He sighed and rolled his eyes, as if I should already be cool enough to know this by now. "We're being sponsored tonight by Unicorn Gold Vodka. Buy one get one free if you re-tweet with the hashtag," he yelled over the music. He held up an opaque gilt bottle, shaped like a phallic unicorn horn pointing straight up. *Someone could get impaled on that*, I thought. Or maybe that was the idea?

"Give them two specials, on the house," said a voice to my left. "My treat." The bartender nodded and reached for fresh glasses.

I turned to tell the guy what I really thought of this horrible publicity stunt, but the sight of him stopped me dead in my tracks.

"It's brilliant, isn't?" he said, smiling directly at me. "It was all my idea. I'm *so* proud of it."

It was my ex-boyfriend.

■ ■ ■

"David," was all I could say. I didn't say it, so much, as the word just sort of tumbled from my mouth, like the last words of my dying breath.

"Hello, Derek," he said, smiling. "It's been *ages*. Are you here *alone*? Where's Bimmy, Timmy and Koo Koo?"

"Bammy, Tommy and Kit," I corrected him, unnecessarily. He was being an ass, right from the start. My stomach began to churn. "They're in Parkville. I'm here with Luke." I leaned back a bit, hoping the sight of my boyfriend would shoo my evil ex away. No such luck.

"Luke. Of course," he said, still smiling that frozen grin. He wasn't too happy to see us, that much I could tell. I had the feeling he was just sizing up the situation, deciding how and where he could inflict the most damage. He took the final sip of his gold hued vodka and set the glass down on the bar. The hunk behind the counter in the unicorn horn lay down three fresh drinks for us, puckered his lips in David's direction, and then moved over to service the next customer.

"David, I," I started, but I didn't really know where to go from there. It was inevitable that I would run into him here in the city. My nightmare had made sure of that. But even though my psyche had tried to warn me, I was still clinging to the hope that I could escape New York without a sighting. Too bad for me.

"Oh, Derek, you always *did* let me take over the room," he sighed. Like anyone ever had a choice? "Tell you what. I'll just jump in here, okay?" He leaned over me and thrust his right hand towards Luke. "Hi, Luke. I'm David. But you know that. We never really met, of course. You were in, then you were out and I was in, then I was out and you were back and I was gone. *Whew!* Confusing, right? As if this guy here can't make up his mind or something. *Ha!* Well, anyway. It's a pleasure to actually meet me, right? Congrats on the win and all. Go, team! I'd throw in some other sports analogies, but I don't really care."

Luke ignored the shade and turned to place his elbow on the bar to get a better view of the crowd. "You got this babe," he said to me, subtly. "I'll be on the dance floor, if you need me. Take him down." He gave me a passionate full-mouth kiss, grabbed his free Unicorn Gold and headed towards the fun.

I strengthened my back. "Oh, I can make up my mind, all right," I said, finding my voice. "I definitely chose the right guy. Speaking of losers, though, where's Marcos? Or is he off auditioning a new third wheel for your bed tonight?"

"Marcos? Marcos, who?" said David, cooing. "Oh, *that* Marcos. He and I had a fun run, but I booted him from the bed months ago. Let's see, first there was Sergio. Then Javier. Then the twins, Ricky and Rocky, and a few whose names weren't even important. There were so many, you know. I'm quite popular. Did you see that hot muscle twink on the pole?" He pointed towards the back of the room. "Of course you did. You can't miss him. No one can. That's Benji. He's *mine*. Well, mostly mine. I share him. *Ha!* He does things to me that you couldn't even imagine, even if you were watching a step-by-step porn tutorial. You were so *boring*, Derek. It was awful. I have no idea why I hung around so long. And to think, I even went *back* for you. *Ha!* I'm so glad I came to my senses. I mean, *look* at me. I can do so much better, right? You have to agree. I mean, you may have been completely wrong for me, but you *know* me. You know I'm right. You do. You *get* me. Unshackling myself from you was the best thing that ever happened. My ball and chain. *Ugh*. So happy I gave up on that idea. *Marriage*. What were we thinking? Are you kidding me? We fought for years to be gay, why on *Earth* do we want to be straight now? All that picket fence crap? A wedding! Kids? A happy little heteronormative life that the breeders can understand? What's with all this whitewashing? Who needs it? Where's our pride in who we really are? Seriously. The moment I realized you'd snowed me into all that nonsense, that was the moment I was free again. I *found* myself, Derek. Me. I found *me*, again. I'd been buried for years in all your pathetic little Southern drippings. Family life and ho-hum sweaters and grown men hiding in the closet with their secret ball gowns. *Ugh*. Here I am now, at the top of my game. My PR company has really taken off. Huge. I'm *huge*. I have so many clients that I have to turn people down. Can you believe it? Of course you can. Everybody knows how driven I am. They can just feel it when they meet me. I'm something special, you know? I was meant to do great things in this town, and finally I'm coming into my own. Unicorn Gold is just the tip of what I can do. And I'm doing it all by myself, without you or anybody else to screw it up for me. All you pathetic, needy gays. When are you going to realize that your fake relationships are doomed?"

My eyes were locked onto his. I had zero plans to walk away with my tail between my legs.

"Nice speech," I said, my jaw clenching. "Did you practice that in the mirror every morning until it felt like you meant it? I may have been the actor in our relationship, but you were always the one who needed that extra hype to really believe in yourself. Something tells me you've just been waiting to run into me. I mean, I'm flattered and all, but you shouldn't have. Since you brought it up, though, let me give you my two cents, Mr. PR Genius. I'll tell you who's doomed. Assholes like you who don't believe in improving this crazy city, or caring for other people, or actually falling in love. It has nothing to do with being straight or gay or adhering to 'society's norms' or any of that other anti-marriage crap you're spouting. The David you've become isn't the David I once knew. And you say that's better, but I have to disagree. Because you were once a real person, or at least I thought you were. But somewhere along the way you became a caricature of a parody of an 'angry gay man,' turning against his own community. You're a follower, not a leader, David. In fact, I feel sorry for you. You say you've found the *real* you? I think you still don't know who you are. Now, if you'll excuse me, I'm going to join my boyfriend. He's not afraid of who he really is."

"Oh, you mean he's a slut, right?" David was fuming, his face a bright pink. "Because from what I can see, you just traded in one for another."

I turned to see what the hell nonsense he was talking about.

I scanned the crowd, but it wasn't hard to spot Luke at all. He was dancing in the middle of the floor, hands raised high in the air. He'd taken his shirt off and he was surrounded by men of all ages, sizes and ethnicities: young, older, muscled, short, tall, Latino, Asian, Middle Eastern, and garden variety white. Every guy in the place wanted a piece of my boyfriend, and boy, he was putting on a show. I pushed through the crowd and charged forward without looking back. It took a lot of elbowing and maneuvering to make it to the center of the ring, but I was on a mission.

"Luke?!" I yelled over the music. "What the fuck?"

"Derek!" he screamed back, a look of pure joy on his face. He held his empty glass up. "This tastes like gold! Haha! *I love it.* Get me another, will you?"

Before I could say anything, some random guy had shoved a fresh glittery cocktail into his hand. He swallowed it down in one gulp and tossed the glass back. Another quickly took its place and it was down and out in seconds, as well. *Oh, God, Luke. What are you doing?* I thought.

"I love this stuff!" he yelled, again. "I love *you*, Derek! Come dance with me, babe!" He reached over and grabbed my face and kissed me passionately, his hands circling around to travel down my back, then around to the front and straight down into my jeans.

"*Whoa*, there, babe!" I said, stopping his hand. He began to fumble for my zipper, and I reached down to try and stop him. "Luke! Stop! What's gotten into you?"

"I'm free, babe! I'm free! It's beautiful. You're so beautiful! Everything is so beautiful!" He was writhing and twirling, hands reaching out from every direction, touching him, caressing him, sliding their fingers across his sweaty body. The lights were flashing and the music was pumping and I was starting to freak out.

"This is amazing! I want to live here. Can we live here? Please? I want to live here!" He reached over and put both his hands on my waist, lifting me high above the cheering crowd.

"Luke! What the… put me down! We need to get you some water. You're drunk."

"Water! Yes! Water. Great idea!" He began to place me back down, but he was gone before my feet even touched the floor. The crowd parted as he made a beeline for the stage in the back of the house. "Move over twinkie," he said to Benji. He flipped his shoes off, reached down, unbuttoned his pants and was down to his boxer briefs in record time. I was trying to get to him, but there was no way, now. He had the attention of the pulsing crowd and I couldn't get through. He reached for the fire hose on the back wall and placed it between his legs, pointing towards his hundreds of admirers.

"Who wants a taste of me?" he screamed to the crowd. They roared back their approval, men and women alike. He toyed with the nozzle on the end, suggestively. There's no way the new owners would have actually left the fire hose active, right? Wrong. No one expected the pummeling spray of water, of course, and the intensity was fierce and instantaneous. The crowd's approval quickly turned to anger and fear. Two security guards dressed in black appeared from nowhere, stormed the stage and threw themselves on my boyfriend's body, taking him down in one swift tackle. In what felt like seconds they subdued him with plastic zip ties and dragged him from the platform, through the crowd, and out through the front doors.

I was helpless watching them, screaming for them to stop. They were hurting him, but they didn't care. I looked over at the bar and saw David staring at me, smiling an evil grin. He waved a tiny plastic bag in his fingers, then turned and disappeared into the crowd.

That piece of shit. He had drugged my man.

6

THE MAGIC IN THE MIRROR

I realized afterwards that I had been so busy arguing with David that I had ignored the free drink the bartender had placed in front of me. I didn't drink mine, but Luke hadn't been so lucky. My nightmare had come true, in a way, but making sure he avoided arrest was an even bigger nightmare.

I ran out to the curb to find two hulking security guards lording over Luke, his hands zip tied behind him, his shirtless body splayed on the sidewalk. They were trying to calm him down, but it was obvious he was on drugs. Well, drugged. But they couldn't have known it wasn't his choice. I reasoned with them and invoked Reggie's name more than a few times. They agreed not to call the cops, but we were definitely not welcome back to the Hoze any time soon. Not a problem. I wanted to get us as far away from here as possible.

I picked up a few bottles of water at the corner deli and made him drink them quickly. Thankfully he wasn't so bad that we had to go to the hospital. I then convinced a cab to speed us back to Reggie's place so I could get him into bed to sleep it off. The driver helped me get Luke up all six flights of stairs, and I gave him a hefty tip. Luke was passed out most of the night, but he woke up the next morning with sore wrists and an even worse headache. He had so many questions. He didn't remember much of anything after he left me standing at the bar. Whatever drug David had the bartender slip into our drinks had rocketed its way through Luke's system pretty fast. He always drank beer, not spirits, so that plus the crappy gold vodka did a real number on him.

"If I ever see that little shit again I'm gonna pound him into next week," he said, after I filled him in on the details of what really happened.

"I'm counting on it, babe. And after you're done with him, it's my turn."

I went down to the Jewish deli and bought him some matzah ball soup and a pastrami on rye. It wasn't Saul's, but it would do. He needed some comfort food to get his energy back. It took practically the whole day before he felt any better, but I was grateful he was improving. It could have been a lot worse.

We were a few days into our trip and I hadn't even tried to find my Uncle Barry's old friend, Chinois Zarée.

New York drag queens work their cabarets and shows all week long, and Sundays were a very popular night, so I knew I had a decent chance of finding her. If she was anywhere near as celebrated as Barry said, it shouldn't be hard. So far, my internet searches hadn't turned up anything at all, though. I was surprised. Maybe she went by another name, now?

Luke and I stayed in bed and had our takeout food while watching some trashy reality TV up in the greenhouse. I had cancelled our Sunday brunch plans with Reggie, so he had taken off to meet some friends of his own. The sun was just beginning to set over the Manhattan skyline as Luke and I stepped outside onto the roof and huddled together to take in the view.

"I'm glad you're feeling better," I said, my arm around him. "But I'm so sorry. I really am."

"Babe, it's not your fault your ex is a psychopath. I've taken worse hits on the field. I'll be fine. I just need a quiet night."

"I hate to leave you here all alone, but if I'm going to find that friend of Barry's, I really need to get going on that. Are you sure it's okay that I take off for a few hours?" I asked.

"As Reggie would say, 'All good, all good.' Do me a favor, though?"

"What's that?"

"Just avoid any of that shitty gold vodka, okay?"

■ ■ ■

I pulled out my phone and booked a car down to Chelsea. I couldn't deal with the subway or a yellow cab today. Last night was tough enough, and I didn't have the energy to force my way through the hordes of tourists. The driver dropped me off at 23rd Street and Sixth Avenue, and I started wandering around the neighborhood, reminiscing. Seeing so many familiar restaurants and shops sparked memories in me that I had long forgotten, but the plethora of new boutiques and places to eat reminded me that I was now a tourist in the city that I had once called my home. They say you could eat breakfast, lunch and dinner in a different place in Manhattan every single day of your life and never eat at the same place twice. Businesses were always opening and closing, living and dying. New York was a city of constant change, and if you didn't run along with the crowd you could get left behind in a heartbeat.

It was only a little after ten at night as I stepped into the first gay bar that I ran across. There weren't that many people out yet, but I asked around about Chinois, and nobody had heard of her. I reached peak discouragement after four bars and no luck. Maybe I was aiming for too young a clientele and I should hit some of the older, more established bars in the West Village? I walked over to Seventh Avenue and hoofed it down to the corner of Christopher Street at Sheridan Square, home of the famous Stonewall riots that started it all in 1969.

I stepped into the Stonewall Inn and immediately felt the sense of history. The bar was still rather quiet, as if the crowd hadn't moved on to this place, yet. There were a few older men seated at the bar and a couple in the back, but it seemed like I was out of luck tonight. I figured I might as well have a cocktail, right?

"Could I get a vodka and soda, please?" The bartender nodded and placed my drink on a bar coaster in front of me. "Thanks. Hey, I was wondering if you could help me out?" I asked. "I'm trying to locate a friend for my uncle. She's an Asian drag queen called Chinois Zarée. My uncle says she's super popular, but I can't seem to find anyone who's heard of her."

"Sorry, pal. Maybe you should try some of the karaoke bars?"

He was disinterested and moved on down the bar. Discouraged, I decided to enjoy the drink and plan my next move.

"Hey, buddy." The voice came from the end of the bar. He was an older gentleman, around my uncle's age, not particularly well dressed, but he wasn't down on his luck either. He blended so well into the bar that I actually didn't see him when I had entered. "You say you're looking for Chinois? I know her. At least I did, back in my younger days. She was pretty popular. Not so much, anymore. That older style of drag went out years ago. These young ones want to look like real women now. Not my thing, if you ask me. I kind of miss the spectacle."

"You know where I could find her?" I perked up. "I promised my uncle I'd say hello."

"Last I heard she was at Suki Su's. Run-down place between Chinatown and the East River. She runs some kinda bingo game on Sundays. Sorta low-key. Older folks, not a late crowd. If you hurry, you can probably make it."

"Thank you so much, sir! Next drink is on me!" I slapped a twenty on the bar and ran out the door.

■ ■ ■

Suki Su's had definitely seen better days. I'd never even heard of it, but the flickering red neon sign was easy to spot as I stepped out of the taxi at the corner. A light summer rain had begun to fall, but this neighborhood was so deserted that there was no one but me running on the sidewalk to escape the drizzle. I reached the glass front door of Suki's and pulled the metal handle, quickly glancing at the laminated menu that was taped to the window from the inside. The unflattering images of pupu platters and fried rice looked as if they had been fading in the sun for decades. Most of the menu prices were amended with small orange stickers and handwritten numbers in an imprecise scrawl.

I stepped inside, wiped the raindrops from my face and ran my fingers over my hair to shake the wet chill. There was a circular red vinyl banquette in the window with large stripes of peeling grey duct tape zigzagging along the back. The booth was empty, so I walked over and slid in. A few people were seated at the scattered tables in the room, as well as two older men seated at the counter eating soup, but for the most part the place was definitely not hopping. Unless you counted the spectacle taking place at the front of the room.

"O, sixty-nine. O, sixty-nine," she teased, her lips too close to the microphone. "Why, I haven't heard anything that exciting since Tuesday night when the Chan twins came over. Each other. Not me, unfortunately." I heard the imaginary rimshot in my head, but the room remained silent as a few sets of hands at scattered tables dutifully scanned their bingo cards.

That had to be her, Chinois Zarée. The drag queen was standing next to a small folding card table with a bingo machine and a flashboard set up in the back corner, near the entrance to the toilet. Microphone in her left hand, right hand ready to pull another number, she was every inch the over-the-top Asian cliché. She was wearing an enormous black geisha wig decorated with a half dozen yellow plastic chopsticks and Chinese lanterns, glowing with what appeared to be battery powered tea lights. Her face was powdered to the whitest degree possible, with thin, red vertical lips, circular rosy cheeks and matte black painted-on eyebrows, arched as high as the heavens. She wore a tight red satin dress embroidered with golden dragons, and the slit on the side came all the way up to her thigh, one long fishnet-covered leg escaping the void. To complete the look, I spotted fish tank heels. I'd only heard about those in stories of old, but here they were in real life: plastic stripper heels with a massive see-through platform filled with water and fake goldfish. At least, I hoped they were fake.

"I, twenty-one! I, twenty-one!" She called out the next number. "I swear that's what he said, officer. I don't know if he was telling the truth, and girl, I could care less. I stopped asking for ID years ago. At my age, if I can hook 'em, I take 'em, know what I mean, Miss Thang? Sorry. *Mrs. Chang?*" The woman seated at the front table looked up from her noodles, puzzled. She may be bombing, but she was going to get through this her way.

"Don't let me take you away from sucking those noodles down, Mrs. Chang. From the looks of your technique, I'd say Mr. Chang's a lucky man." I chuckled to myself as she spun for another numbered ball. "B, twelve! B, twelve! I take my vitamins orally, of course. Every chance I can."

"Bingo!" An older lady along the sidewall raised her hand and waved at Chinois.

"Well, congratulations, Mrs. Chow. For your prize, I won't tell my next joke. Bring that card up here and let's get you verified." She stepped over and they huddled over the card. A few moments later she announced, "We have a winner, comrades." The few people in the restaurant who were actually playing clapped their hands, Chinois handed her a cardboard Chinese takeaway box, and she sat back down at her table.

"Thanks for coming out tonight, lovelies," she said, as she surveyed her lackluster crowd. "I'm your host Chinois Zarée, and I'm here every Sunday night, just like that funny itch that doesn't seem to go away no matter how much cream you put on it. Don't forget to tip your waitress more than a penny. That coin has been out for a few decades longer than me. Sayonara!"

She switched the microphone off and walked slowly over to the counter. "I'll have a saké, Suki, and don't be stingy." Now was my chance, so I slid from the bench and stepped up quickly beside her.

"Excuse me, Chinois? I loved your show and I just wanted to say hi. I'm Derek. My uncle sent me here to say hello to you, actually. Barry Henry? Maybe you remember him?"

If she had been a tall man she would have towered over me in that wig and those platform heels, but Chinois was definitely shorter in stature, hunched over the bar top, drink held firmly in her hand. As she was, we saw eye to eye.

"Barry Henry," she said slowly, recognizing the name. "Holy shit. Are you trying to give me flashbacks? I haven't heard that name in years. What's Barry up to these days?"

"Well, I think that's why he wanted me to look you up, actually. You probably don't know it, but you were really an inspiration to him. He'll always be my Uncle Barry, but he's better known as Beret, now. Here, I have some pictures." I pulled out my phone and scrolled through some photos, and she smiled softly.

"Well, I'll be," she said. "I knew she had it in her. Barry and I had some fun times back then. She's okay?" She looked at me with concern. By "okay," I knew what she meant, and my heart broke just a little.

"Yeah, she's doing well," I said. "All negative. She could stand to lose a few pounds and cut down on the drinking, but overall she's good."

"Cut down on the drinking?" she said with a shocked look on her face. "What kind of a sadist are you?"

"You sound like my uncle."

"Good to know some things haven't changed," she said, and threw back the rest of her drink. "Derek was it? Come on back to my dressing room and we can chat while I get out of this get-up. These heels aren't as comfortable as they look. Grab us some fresh ones?" She turned and walked away towards the back of the room, leaving me to get the next round.

"A vodka and soda, please, and whatever Chinos is drinking. Thank you."

The bartender made my cocktail and then handed me a small bottle of chilled saké and a cup. I paid the tab and went in search of Chinois, drinks in tow. The restaurant was so small that it didn't take me long to realize her "dressing room" was actually the men's bathroom. The door was slightly ajar and I pushed it the rest of the way with my hip. She was seated on the toilet, lid closed, in a black silk bathrobe and red marabou slippers. There was no mirror above the sink, so she had propped a small one with a pink plastic frame on the toilet paper holder. The roll was unwinding in her hand as she used cold cream to remove the heavy makeup from her face.

"Welcome to Shangri-La, pull up a golden throne," she said, not looking up as I entered. "Just set that drink on the sink."

I put the saké down beside her makeup kit. A plastic sandwich bag filled with bottles of prescription medications lay next to it. I spotted a metal fold up chair behind the door, so I brought that out and took a seat. Her makeup was almost gone and I could finally see the face behind the mask.

"Wow, you're not…"

"Chinese? No. I have the short part down, but the eyes, not so much. Thank God for eyeliner and the art of shadowing."

"I feel so stupid," I said, laughing to myself. "Barry didn't tell me your real name, so I just assumed you were Asian."

"That's funny," she said, finishing her cleanse and turning to pour her drink. "No, we were much less politically correct in our day. They call it 'racial stereotyping' now, but if it was good enough for Mickey Rooney, it was good enough for me." Rooney's cartoonish portrayal of the Japanese neighbor in the film *Breakfast at Tiffany's* had cast a dark shadow on his career for years, but apparently Chinois had used it for inspiration. "The name's Charlie Zaretsky. Russian Jew, if you must know. But nobody's called me that in years."

I heard a calendar alarm and Chinois reached for her phone to shut it off. Her press-on nails were so long that she used her knuckle to slide across the screen. "Cocktail time!" She pulled the plastic baggie from the counter and fished out her pills, counting to herself from one to six as she placed them in her palm, finally downing them all with her drink.

"Is it okay to take those with alcohol?" I asked cautiously.

"Darling, if the HIV can't kill me, I doubt the saké can. Oh, don't make that concerned face. I get enough of that from my doctors. Listen, there's nothing to feel sorry about. I lived my life to the fullest and I had a great time. But I did stupid things before anyone knew they were stupid. Someone has to be ahead of the curve, right? The way I see it, I'm a trailblazer. And, my dear, I'm still here."

She was right. Someone had to be first, and Chinois had led the pack. She began to tell me tales of her crazy days and nights at the Hotel Chelsea. She had stories of discotheques and nightclubs, late night drag shows and pageants, drug-filled orgies and passionate trysts in dark rooms and alleys. Her fortunes had been high and her star had been on the rise, but as the years passed, the lights began to dim and her dreams faded along with them. Younger queens began replacing her on the circuit and her name recognition fell to an all-time low. Her current gig at Suki Su's was the best she could do, and it barely paid her bills.

"Listen, darling, promise me you won't tell Barry? It's better that he remembers me as he did. No reason to crush any more dreams than we have to." She reached in her bag on the floor and pulled out a glossy 8 x 10 black and white photo of herself and inscribed it with a black marker, *To Beret with love, Chinois*. She handed it to me and said, "We'll just leave it at that, okay?"

As I left, I couldn't help but feel a little sad. Barry had built up Chinois to an impossible standard to maintain, of course. I should have known better. We both should have. I held the picture tightly in my coat as I hailed a cab. Right now I just wanted to get back to Reggie's and count my blessings in the reassuring strength of Luke's arms.

■ ■ ■

The next few days found me playing the role of New York tour guide extraordinaire. We hit every monument from the Cloisters to the Statue of Liberty, and Luke was having the time of his life. We put the incident at the Hoze behind us, and his smile was infectious, even to the most jaded of New Yorkers. We woke up early Wednesday morning and jogged across Columbus Avenue and Central Park West to Central Park. We ran the track around the reservoir, spotted the Guggenheim on the East side, curved north, and finally made our way back around to the Upper West Side. We kept pace with each other, our competitive natures taking a break while we were on vacation, but not everything was running as smoothly as our jog. There was a strange sense of unease in the air, and I wasn't sure if it was just my classic overanalyzing, or if I had something more to worry about.

I made the decision before we left on this trip that I had had enough of the way we were treated at the school. We were both very stressed out from all the social upheaval over our relationship, and I had started to not so subtly pressure him to quit his job. But would I ever learn? The last time I pushed him to come out, he broke up with me. This time, I needed him to realize on his own that leaving Parkville High was in our best interest.

Sometimes I could be my own worst enemy. But now that our vacation week was coming to an end, I was getting antsy again. We hadn't even discussed taking over Lloyd's Catering at all. Nothing. And we had a meeting scheduled with Lloyd the day after our return. To make things worse, every time I looked over at him, it seemed like he was texting Fletch. It drove me crazy, and I'm not afraid to admit I was feeling a little hurt. Luke *never* texted me, yet here he was giggling like a school girl every few minutes, his head facing down, staring at his phone as we walked down Broadway. They had really bonded on this trip. Maybe too much?

It was our final day in the city, and Reggie was going to meet us for a farewell dinner that evening. We hadn't been able to spend nearly as much time with him as I would have liked, but I was grateful to pass a few hours with him. I hadn't stayed in touch with him as much as I should have after I left New York. I regretted that, but the world is constantly moving us all in different directions and it's up to us to keep the connections alive. I only had myself to blame.

"Hey, babe!" I called out to Luke in the shower. "Reggie is meeting us at the restaurant at eight so we have plenty of time. Want to take a slow walk there and take in some more sights?"

"That'd be great," he said, coming out of the bathroom, a towel wrapped around his waist, "but I just got a text from Fletch and he wants to meet up for a quick drink before I head to dinner. Is that cool?"

"Oh, yeah, sure. We can do that." Clearly I couldn't say no or I'd look like an ass, but I was looking forward to getting back home to Parkville and leaving Fletch right here in the city.

"Actually, babe, I was kind of hoping I could hang with Fletch alone? It's just...I'd like to hang with my buddy, you know? Kinda like you and Tommy. It's a guys' night kind of thing, like we used to have in college. We're just going to catch up on old stories and stuff and you'd probably just get bored. I'll catch you and Reggie at the restaurant, okay?"

"Um, yeah." Damn it. *Quit doing that thing with your face*, I thought to myself. *You're trying too hard to be "cool" with this. Just think before you open your mouth.* "Tell him it was nice meeting him and say good-bye for me."

They say honesty is the best policy, and I was definitely ready to say good-bye to Fletch Powell. For good.

7

THE SOUND OF SILENCE

Reggie and I met up at our favorite comfort food restaurant down in the West Village. It had changed a lot over the years since it had been "discovered" by a cooler crowd, but we were regulars from its not-as-popular past. As we walked up to the entrance we sailed by the long line of hipsters waiting in vain for a table and the hostess greeted us with a friendly smile of recognition. They didn't take reservations, but they always held a few tables for their favorites, and thankfully Reggie was still on that magical list of names. We climbed the stairs and they placed us at the best table in the corner, by the window. We ordered a round of drinks while we waited for Luke to arrive, and the catching up began.

"So, he's out with this Fletch guy?" asked Reggie.

"Yep," I said, not too happily. My mouth was tense and I had glanced at my phone way too many times in the last thirty minutes. "I sent him a text message, but he hasn't answered. He should be here soon, though. He's usually pretty punctual. I'm the one always running around trying to get out the door in time."

"Didn't you say he doesn't really do texts? Maybe you should call him."

"I tried. No answer. Maybe he's in the subway? I have no idea where he and Fletch met up. Is there a Hooter's on Manhattan?" I said, joking.

"Yeah, there is," said Reggie. "It's over near Penn Station."

"I'm not sure which scares me more," I said, staring at him. "The fact that you know that, or the fact that New York has changed so freakin' much since I left."

"Well, the concrete jungle is more of a suburban playground these days."

"You planning on staying?" I asked. We had both moved up here within months of each other, and I remembered eventually feeling the itch that it was time to move on. People told me it would take about five years to get to know the city, and then another five years to enjoy it. After that, there would be a risk of growing too hardened to live anywhere else.

"I've been bouncing ideas in my head," he said, "but I don't see myself happier anywhere else. New York has everything I need: great food, awesome nightlife and a steady stream of very hot women. That's pretty much heaven for me."

We laughed. I understood him. I knew that New York was my past and it had been time to move on when I left, but I never imagined I'd find what I needed in Parkville, Tennessee. Somehow, I did.

"You wanna give him another shout?" he asked, pulling me back to the present.

"I'm sure he'll get here soon. I just need to chill, right?"

"Are you asking me, or telling yourself that?"

Honestly, I wasn't sure. Both probably. It seemed that every time Luke and I got too close to perfection, something or someone stepped in to steer us off course. First, there was David, then Jett and the protests at the high school, and now Fletch. But I knew I had nothing to worry about. I definitely needed to relax.

"Let's order another round and get some appetizers," I answered. "He's a big boy. He'll be here when he gets here."

The second round of drinks was gone in no time, as were the appetizers. I excused myself to the bathroom and made another call to Luke, but it went unanswered, as before. Wherever he was, I hoped he was having fun and it was worth it, because I was getting really pissed off.

Reggie and I went ahead and ordered our meals and he filled me in on the many beautiful women he had dated since I left. None of them had hung around long enough to be a girlfriend, either through his own choice or hers, but he was having fun and enjoying life. His career was going so well that a producer wanted to send him out on a DJ club tour, but he turned him down. He was happy with his current level of success and didn't want it to go too far. "Man, if I had groupies I don't think I could get anything done," he said, by way of explanation. The waitress had just finished clearing our plates when we heard a loud male voice shout from the top of the stairs.

"There y'all are! *Let's get this party started!*" Fletch yelled across the room and pointed in our direction. The other patrons looked up, clearly disturbed that some obnoxious drunk had shown up to ruin their night. He had his arm around Luke, and it was obvious that they were wasted. Their party had already come and gone several times, by the look of it. They sloshed their way over to our corner and looked down at us. Fletch's left hand landed heavily on the edge of the table and I immediately wanted to apologize to Reggie, but I was so angry I couldn't even look his way. I was saving my evil eyes for Luke.

"*Ooooh*, Lukey, looks like the boyfriend's pissed," Fletch bellowed. "Am I right?" He made an exaggerated face, his right arm still snug around my boyfriend's shoulders. Luke was holding on so tight he was practically buried in Fletch's chest. I couldn't tell if that's where he wanted to be or if he just needed the support to stand up. Either way, he had a drunk, goofy grin plastered on his face.

"*Will you two sit down, please?*" I hissed through clenched teeth. "You're making a scene."

They made a big show of making those *oh, no, we're in trouble now* faces as they noisily pulled two chairs from the table and flopped down on the seats.

"See, I told you he wouldn't mind if I crashed your party!" Fletch said in a rowdy stage whisper. He called out to our waitress. "*Yo!* Darlin'! Can we get some drinks over here?"

"Haven't you two had enough?" I said, trying to keep my voice calm. But I was failing, badly. "I know I have." I was still angrily staring at Luke, but he had barely glanced at me since they arrived. He only had eyes for Fletch right now.

"Oh, we're just gettin' started!" said Fletch. "Lukey and I are on a roll." His right arm was hanging over Luke's shoulder and he reached down and gave my boyfriend's pec a clumsy double squeeze. "Muscle boy over here wants to have some fun on his last night. Ain't that right, buddy?" Luke just nodded, adoringly. So far he hadn't said a word, but it appeared he was having the best night ever.

"Maybe we should pay the bill and head somewhere else," said Reggie, trying to help me out. He threw a nod over to our waitress.

"Good idea," I said, grateful that I wasn't in this alone. "Come on, Luke. Let's get out of here."

"I see what you mean, number one," said Fletch, digging in. "He *does* like to tell you what to do." He flashed that million-dollar grin at me and it took everything I had to hold back. At this point I couldn't decide who I wanted to kill more; Fletch, for unduly influencing my boyfriend, or Luke, for being friends with this jerk in the first place.

The waitress walked over and said, "Here you go, Reggie. We'll see you another night, okay?" It was a pointed suggestion to pay the check and get out of there quickly.

"There you are, baby!" bellowed Fletch. "My buddy and I are gonna need a few beers and some whiskey. Y'all do pickleback shots here?"

"Sorry, guys," she said, clearly annoyed. "I think your night is over."

"Oh, I can go *all night*, baby!" said Fletch, turning to Luke and laughing. He put up his hand and they high fived.

"Thanks again, guys," she said, ignoring Fletch as she handed Reggie the credit card receipt and turned to leave.

"Aww, don't go, baby," said Fletch. "I shaved my balls just for you. My buddy Luke said everybody's doing it." With that, he stood up, unzipped his jeans, reached in and pulled them right out through the zipper. I was dumbfounded. This wasn't happening.

"*Whoa*," said Reggie. "Derek? Maybe we should..."

"Damn it, Fletch!" I said. "What the *fuck* are you thinking?"

"What's wrong? They're all smooth, now, just like you like 'em. See?" He tried to reach over the table for my hand, but I pulled back and he lost his balance, crashing down on top of Luke. The two of them ended up on a pile on the floor, Fetch's balls still hanging out for the world to see. I froze in disbelief, but Reggie was up in a flash, taking charge. He pulled Fletch up, and I quickly snapped out of it and followed suit with Luke. We hauled them past the gaggle of shocked diners, down the stairs and out into the street, the two frat boys laughing up a storm the entire way.

Reggie and I stood out on the corner, my hands over my face, not believing what had just happened. Fletch was lying on the sidewalk with Luke rolling on top of him, wrestling and laughing like two jocks in the locker room, high on life after a winning game.

"Derek, I'm sorry, man," said Reggie. "I had to get them out of there. Let's get a cab and pour these guys in."

"I'm the one who's sorry," I said. I was so angry I could spit nails. "Luke, get up *now*. We're going home."

"Aww, don't get your panties in a wad, there, sister," said Fletch. "Lukey's not ready to go home. Am I right, buddy?"

I stared furiously at Luke. Sure, he was drunk, but he'd better sober up fast and fix this. So far, he hadn't said a single word.

"Are you gonna let him talk to me like that?" I spat, fed up.

"Yeah," said Luke, finally speaking up. "I am. I'm having fun. What's your problem, buddy?"

"Buddy?" I repeated. "*Buddy?* You've *got* to be kidding me. Do you even *see* yourself? Do you know how much of an embarrassment you are right now? Up in that restaurant, in front of Reggie? We're going home. *Now.*"

"*Ooooh*, someone's in trouble," laughed Fletch, saying the words like a singsong schoolyard chant.

"Maybe I don't want to go home," said Luke, his face taking on a manic expression, eyes wide. "Maybe I'm having fun without you, and you can't handle that?" He put his arm around his buddy, staring me down as if to dare me to try and stop him. "Come on, Fletch. I need another drink. Someone's killed my buzz."

Fletch grinned and looked at me like he'd just won the top prize at the county fair. With his arm firmly on Luke's shoulder, they turned to stumble down the block, and I stood there not believing what had just happened.

"Should we follow them?" asked Reggie, clearly uncomfortable, but trying to help.

"No," I said, fuming. "Let him go. He made his choice."

■ ■ ■

Reggie and I took a cab together back up to the Upper West Side, but we barely spoke. I was shocked and embarrassed, and I'm sure Reggie really didn't know what to say, anyway. We walked slowly up the six flights of stairs, and he unlocked the door and turned on the kitchen light.

"You gonna be okay, man?" he asked.

"I don't know," I said, truthfully. "I really don't. That definitely wasn't the night I'd expected. I'm sorry you had to see all of that."

"All good, all good," he repeated, and he meant it. Reggie wasn't the type to bear a grudge or hold Luke's actions against me. "You want to talk about it?"

"No, thanks," I said, wearily. "We have an early flight, so I'm going to try and get some sleep. I arranged a car service for tomorrow morning. We'll try not to wake you.

Thanks, again, for letting us crash here. It was so great to see you." I meant it.

"Any time, my friend," he said. "I hope you can get some sleep." He reached over to hug me, and then gave me a few reassuring pats.

I walked over to the spiral staircase, headed up to the greenhouse and sat on the edge of the bed. I was seething, bewildered, close to tears. This didn't make any sense. It was clear to me that Luke was mesmerized by this guy, this jerk who held so much sway over him, but had he meant what he said? Was I keeping him from having fun? I pulled back the covers and crawled into the sheets, knowing there was no way I would be able to sleep. The bed felt so empty. It wasn't even midnight yet, and not knowing if Luke was safe or not was killing me. Even if I was angry with him, I still loved him. A few hours passed, and I drifted away ever so slightly before the heavy footsteps on the spiral staircase woke me from my light sleep. I had my back to the stairs as he sat down clumsily on the bed, removing his shoes and clothes. I didn't say hello. I didn't say a word, actually, and neither did he. My heart was racing with outrage and despair. This was a stupid fight and I was being stubborn, but I chose to stand my ground and remain cold. He pulled the sheet back and got into the bed, but positioned himself far from my touch, seemingly on purpose. There was no kiss, no spooning, no words of regret. Nothing. I feigned sleep, hoping that this night would just end, and we could start fresh in the morning. My eyes were shut, but I could hear him clumsily fumbling with something. The glow of his cell phone lit up the ceiling and I opened my eyes, ready to tell him to shut it down, that I needed to sleep. I sat up in bed and turned towards him, prepared to yell, but he didn't even see me.

He was too busy checking out guys on Huntr.

■ ■ ■

The alarm went off at seven the next morning, just a few short hours after he had come home. Our car would be downstairs in thirty minutes, and we would have just enough time to clean up. The silence continued, but now everything felt even worse. We were both being stubborn as we lumbered about the room, quietly packing and not saying a word to each other. He looked like he'd been run over by a truck and I could tell his head was pounding, but I offered no aspirin and no words of support. He dug this hole, and I wanted to see if he could dig himself out. But would he even try? We took the bags down the six flights of stairs, carried them outside and loaded them into the car, then rode in silence to the airport, me looking out my window, Luke looking out his. When the car stopped at the terminal and the driver popped the trunk, I grabbed both of my bags and walked into the airport, not waiting for him and not looking back. I was going too far, I could feel it. But I couldn't stop. It was like a game that I wanted to win, but even then I knew that if I won, I would lose.

We chose separate check-in lines. Everything here was do-it-yourself, just like the flight up. I chose my seat, realizing that there was a chance he wouldn't be seated next to me. I froze for a moment, but pressed the "finished" button anyway, then left my big suitcase at the baggage drop. I could feel him behind me, near me, somewhere within earshot, but we had both already gone too far to fix this, just now. It would have to wait until we got home.

He didn't wait at the same gate with me. When it came time to board, he was nowhere to be seen, and for several uncomfortable minutes I wasn't sure what he was planning to do. The air on the plane felt colder than usual and I was sick to my stomach. I tried to scan the aisles without looking too desperate, when I finally spotted him boarding the plane. He walked right by me, one of the last passengers to get on. The seat next to mine was empty, yet he chose to stare forward and march towards his place in the back. I tried to catch up on my sleep on the two and a half hour flight, but that was not going to happen. My mind was racing. I needed to say something, but I wasn't even sure how to start. When we landed back home in Parkville I disembarked first, and then headed towards baggage claim to pick up my suitcase. Luke shot past me in the terminal, pulling his wheeled carry-on behind him.

"Hey," I called out. He kept on walking. "*Hey!*"

"*What?*" he said, spitting the word out. He stopped, but didn't turn around.

"I have to get my suitcase," I testily reminded him. "Are you planning on waiting for me?"

He paused. "I'll be at the car," he said, his voice betraying no emotion. He continued on, still not turning.

Time seemed to stop at the luggage carousel. I waited for what felt like an eternity. I'm positive my suitcase was the last one to come flying from the chute, and I heaved it from the circular belt, and then wheeled it and my carry-on out towards his Jeep. He was already in the driver's seat, staring forward, and he made no move to help when I approached. The car was idling as I opened the back and placed my heavy bag inside, and then took my seat next to him. We drove home in silence, and the tension became unbearable. When we arrived at the house he stepped out of the car, unlocked the front door and headed straight towards the refrigerator to grab a beer. I stood there in the living room with my bags, watching him as he walked back into the room. I couldn't take it anymore.

"Oh, because getting drunk has worked out so well for you in the past few days?" I couldn't help myself.

He just stared at me, his nostrils flaring.

"Why are you even mad at me?" I asked, frustrated. "I'm the one who should be mad at *you*. I don't get it. *You're* the one who made a fool of himself in that restaurant. All that hanging on to Fletch? It was embarrassing. And it was disrespectful to *me*, especially in front of my friend. And then Huntr when you got home? Did you think I didn't see that? What were you thinking? What *are* you thinking? We have a business meeting with Lloyd Barton tomorrow, did you forget that? You can be as pissed off as you want to be at me, but we need to put on a unified face tomorrow if we're going to convince him to sell us his catering company."

He took another swig from his bottle and stared at me, coldly. "I *like* my job. I'm good at it. I don't want another one." He turned and walked down the hall towards the bedroom, then firmly shut the door.

So. That was that. It looked like I was going into business by myself.

■ ■ ■

"Good morning, Derek. Is Luke not joining us?"

Lloyd Barton looked like the proper Southern gentleman with his perfectly combed grey hair and seersucker suit. Seated on the terrace at his establishment, he was having a continental breakfast and reading the *Parkville Post*. Simply called Lloyd's, the white building with imposing Grecian columns sat stately on a side street in downtown Parkville near the business district. Before finally settling into its current incarnation as an event space and wedding site, the building had a storied history as a manor house, a nightclub, and even a house of worship. Through the years the facade was repainted white too many times to count, and the interior remained much the same as it did from its last incarnation as a church, with a few decadent additions. The entryway was small and led to an expansive main floor, with a long, dark oak bar placed to the right. Ornate gold mirrors covered the walls and a small proscenium stage stood at the back of the room. The focal point was the high curved ceiling, painted blue with white fluffy clouds floating above the balcony that looked down on the black and white tiled floor. The room exited towards the back right, into the library with its high wooden bookcases and fabric lined walls, just before leading out to an urban garden filled with moss-covered statuary and rose bushes. The city had grown up around it, however this terrace felt like a private sanctuary with the beat of the workers surrounding it, humming on the outside but never threatening to encroach its tranquil beauty.

"There's been a slight change of plans, Mr. Barton," I answered, a serious but friendly look on my face.

"Oh, please, call me Lloyd. Your uncle is practically *family*, after all."

"Thank you, sir." I took a breath and steeled my gaze. "As it turns out, Luke isn't ready to leave coaching, after all. He's going to stay on at Parkville High. But I'm ready to take on this challenge. It's not like I'll be alone, of course. You know I have ties to the *community*." I paused, extra emphasis on that word, community. Lloyd was old school Southern, and gay life wasn't discussed in the open. I continued. "With my uncle's connections, and the Walcott's, of course, you know that I'm in a position to ensure that the standards which you have set will be upheld. I worked in my fair share of restaurants and bars in New York, and I definitely know my way around a kitchen. I haven't managed a staff before, but I'm sure I can learn. I'd like to take this on, Lloyd. I'm ready."

He looked at me quietly, a crooked half-smile on his face. He then removed the folded newspaper from his lap, placed it on the table, reached for his coffee cup and took a long sip. He was making me wait, and enjoying every second of it.

"So, Luke's *out*, eh?" he said, finally. The play on words was smart, but subtle. "Well, I don't see that as a problem, Derek. That ole high school would never forgive me if I stole their winning coach, now would they?" He smiled broadly and I felt relieved. "I *do* have one request, though, and it's a deal-breaker."

"What's that?" I asked, nervously.

"I'd like to keep my name," he said. "It *is* mine, after all. You can have my client list, of course, and all my business connections, but you're going to have to build a new reputation all on your own. No more Lloyd's. How do you feel about that?"

"That's a deal I can live with, sir."

He smiled again. "So, 'Derek's Catering' it is, then?"

"No, sir," I said, resolutely. "I actually had something else in mind."

I had decided to call it the Duke.

8

LIKE A BEACON SHINING BRIGHT

I felt like I was truly home the moment I stepped into the Firelight. "The Man I Love" by Billie Holiday was barely audible over the sounds of a cue ball finding its mark on the scruffy pool table in the back room, but the lyrics quickly found their way into my ears and stung my heart. My friends were camped out in our favorite booth, as if we could never belong anywhere else quite like we did here. Kit was the first to spot me and her back shot straight up as she waved her hand high in the air and flashed a bright smile. Oh, Kit! I missed you.

"Baby!" she squealed. "Get over here and give us some love! *We. Missed. You!"*

Kit, Tommy, Bammy and Michael stood up as I approached the table and we all hugged as if we hadn't seen in each other in months, but the truth was, Luke and I were only in New York for a little over a week. It did seem like an eternity though.

"Where's Luke?" asked Bammy, right out of the gate.

"He decided to stay home tonight," I said, not lying. But my face betrayed my feelings, as usual. She looked to Michael for an answer, but he didn't even react. Well, good to know Luke hadn't called his half-brother to offload. Yet.

"Okay..." Bammy said slowly. We'd get to that later, I knew. She was just giving me a moment to prepare my forthcoming lame excuse.

"What about Meredith?" I asked Tommy, eager to change the subject.

"Yeah, she wanted to be here to welcome you back, but she's in North Carolina this weekend," he said, beer in hand. "There's an artist who works with glass over in Asheville she wanted to check out, and this was his only free time. She's trying to represent him."

"Oh, cool. How are things going at the gallery?" I asked Kit. I was so proud of her. The business she shared with Tommy's girlfriend Meredith was quickly becoming the epicenter of downtown culture.

"*So. Good!*" she said, smiling. "Your dad's sculptures sell before we can even get 'em in the door. Johnny has this huge following, and we have people calling us every day to get in line for something new from him. His prices just keep climbing higher and higher. *We. Love. It!* We're getting a real reputation now for being a quality art gallery. He's *great* for business."

"I'm so happy for you, Kit," I said, and I meant it. "But I get a cut, right?"

"Baby, for you? *Anything. You. Want.*"

"Well, what I want right now is a drink. Pass that pitcher over, Tommy."

"Are you feeling all right, man?" asked Tommy as he poured me a glass. "You do know that beer has carbs, right?"

"Trust me, a few beers aren't going to do much more harm than all those bagels I ate this week."

"*Tell. Us. Everything!*" said Kit. "What was it like being back? Did you want to stay? Please tell me you two aren't thinking of moving away from us."

"No, nothing like that," I said. But exactly what did happen, I wasn't ready to elaborate just yet. Bammy was keeping quiet, so far, but that spark of recognition was just dying to travel from her mind to her lips, and I had to stop her quickly before I told them everything. "We had a great time, really, but I think we just exhausted ourselves. We were triple booked every day with meeting friends, going to restaurants, sightseeing, clubs."

"Oh, I bet Luke *loved* that!" said Kit. "I've imagined a dream trip to New York so many times. I'm sure he was all over the place, wasn't he?"

"Uh, you could say that," I said, my voice starting to betray the very real feelings I was keeping bottled inside. Shit. I hadn't planned on doing this.

"Derek, honey?" It was Bammy, and she was looking right at me. "Spill."

"What?" I feigned. Would she let me get out of this? Please, Bammy?

"Do *not* play this game with me, my friend," she started, before I could even begin. "I have known you too long and you can't hide anything from me. Somethin's just not right here. Where's Luke? And tell us the truth."

"He's at home," I said, a bit too forcefully. "He was just tired. Honestly, it's nothing, really." I had to stop this before it escalated. How about a change of subject? "This song *sucks*, right? Who played it? Let's go fill the juke-box with quarters and reclaim the atmosphere. Come on, Bammy."

I started to get up, but no one else followed suit.

"Bammy?" I said again, trying to nudge her into action, but she didn't move. She was staring at me with both eyes focused intently upon me. She took a sip from her glass, placed it methodically in front of her, and then folded her fingers on the table, like the principal that she was. She meant business, and everyone else had ceded the floor to her and her alone.

"Derek, honey," she said slowly, as if talking to a child, "I love you. I do. You now that and everybody here knows that. Hell, even Michael knows it, and he sleeps with me every night. You're pretty much closer to me than my own family. But honey, you are the *worst* liar I know, and even worse at keeping secrets. That face betrays everything, my friend, and we all know how this is gonna play out. You're gonna grab my hand and walk me all ladylike over to the jukebox, we'll put on some Patsy Cline and you'll pull me into a tight two-step and we'll dance lightly over a few lame conversation starters before we get to the real meat and potatoes part of the problem. Finally, you'll spill your guts, I'll give you my advice, you'll tell me how much you value my friendship, but you'll vow me to secrecy and we'll waltz over here like nothing much happened. Then, one by one, we'll all find out whatever you didn't want us to find out. Michael will talk to Luke, then he'll feel weird about talking to me. You and Tommy will grab a drink and you'll get all talky-talky, like you always do. Kit will overhear something that Meredith shouldn't have said, and before you know it or planned it or meant for it to happen, we'll all be up in each other's business, like we always are, like we're meant to be. We're not just friends, Derek, we're your family. So, instead of all that tiptoeing, secret room bullshit, let's just cut to the chase, waddya say?" She reached for her drink again. "Now, like I said...*spill*."

Damn it, Bammy.

"Well, shit," I said, my chest deflating. I was defeated, and I hadn't even started. So much for my subterfuge. There was definitely no way out of this one. I slunk back into the booth and looked down at the table. I couldn't even face them. She was right. I took a deep breath and waited for something to happen, but I knew that it was up to me. This was my problem, and I *did* need my friends, so I gave in to the momentum.

"Before we start, we're gonna need some vodka," I sighed.

"That's my boy," said Kit, and she reached out to hold my hand.

■ ■ ■

It wasn't as hard as I thought it would be, and Bammy was right. I needed to get this off my chest. My Scooby Gang was my family, and anything I wanted to tell her I could share with all of them, at once. Even Michael. I recounted the whole story, from meeting up with Reggie, to that strange night in the hot tub at Fletch and Brandee's place, to the horrible throwdown with David at the Hoze. I told them how he had drugged Luke, how we had barely escaped being arrested, and that it had actually brought us closer together. Or, so I had thought. Because I wasn't expecting Fletch to land on the scene as hard as he had, and I certainly wasn't expecting him to keep coming back for more, or for Luke to get so caught up in his past, again.

"It's like he has this magnetic hold on Luke," I said, my hand cradling my glass. I emptied the last drops of vodka into my mouth and Kit quickly poured more from the bottle. The Firelight doesn't have bottle service, but somehow she had convinced the bartender that it was a *drinkmergency*, so he set us up with a bucket of ice, orange juice, cranberry juice, limes, the works. I skipped all the bells and whistles, though, and just sipped it straight.

"I mean, I can understand it, in a way. He's Fletch Powell, for God's sake. He's fucking *every*thing. Handsome, charming, built like a truck. I get it, you know? But I just thought Luke was stronger than that. I thought *we* were stronger than that. I really thought he loved me."

"Baby, Luke *does* love you," said Kit, holding my hand tight again and shaking her head. "We can *all* see that. So just get that idea out of your head, now, okay?"

"She's right, man," said Tommy, leaning in. "That guy would move mountains for you. Hell, he already has."

"Derek, you're more of a Walcott than I am, and I'm his half-brother," said Michael, speaking up. "Red parted the seas for you and made way. That's something you can't deny."

I looked up to the ceiling and exhaled. "Damn it, Bammy. I didn't want to do this tonight." How many times was too many times to cry in front of your friends?

"Well, too frickin' bad, my friend," she said, "but we've already started, so let's figure this out."

"Maybe it was just a wild hair, you know?" asked Kit. "Like, Luke is a different person now, but seeing Fletch made him revert or something? Fletch was his hero, after all. Maybe he just needed to get him out of his system, once and for all? I don't know. All that male bonding stuff just mystifies me. I'm so grateful Shawn has his band as a hormonal outlet."

"It's more than that," I answered. "It wasn't just seeing his hero, it was seeing his hero and not being afraid of himself, anymore. He's free, now. He's out. It was like two friends who finally decided to date after years of ignoring an obvious mutual attraction. The energy was intense. And it wasn't like I was *kind* of left out, I was *completely* left out. I just wasn't even there. Luke didn't even see me anymore."

My circle grew quiet. No one had any real answers. We would just have to wait and see what would happen next.

"I'll talk to him," said Michael, finally. Bammy had her arm intertwined with his. "Maybe I can get some insight that you can't."

"Thanks, Michael," I said. "I'd appreciate that. Because I'm at a loss. We pretty much came back to town in silence. He didn't sit with me on the plane, he didn't wait with me at baggage claim. I'm almost certain he would have driven home alone if one of you had been there to pick me up instead."

"Well, he can't lock you out forever," Bammy reasoned. "Sooner or later you're gonna have to talk this out. School starts in six weeks, and we just can't handle anymore drama this year."

"Uh, yeah... about that," I started. *Shit*. I hadn't told her about Lloyd's yet. "When it rains, it pours, right y'all?"

"Derek Walter, don't you dare," she said. Her eyes widened and she dropped her shaking head into her hands, and then looked up once more. "Again?"

"I'm sorry, Bammy," I winced. "I love you, I do. But... Parkville High. It's just not for me, anymore. Especially after all that chaos this spring. Jett, the CCCP, Mayor Bellman. Honestly, the thought of facing all that again. It's too much. I need to be able to be myself, without worrying about every word I say, every action, every glance towards my boyfriend. I'm not even allowed to hold his hand, anymore!"

"Well, if y'all keep fighting, maybe that will solve it-self?" she said, smirking, and I had to laugh at the thought of it. "Just trying to keep it real, you know?"

"What about *Love All*?" asked Kit. "We won!"

"I know we won, Kit, but in a way, we lost, too. So much was brought up in that fight, that I just can't suppress it all again. I can't *not* be me. I did that for too long as a teen, and I refuse to do it anymore." I turned to Bammy. "I can send you my formal resignation in the mail tomorrow. You'll have to find a new theatre teacher. I'm really, really sorry. I am." It wasn't a lie. I had had a great time teaching the students, but the drama of the last year had just been too much for me.

"And Luke, too?" she asked. "Gay or not, that Booster Club will have my ass if my winning football coach quits. What am I gonna do? Oh, Lord." She held onto Michael even tighter.

"Not so fast there, Principal Talbot," I said. "You're keeping your coach. We were supposed to leave together, as a team, but that's all changed since New York."

"*Whoa*," said Tommy. "You're leaving out something here. What were you two planning to do?"

"You *promised* me you weren't going to move back to New York!" Kit said, clearly unhappy.

"No, no, no. Slow down," I said. "It's good. I promise. I need y'all on board with this. I'll need customers, after all."

"Customers?" asked Kit.

"I was planning on telling you tonight, but we got sidetracked with the whole Luke thing. So here's the deal. Y'all know Lloyd's Catering, right?" They nodded, but I could tell by their faces that they didn't see where this could go. "Well, Lloyd's business is still going strong, but he could use a boost of younger energy to bring in some new clients and upgrade his offerings. That old building of his has seen better days, and frankly, I think it could be used more, for events, parties, weddings, music, you name it."

"You're partnering with Lloyd?" asked Tommy.

"Nope. Even better. We're buying him out. Well, I am. It's just me now. Luke and I were planning on running it together, but it's not something he sees himself doing. He's a football coach, and I get that. That's what he loves, and he's great at it. I wanted a new challenge, and this presented itself. It just felt right."

"*I. Love. It!*" said Kit, and she threw her arms around me. "Baby, you throw the best parties ever! This will be amazing!"

"You're keeping the name, I assume?" asked Michael, ever the businessman. "Lloyd has a pretty deep roster of clients, I imagine. You can't rock the boat too much."

"Well, you're right there," I answered. "I have to keep his older clients happy, but I hope to change a few things to inspire a new group of clients to come on board. I hope I can count on you for some advice?"

"Absolutely," he nodded.

"Because I'm going to need everyone's help to make the Duke a success."

"Oh, *Duke*!" said Bammy and Kit, together. They remembered our pet name for me and Luke, of course.

"Derek, honey, I'm so glad we met up here tonight," said Bammy. "Maybe you told us more than you wanted to, but I have a feeling this will all work out. Here's to friends." She raised her glass and we downed one more shot.

"To friends!" we shouted, together.

■ ■ ■

We switched gears and took the spotlight off me for a change. Bammy and Michael had taken a trip to New Orleans while Luke and I were in New York City, so they caught us up on their adventures there. They had rented a house in the Garden District, and Bammy loved it, of course. They rode the streetcar down St. Charles to the French Quarter, drank café au lait and ate beignets at Café du Monde, and perused the art galleries around Jackson Square. She couldn't stop talking about the piano bar at Pat O'Brien's and the muffuletta sandwiches at Central Grocery. They enjoyed their time in New Orleans so much that Michael was considering buying an investment property there. His financial situation was considerably better than before, now that he was working solely for his biological father, Red. They were both secure in their relationship, too, and it showed. I wasn't jealous. They both deserved it. I just wished that Luke and I could get back on track.

Tommy had a few more weeks of construction scheduled at Uncle Barry's place. The extended terrace with the barbecue pit and hot tub were coming along well. I didn't tell them about my pre-New York nightmare, but it was all still fresh in my mind. I could already picture Barry's place before Tommy filled in all the details. According to Tommy, Barry was a hoot to work for and he was keeping all of the construction guys on their toes. I could only imagine.

It took about an hour before everyone sobered up enough to be able to drive home. Tommy offered to give me a lift, but I felt fine. We all kissed and hugged in the parking lot before we headed to our separate cars. I unlocked the door to Willie Nelson and climbed inside my beat up old ride. I decided to take a late night drive down the familiar back roads of my youth, before I headed on home to Luke's. These were the same roads that he had driven on that first fateful night when we met at the Firelight, just over a year ago. So much had happened since then and I wanted to take some quiet time to decompress. To be fair, I wanted to enjoy this chosen silence before returning to the unwelcome silence of an argument. I drove Willie down by the lake where Luke and I had run so many times together and parked by the swing set on the big grassy hill that looked down towards the water. The night was calm and eerily quiet. I sat on the hood of my car and watched the fireflies dance in the nighttime sky.

"Time to get going, Derek," I said out loud to myself, breaking the silence. I couldn't avoid him forever, and I didn't want to. Maybe if I just crawled into bed next to him he would wrap his arms around me and everything would be okay again? Why did I even care about Fletch? He wasn't a part of our lives at all. So Luke had a crush. None of that really mattered, right? He still loved me. Of that I was certain.

Go home, Derek. You want to fix this, I thought.

Or did I?

9

COME AND KNOCK ON OUR DOOR

I pulled Willie into the driveway and silenced the engine with an anxious flick of my wrist.

My heart pounded as I walked towards the door. Our door. Bammy was right. I wore all of my emotions on my face, so there was no sense in hiding from the fight that was about to ensue. But did it *have* to be a fight? Sometimes things happen that are out of our control, but other times the result occurs from our own poorly chosen words or actions. Who's to say I couldn't choose better words and kinder actions?

I immediately heard Ella playing from the stereo as I opened the door. We had begun to pick up the odd piece of used vinyl here and there at thrift stores around town, and we had amassed enough records to warrant bringing over my dad's old hi-fi. It was an enormous piece of furniture that took up most of the wall facing the couch, but it looked oddly at home with the flat screen TV hanging on the wall above it. We both had a soft spot for '80s music so we mostly stuck to that theme, but I had recently turned him on to the jazz greats, Ella Fitzgerald and Louis Armstrong.

The familiar pops and scratches of the record wormed their way into my soul, and I knew he was playing this just for me. Suddenly the storm in my head stayed on the other side of the door as I closed it gently behind me.

"Luke?" I called out.

"Back here, babe," he answered.

I walked through the kitchen and pushed the screen door open and out onto the old wooden deck. He was seated in a sturdy chair under the porch light, a few empty beer bottles on the table, but not so many that I needed to be worried again. He had laid out a plate with fresh cut vegetables and hummus.

"I figured you'd be snacky when you got back," he said, by way of explanation. "Peace offering?"

"So, I guess we're not breaking up, huh?" I smiled, meagerly.

"Not just yet. There's still hope, though," he teased, raising an eyebrow as he lifted the beer to his mouth to take another sip.

"Well, if I stick with you, at least I won't die alone. Somebody will be there to call the authorities." I pulled up a chair, sat beside him, and then began picking at the snacks in front of us.

"Not if I'm the one who did it," he deadpanned.

My jaw dropped. "You wouldn't!"

"Get over here." He nodded his head in such a way that made me melt a little on the inside. I got up from my chair and dropped myself in his lap for a kiss.

"*Oof,*" he said, bouncing me. "Someone ate a few too many carbs in New York."

"*Hey!* Not fair! I'm not the one who rediscovered his love for pizza."

"Well, we'll get back on our routine tomorrow. How about a run at the lake in the morning, and then a workout here at the house, after?"

"Your workouts are *so* not fun," I said. "You know I hate burpees more than my 7th grade math teacher."

"That's not the kind of work out I was referring to, champ."

We were going to be just fine.

■ ■ ■

I woke up the next morning to find Luke had already left the bed and jumped in the shower. I'm usually the one who wakes up first, but I guess my drinks from the night before had a greater effect than I had intended.

I dragged myself to the doorframe of the bathroom and called out a sluggish greeting. "Good morning," I said, clearing the sleep from my eyes.

"Morning!" He sounded so chipper.

"Seriously? Are you that excited to go running? Why don't you come back to bed? God gave you two hands and a mouth for a reason."

"There's time enough for that later, babe. Besides, I always get horny with all that extra testosterone pulsing through me after a run."

There was no fighting this one. "I liked you better when you were touching my penis," I mumbled.

"What's that?"

"I said, *I'd like myself better after refilling my caffeine*," and I turned to leave.

"Make it quick," he said, sticking his head out from the curtain. "I want to get out to the lake before all the kids start using the running path."

I was sitting at the kitchen table enjoying my second cup of coffee and reading the *Parkville Post* when Luke appeared in his running gear, all set to go.

"I'm glad we talked last night, babe," he said, as he leaned over and kissed my cheek. He was still wet from the shower and he smelled soapy.

"Me, too. I guess we didn't solve everything, but we'll figure it out, right?"

"That we will," he assured me. "Anything in the paper?"

"Old Hester Fay called the police on her husband last night. Seems they had a fight over the TV channel. They made the front page."

"See? Things could be a lot worse. At least we haven't made the *Post*. Again. Come on, let's get a move on. Get in the shower so we can go."

I thought I heard voices as I was soaping up, but I figured it was just my imagination. Then I realized I wasn't making it up. Who was Luke talking to? I turned off the shower, wrapped a towel around my wet waist and walked down the hall to the living room, leaving a trail of liquid footprints.

"Derek, buddy, am I glad to see you!"

Fletch jumped up from the couch and grabbed me in a bear hug. The towel that I had been gingerly holding with my fingers dropped to the floor as I tried to catch my breath. I looked over Fletch's shoulder to see Luke sitting on the couch, holding up his hands and making that *hang on a minute, don't get mad at me* face.

"Fletch, I can't breathe," I gasped, feeling awkward as my naked body pressed up against his massive frame.

"Sorry, buddy." He released me and I hastily reached down to snatch my towel, modestly covering up once more.

"What's going on?" I asked. Luke was silent.

"It's Brandee," said Fletch. "She left me, for good this time."

■ ■ ■

I never imagined I would see a man like Fletcher Powell cry. Even stranger, I never imagined I would enjoy it.

He looked despondent, lost, like a little boy who had just seen his new puppy get mowed down by a passing truck.

"I didn't know where else to go. I had to come see my number one. What am I gonna do?" he cried.

"Tell us what happened, Fletch," Luke said, his arm around his idol.

And just like that, the tears were gone.

"I was out with my boys the other night, like I normally do on Fridays and Saturdays. Sometimes we start on Wednesday or Thursday. Every now and then it's Tuesday. But we always take it easy on Sunday. A man needs a break, know what I mean?"

No wonder Brandee self-medicated. Fletch kept the party going non-stop.

"Like I said, I had my boys over. It's usually me and like three or four guys. Maybe six, at most. But like no more than ten, you know? It was Sunday, so we were just taking it easy, chillin'. We were grilling steaks out on the terrace, watching the game on the big screen. Some hot tubbing, some weed, a little music. Nothing major. Guy stuff, you know? Brandee had been out earlier with some of her gal pals having brunch, like always. Them ladies love brunch, I tell ya. Well she came home with her arms full of shopping bags, threw 'em all on the floor in the foyer, then went off to her bedroom to sleep it off. I didn't figure anything of it. Well I guess we went a little later than we normally do for a Sunday, but hell, I didn't know it was after four in the morning. What am I supposed to do, keep looking at my watch when I'm having fun? Am I right?" He held his arms out for approval.

I zeroed in on Luke, still sitting on the couch, nodding sympathetically. Were we supposed to agree with this?

Why was he reacting like that? Or rather, why wasn't he reacting like I wanted him to?

"Next thing I know," Fletch continued, "Brandee comes straight outta her bedroom like a crazy woman. Like Medusa. Remember that story we read in high school English? Well, I didn't read it, but you wrote me a paper on it and I read most of that. Anyway, she was all like snakes in her hair and shit, screaming bloody murder 'bout how I don't respect her and how she needs her beauty sleep and how this isn't the life she wanted and she always dreamed of having a baby and shit. And I'm like, a *baby*? I'm having too much fun to have a baby, know what I mean? Then she starts screaming at my guys, tellin' 'em to put their clothes back on and get the hell outta her place. *Her* place? Who does she think paid for that place?"

This was getting good, but I was still standing there dripping wet in my towel. Dear Lord, please tell me this ends with Brandee on a jet to fetch Fletch?

"I mean, I eventually had to put my beer down to try and calm her ass, you know?" he said, laughing.

Crap. There was zero chance that she would chase this man to Parkville.

"Well, next thing I know she stomps off to my bedroom and starts throwing my things into a suitcase. At least she didn't throw them off the terrace like last time. That cost me a fortune. I was lucky that taxi just crashed into a pole and not a tourist, am I right? I didn't want to inconvenience my boys, I mean it was bad enough she broke up our party, so I decided to check into a hotel, you know?

Just let her burn off whatever crazy she had cooking. But I don't think she's comin' 'round this time. She actually went to the lawyer. *My* lawyer! She served me divorce papers and everything. That damn guy tracked me down in the steam room at the hotel spa. Can you believe that?"

"No, Fletch, I could never imagine you naked in a room full of hot, sweaty men." *Shit. Did I say that out loud?*

Luke shot me daggers. "Derek, you think you could leave me and Fletch alone for a bit?" he said through clenched teeth. "I think he just needs the comforting shoulder of a friend, okay?"

"Yeah, thanks buddy," said Fletch, holding tighter to Luke. "I just need my number one."

"Sure, no problem," I said, and turned slowly. "I was getting ready to go for a run anyway. Been looking forward to that. Real excited." My voice trailed off as I walked back towards our bedroom. I didn't know what the hell Luke was planning, but I hoped that Fletch would be gone by the time I came back. If not, we'd be looking at a world of trouble.

■ ■ ■

I changed into my shorts, put on my running shoes and walked back into the living room to say good-bye. Luke and Fletch had already moved on to the back porch, so I just quietly left through the front door. I drove Willie Nelson down to the lake and parked by the swings, where I had first left that mean note on Luke's truck, before I knew it was him of course. I didn't feel like running, literally or figuratively, so I let my instincts guide me. I opened my phone and dialed.

"Hey, Mom. It's me, Derek."

"Hi sweetie! Where are you? Are you boys back?"

"I'm in Willie Nelson," I said.

"Well, that doesn't sound good no matter how you phrase it, but I understand."

"Sorry, I guess that sounded creepy. What I mean is, I'm down by the lake. I was going to go for a run but I don't really feel like it anymore."

"Is Luke with you? How was New York?"

"No, he's at home," I said, but didn't offer any more. My mom was smart, though. She could read volumes in the silence.

"Anything you want to tell me, sweetie?"

"No."

She paused. "All right, then, how about if I talk?"

"Perfect."

"You'll be happy to know I'm driving your dad crazy with all my knick-knacks. This place wasn't very organized to begin with, but it's in an even greater sense of disarray now."

"At least it's colorful chaos, right?" I had to laugh, imagining Mom's things taking over the farmhouse where Dad grew up.

"Oh, definitely!" she giggled. "But when I can see that he's had enough, I just ship him off to that yoga studio you took him to. I think he likes the attention."

"Yeah, Peaches and the Chesty Cheese girls have taken a liking to him," I said. "They say they can see my future in his face."

"What do you think's in your future, honey?" She was digging, and not so subtly.

Now it was my turn to pause. I inhaled deeply and then asked, "Mom, do you think I'm happier when I'm unhappy?"

"Well, isn't that the $64,000 question?"

"Dated reference, Mom."

She didn't waste a beat. "You know exactly what I'm getting at. You've always been like this. You think and think and think yourself into a deep, dark place, but you never give yourself a break. You know, your dad and I are very different people, but I can appreciate that he gives himself the chance to breathe every now and then. We'd both be better off if we could follow his example."

I smiled softly. "I'm going for that run, Mom. Time to clear my head."

"You do that. Dinner next week? Barry's coming, too. He's chomping at the bit to tell us about the renovations at the house."

"We'll be there. I love you, Mom."

"You, too, sweetie. You, too."

■ ■ ■

Luke's Jeep was gone when I made it back to the house, so I figured he and Fletch went off somewhere to have a few hundred beers. Even better, maybe Luke drove him to the airport to catch the next flight back to New York?

It was quiet when I opened the door, but as I took my shoes off I heard moaning coming from down the hallway. Not sad moaning, like you hear when someone is crying. It was more like…sex noises. What the *hell*?

I stormed down the hall towards our bedroom, ready to pull Luke off Fletch and tell him I'd had enough of this bullshit, when I passed the guest room on the right. Fletch was sprawled out on the bed, covers pushed to the side. His clothes and underwear were in a pile on the floor, and he was pleasuring himself to a threesome on the TV screen.

"*Oh, my god!*" I yelled, wide-eyed.

"Oh, *shit.*" Fletch looked up at me and made that all-too-familiar face. It was too late for him to turn back, but I still had the chance to turn *my* back and hightail it out of there as I heard him gasp and cry out his final wails of pleasure.

This wasn't happening. Holy *fuck*. I ran back into the living room and sat on the couch, my head in my hands. I couldn't unsee what I had just seen.

I heard Fletch walking down the hallway, and could only imagine he was as embarrassed as I was.

"Dude! That was awesome!" he exclaimed.

I looked up. Fletch was standing in front of me, naked, his fist pumping the air in triumph. "I just couldn't get there, you know? I'd been tryin' for like twenty minutes, but then you walked in and *BAM!* That was all I needed, know what I mean?"

"Are you *kidding* me right now?" Of course he wasn't embarrassed. He loved it.

"Hell, no! Thanks for helping a brother out, man. Reminds me of good times, you know?"

"I can't believe this is happening." I buried my face in my hands again.

"Believe it, man!" he said, oblivious. "Luke went out to get us some steaks and more beer. Told me to make myself at home, so I did. Y'all got a great Wi-Fi connection here, by the way. I just needed to burn off some heat, you know? I was so close and I needed my number one, but he wasn't here for me, man, so I appreciate you steppin' up. That was awesome!"

"This isn't real," I said, looking at him once again.

"Oh, it's real, all right." He pointed a finger gun at me, then said, "I think you just made yourself my number two, Derek."

He then turned to walk down the hallway, his naked football ass bouncing the whole way.

10

THE DUKE

Fletch didn't leave.

To quote Chinois Zarée, he was like that funny itch that didn't seem to go away, no matter how much cream I put on it. As I found out that first night, Fletch didn't believe in clothes. Or closed doors. Or shower curtains. Or "private time." No telephone call was too personal, no bathroom moment was too indelicate to share, and no joke was too inappropriate for mixed company.

"Hey, Lukey," he said, one night over a massive meal that Luke had meticulously prepared on his own and presented to his idol like a hero's feast. "What's the difference between a joke and two dicks?"

"I don't know, Fletch. What?" he answered eagerly.

"Your mama can't take a joke," bellowed Fletch.

I froze, my wine glass at my lips. Did he just insult the memory of Luke's saint of a mother, Posy Walcott? Why, yes, he did. And they laughed and slapped their hands on the table like there was nothing funnier in the world.

I learned more about Fletch that week than I ever cared to know. Fletch tanned in the nude in the back yard. Every day. He clipped his toenails at the kitchen table. His love of porn was so strong that even I had become immune to the sight of his manhood.

"If I never see that man's erection again it will be too soon," I said to Luke one night as we were getting into bed, the sounds of yet another threesome emanating from the TV screen down the hall.

"Keep your voice down. He'll hear you."

"Oh, dear Lord, *heaven forbid* I make Fletch feel uncomfortable," I sighed.

"He's lonely," countered Luke. "He misses Brandee."

"Are you kidding me?" I sat up in bed. "There's nothing about Brandee he misses *at all*. You've taken care of his every desire."

"Hey, he's my buddy. He *needs* me right now, and I'm gonna be there for him."

"Well, I think he needs you a little too much, if you ask me."

"It's a good thing I didn't ask you, then." And with that he turned his back to me, reached for the light by the bed and covered us in darkness, once again.

■ ■ ■

Luke had his hands full with Fletch, and I wanted to spend as much time as possible away from the house. As it turned out, taking over Lloyd's catering business was exactly what I needed to occupy myself.

Lloyd Barton wasn't meant to be a caterer. He came from old money so he didn't have to work. The way he told it, he just loved to throw parties and the business simply sprang up around him. The Walcotts and the Bartons both lay claim to being founding families of Parkville. Whereas the Walcotts created wealth through land deals, the Bartons found their livelihood in the world of hotels. They preferred, however, to call themselves "hoteliers," rather than say they were in the "service industry." That just smacked too much of a lower class with which they preferred not to be associated. As the years passed, the hotels were sold off, and the firstborn sons of the firstborn sons used their family money to create more and more money. That in itself was the only job they needed. Lloyd married well, as was expected. When he and his wife had no children, well, that was expected, too. No one was really sure what became of his beloved. No one I knew could even recall her name. The story went that she just left one day on "a trip," and decided not to return. Some people have suggested that she's living out her golden years on a plantation in the Caribbean. Others believed she finally found a man who would love her for herself, and not for her bank account. If you listened to the darkest of whispers, however, you would have heard the story of a madwoman rocking away the sadness of an unfulfilled life in a distant sanitarium.

Regardless, whatever happened to Mrs. Barton didn't alter the course of Mr. Barton's life in Parkville one little bit.

Lloyd's Catering was the elite party and event planner in town. As Lloyd had no children, he was faced with two choices. He could let the business die with him, or gracefully step aside to allow a new generation to succeed where he had so artfully sown the field.

Lloyd and I spent my first week together at the Duke carefully going over the books, learning his trade secrets and meeting the core staff. I was grateful for his guidance, as I wanted to glean as much information as I could from him before he handed over the keys for good. He made it clear that this would be my business, not his, and after he left he would simply be a guest at events, and not running them. It was up to me to sink or swim, and I planned on going for the gold, with or without Luke's help. I had a lot of roles to cover: owner, manager, salesman, and the all-important public face of Duke Catering and Events. I was excited to get started.

There were only two kitchen workers on permanent staff and they had been with Lloyd for years. Thankfully they chose to stay on with me at the helm. The bartenders and cater waiters were mostly university students who worked shifts when they could around their class schedules. Lloyd had picked most of the men for their handsome looks, of course. The ladies were secondary, in his view. The roster was small, and the students would drop in and out during the year, depending on their course loads. I definitely needed to refill the ranks, and quickly, so I placed an advertisement on the bulletin board at the student union, as well as a few job sites online.

Lloyd's reputation was solid, and the applicants turned out *en masse*, as the perks of the job were well known. Not only did Lloyd pay well, but who wouldn't want to hobnob with the wealthiest citizens of Parkville every now and then, all the while copping a free drink or two (or three) from the bar?

I was surprised, though, when two former students paid me a visit that first week. I was sitting in my office upstairs on the second floor in what used to be a bedroom when the Duke was a residence.

"Hey there, Mr. Walter."

I looked up from my desk to see two shit eating grins staring down at me.

"Well, isn't this my lucky day?" I joked, pushing my laptop to the side.

Chip Carter reached out his hand to shake mine. Jett Winthrop, meanwhile, had already taken a seat in the leather club chair facing my desk, his left leg flung casually over the arm.

"To what do I owe the pleasure?" I asked. "Or did you boys come by to apologize for that mess you created this past spring?"

"Aw, shoot, D-man," said Jett. "That's all in the past, you know that."

I gave up. There truly was no winning with this kid.

"We just came on down to sign Chip up for one of those catering jobs. We figured he had an 'in' with you, since we're such good pals and all. Hell, I'd sign up too if I were eighteen. We're just lucky that Chip failed a few grades. Ain't that right, Chip?"

"It's true, Mr. Walter," said Chip, with as much earnestness as he could muster. "I'm trying out for the football team, of course, but I probably won't get much action this season. On the field, that is." He smirked at his own joke. "But I was hoping you'd let me pick up a few shifts here, when I can. I'm a good worker. Yeah, I ain't the smartest guy, but I can lift things, carry dishes, whatever you need. I'm a work horse."

"Besides being hung like one," said Jett, and they both broke up laughing. "But seriously, he ain't too hard to look at, neither, and from what we understand, that counts for a lot around here." He winked at me, still pushing the boundaries, as always, then adjusted himself so both feet were on the floor. "Listen, don't hold my bullshit against him, all right? Chip's a good guy. He won't do you wrong."

What was that old saying? Keep your friends close, but your enemies closer. Damn it.

"Don't make me regret this, Chip," I sighed. "Fill out this paperwork and hand it back to me on your way out. We'll organize a training session next week. And Jett?"

"Yes, sir?"

"I want to see you around here as little as possible, you got that?"

"Oh, you can count on that. I don't need a job, remember? Mom's third divorce left us sittin' pretty. I could use a drink, though. What kinda gin y'all got around here?"

"Get your asses outta here before I change my mind."

"Yes, sir!" in unison, and they were gone.

■ ■ ■

The Duke was in pretty good shape when I bought it, but I still asked Tommy to come by and check out the place. I didn't have any major changes in mind, but I did want to spruce up the walls with a fresh coat of paint, new curtains, and some landscaping around the patio. Most of his guys were busy with Uncle Barry's renovations at Mom's old house, but he recommended a few workers who were available to help us out. Lloyd had anticipated the sale so he had slowed down in accepting new clients. We had about a month with nothing booked before our grand debut. I was grateful for the time, even though I was still working my ass off. And like I said, it kept me away from the "Fletch and Luke Show."

The painters were in and out in a few days and they left the place looking picture perfect. Meredith and Kit came by with a cleaning crew to help me polish off the rooms one by one, hang the new curtains, and place the appropriate pieces here and there, on loan from Parkville's premiere art gallery, of course. We were on our way to making the Duke the best catering and event location in Parkville, and I couldn't be happier. Or could I?

I missed Luke of course. Not that we were apart, but Fletch had become a huge wedge between us. He was everywhere, all the time. We had no privacy and certainly no time for us. It was like we were living in the new frat house on UT campus, *Tappa Kegga Brew*. I was over it, but I was at a loss as to what to do.

■ ■ ■

"Well, I like what you've done with the place, I really do!"

Lloyd Barton walked through the front door of the Duke, nattily dressed in his trademark seersucker suit.

"Why, thank you, Lloyd," I said, smiling. "Retirement seems to agree with you."

"Oh, don't go saying such things," he said. "It's not as if I've been put out to pasture. I'm still active." He winked at me and gave me a knowing smile.

"Yes, I've heard," I replied. "But I don't talk." I sometimes wondered if there was anyone left in Parkville who wasn't in on these little secrets we all carried?

"Speaking of," he started, "I realized that I was remiss in not elaborating one very important detail in our business arrangement. It's alluded to in the contract, of course, but unless you knew what you were looking for, you'd have missed it. We do value our privacy, as you know."

"Go on," I said, intrigued.

"Oh, it's nothing to be worried about, you see, just a monthly gathering we like to call 'Secret Sundays.' It's not advertised, of course, but we have been faithfully lighting the torch on the last Sunday of every month for well over thirty years now. Why don't you fetch us a nice glass of iced tea and we can sit out on the terrace and go over the details."

And with that, he breezed by me and made his way out through the double glass doors in the library and took a seat in the private garden. I went into the kitchen, grabbed a pitcher of tea and took my place beside him, ready to hear more, knowing that nothing he could say would shock me. Parkville was full of secrets.

"May I be blunt?" he asked with a smile, as I poured the iced tea and placed it before him.

"Of course," I answered.

"As you well know, the Bears' Club is an established gentlemen's society here in our fair town, specifically created to fill a gap that needed to be filled. Occasionally we men need an outlet to share similar ideals with other men, who just happen to be dressed as ladies, of course. No matter, it's all in good fun. Heterosexual, homosexual, whatever you're calling it these days, all are welcome, and no one leaves unhappy, as long as our lips are sealed. We bond, hold our cabarets, drink our whiskeys and bet our wives' inheritances, with none the wiser. But eventually, a small group of men like us decided that we needed more. And by 'us,' I mean men like me, your Uncle Barry, and you, of course. The true homosexuals. That's where Secret Sundays come in. Whereas the Bears' Club admits any gentleman of any inclination, we are stricter with Secret Sundays. Oh, they may be married, they may be divorced or widowed or single, but as long as they admire the undeniable beauty and grace of the male form, they are welcome to our private gathering."

"So that's why you hired all the handsome college students. It wasn't just your personal taste, it was for the business."

"Precisely. Secret Sundays is a rather quiet affair. We start promptly at 6:15 pm on the last Sunday of every month. The night is over by 10:00 pm, and you won't need a large staff, just one bartender and one cocktail waiter. *Males* only, of course. I will suggest a few who can be discreet. We do have our favorites, after all. The members pay an entrance fee and the boys will be rewarded handsomely. Have the chef prepare something simple for the members to snack on. Meatballs, a cheese tray, anything you can heat up and take care of yourself. The smaller the staff, the better. Don't be shocked by the goings on, Derek. These men need to feel safe in this environment. There won't be anything too salacious, of course, but hiring the occasional go-go boy or male stripper will certainly be appreciated. Again, I will give you contacts for those."

"So let me get this straight," I said. "You don't have to be gay to be in the Bears' Club, but it's a prerequisite for Secret Sundays?"

"That's right. And your discretion was ensured when you signed the contract. Now, I'm off to play a round of golf at the country club with Red Walcott. Here's an envelope with those names I mentioned. *Oh!* And one more thing. You'll need to hire a driver for the evening to discretely transport those who wish to remain under the veil, so to say. I've placed his card in there as well. And with that, my boy, I bid you adieu. See you at Secret Sunday!"

I watched him get up and drift his way through the salon and out through the front door. The envelope in my hand was a stiff, high quality paper. I felt like I was holding the secrets to another world, and my heart raced a bit as I reached inside for the list of names. As I opened the flap, the driver's card fell out first.

His name was Tucker Matthews. Wait a minute. That name rang a bell. I pulled out my phone and dialed, not really sure what I was going to say.

"This is Tucker Matthews, how may I help you?" He sounded young, early twenties, and polite, with a nice Southern twang to his voice.

"Hi, Tucker, this is Derek Walter. I don't think we've met before. Or maybe we have? Your name rings a bell for some reason. Anyway, I just bought Lloyd's Catering and he suggested that I give you a call to discuss driving for some of our more, uh, discrete events. He said you'd understand?"

The phone was silent, but I could definitely hear him breathing.

"Hello?" I asked.

"Uh, yeah. Sorry. I mean, yes. Sure. I've driven for Lloyd before. Discretion is key in my business. It's a small town, so I rely on repeat service, and Lloyd has always been a great customer."

"Fantastic, good to know," I said. "Listen, I was wondering if we could meet up and discuss details? I'm on my way to a dinner tonight, but how about tomorrow?

■ ■ ■

"Luke? Babe?" I called out my boyfriend's name as I walked through the front door. I had gotten in the habit of announcing my presence, loudly, even if his car was missing out front. I was hoping that Fletch would take the hint and cover up or at least pretend to care that I was even there. A quick jaunt down the hallway and a peek out back proved that neither of them was actually home, which was rare, lately. They had been spending a lot of time horsing around in the living room, drinking beer on the porch, and watching TV and God knows what else together in the bedroom. I didn't want to think about it.

Even though it was nice to finally have the place to myself, I actually felt lonelier than I wanted to in my own home. We were supposed to go to Mom and Dad's for dinner tonight, so at least he wouldn't bring Fletch along for that, right? That's when I spotted the note on the fridge.

> *Derek,*
> *Went out with Fletch. Needed a change of pace to*
> *break the monotony.*
> *Home late.*
> *Luke*

Great. He forgot about my parents. And no more details than that. No info, no specifics, nothing. Just gone. And was I contributing to the monotony? I was pissed, but I wasn't going to give him the satisfaction of calling him and bitching him out on the phone. They expected that. I knew I was playing games, but honestly, this was getting out of hand.

I picked up the phone, anyway.

"Barry? It's Derek. You got a minute?"

"Sure, Dolly, what's up?"

"You're coming to Mom and Dad's tonight, right?" I asked.

"I'm picking out my special pearls right now."

"Funny. Listen, I was wondering if we could have a little private chat out back. I need some advice."

"Sure thing. Clothes or men?"

"Men. Well, one man, in particular."

"Trouble in paradise?"

"I don't think it's gotten to that yet, but we're definitely off course."

"I'm all ears, kid."

"Great. And another thing. Do you remember the name of that limo driver who drove Luke and me to prom?"

"I'm not sure. Why do you ask?"

"I think I just hired him. Or inherited him, at least. I'll explain later."

"All right, nephew. See you tonight, then. Cocktails at eight?"

"It's a date."

11

THE WALTERS

The farmhouse where Dad had grown up had been in his family for generations. When he and Mom were married they moved into their own home, and that's where I was raised. That home was sold after they divorced, and Mom and I moved into the A-frame that my Uncle Barry now called home. Dad came back to the farmhouse where his story began, but this time he had Mom in tow. And she was dead set on making her mark.

Farmhouses weren't built to accommodate modern social gatherings. Today people like to gather in the kitchen to socialize and then spill out into the living room when everything is ready. Few homes today even have formal dining rooms. Rooms were smaller back then, with multiple doors on this side and that side to hold in the heat. Lots of tiny rooms could feel like a maze with confined halls and doorways leading back to the kitchen, the heart of the home.

Like Barry, Dad had decided to initiate his own renovations when he moved back from California and took over his ancestral home. The small kitchen had now been expanded to include the living room, and he had added a nice, cozy screened-in porch behind that. There was nothing fancy or too modern in the changes, since Dad said he wanted to be true to the former space and not alter its *chi*. Mission accomplished. The one thing he did modernize, however, was the plumbing. On the ground floor he expanded the existing bathroom to include a shower, and upstairs he had taken over the second bedroom to create an expanded master suite with a walk-in closet and bathroom with a claw foot tub for Mom. He had been thinking ahead, I guess. There was still one guest bedroom down the hall and Dad used that as his office. Art is not just creativity, it's a business, and he had done well for himself.

I didn't bother ringing the bell or knocking on the front door. This wasn't the Walcott residence. I had prepared myself for chaos when I walked in the door, but honestly, it was nowhere near as bad as Mom had described. In fact, I thought her things fit in rather well. True, she didn't have a real sense of where to place anything, but her old, kitschy vibe felt at home with the antique walls of the farmhouse. She just needed a little guidance, that's all.

"Hi there, sweetie." Mom gave me a kiss as I entered and tossed my keys in the cigar box by the door. Nice to see that she had carried over some traditions from the old house.

"Your dad's in the kitchen making a vegetable curry," she said, as he waved at me from behind her head. "It's vegan, actually, with coconut milk. Honestly, I don't know what I'm talking about. We have food and I hope it's edible. How's that?"

"Sounds great," I said, laughing.

"No Luke?" She cocked her head.

"No Luke. Not tonight, at least. He had other plans." My mind told me to avoid eye contact, but my heart knew better than to try and deceive her. That would have been useless.

"Well, that's vague enough for me to realize I should just shut up and move on, now isn't it?"

"That's probably a good choice." I scrunched up my nose and nodded.

"All right then, you and I have plenty of work to do out here, anyway. Tell me, what am I gonna do with all these?" She pointed to a cardboard moving box filled to the top with dusty old Brownie cameras.

"Well, where are the teacups?" I asked.

"Over there." She pointed to a glass cabinet, already overflowing with china cups and saucers.

"And the cigar boxes?"

"Under there." They were stacked in rows beneath the coffee table.

"And the clocks?"

"Oh, honey, I haven't even started hanging those. I'm not sure we have enough wall space."

"Mom?"

"Yes, sweetie."

"I think it's time you started downsizing."

"I was afraid you'd say that. I guess I could store some things in the barn?"

"Don't you even *think* about it!" Dad bellowed, as he walked over from the stove, his white chef's apron splashed with happy yellow splotches of curry. "That's my art studio, not your storage space."

"Well you don't see me complaining about your heaps of twisted, rusted metal, do you?" she asked him.

"No, and I don't expect you to," he answered, thoughtfully. "Those heaps of rusted metal pay the bills."

"Well, there's that." She looked down at the box and frowned. "Honey, you're gonna have to show me how to eBay."

I exhaled. "Can I at least get a drink, first?"

A familiar voice chimed in from the screened-in porch. "I thought you'd never ask!" said Barry, standing at the doorframe. "Get on out here, kid. I have a pitcher waiting. Audrey, go pretend to help Johnny Ray in the kitchen. Derek and I need a little *me* time before dinner."

"Shouldn't that be *we* time, if we're both included?" I asked.

"Who said we were going to talk about *you*? Kids these days, I swear!" And he shut the porch door dramatically.

"You'd better go join him before he gets too pouty," Mom teased, giving in.

"Dinner will be ready in about thirty minutes," said Dad, and then headed back to his stove.

"We want to hear all about New York," Mom continued. "And I guess you'll leave out the stuff you don't want us to hear." She kissed me on the cheek then practically pranced after Dad, tugging on the strings of his apron. It was so weird seeing them in love again. Weird, but nice.

"I made vodka stingers," Barry said as I walked out onto the porch. "Would you like one?"

"How about three?" I asked, a bit dejectedly.

"What's new, pussycat? Spill! Spill!"

"Have you been saving that one?"

"Of course! Now, really. Tell me everything. Did you find Chinois? I've been dying from anticipation. Is the fabulous Ms. Zarée as fabulous as ever?"

I poured a very heavy vodka stinger and then filled him in on *most* of the story, but left out the fever dream that started it all. I wanted to tell him the truth about his idol, Chinois, but I had already decided that my uncle had had enough fractured fairytales in his life and he didn't need any more sad endings. Besides, Chinois had instructed me to gloss it up a bit, so I did. I told Barry that his friend was doing great, that she had moved around town a bit and had updated her act for her latest gig in an "Asian hotspot." It wasn't exactly a lie. They sold noodles, right? I said that she was really happy performing and that she remembered Barry. I left out the part about the HIV diagnosis. That

wasn't for me to divulge. But I told Barry that Chinois/
Charlie had given me an 8 x 10 signed glossy and her e-
mail address, so it was up to them to take it from here. He
was thrilled, in that way one feels when you've rediscovered an old friend.

I then moved on to cover the rest of our trip to New
York, running into David, meeting Fletch and Brandee,
that terrible scene in the restaurant when Fletch and Luke
showed up drunk, and now the fun of having this interloper in our house full time with no end in sight.

"Well, this is a no brainer," he said after a healthy pause
and an even healthier sip. "You have to get him out of
there. You have to make him think it's his idea, of course.
If you try to push him, he'll plant his feet and grow roots."

"He's not exactly the brightest porch light on the street,
if you know what I mean," I said.

"Even better. I assume he drinks?"

"He's drunk all the time."

"That's impressive."

"Totally," I said. "It's a real commitment."

"Well, then," Barry schemed, "you just have to get him
good and drunk and then make him realize he'd rather be
anywhere but here in Parkville."

"But what if I succeed," I asked, "and I'm still having
problems with Luke? What if I find a way to get rid of his
hyper-sexual best buddy, but he still feels like he's missing
something in his life that I can't provide?"

"Oh, Dolly, that's a tough one." Barry refreshed our
drinks from the pitcher, and then looked up towards the

moonlight cascading through the screens. "I know you love him. You do. But sometimes, just sometimes, the person we love… it's not that they *don't* love us, it's that they *can't*."

"But I don't like that answer. I'm not accepting that." I placed my drink on the table between us and put my face in my hands, then looked up at him again. "He loves me. I know he does. I'm like this puzzle that he keeps trying to figure out, moving the pieces around until they fit."

"Well, maybe that's it, kid. Sure, you're a puzzle, but maybe you're just not *his* puzzle."

I couldn't say any more. My heart hurt too much to beat properly. Barry put his hand on my knee and we waited in silence until Mom called us in.

■ ■ ■

Dad's vegetable curry was awesome. Mom couldn't serve an entirely healthy meal so we finished the evening with several helpings of banana pudding and store bought whipped cream. Even Dad had to admit it was good. He said he'd just have to make a few extra trips to yoga class and he gave me a knowing wink. I imagined that Peaches and the other Chesty Cheese girls were making him feel right at home.

We all helped to clear the table and then made our way to the door to kiss our good-byes. Mom pulled me to the side before pushing us out and whispered in my ear, "Remember, Derek, it's all about communication. That's the key." But in a town full of secrets, I wondered if that was even possible.

I didn't want to go home alone and sit in bed pretending not to wait for Luke, so I asked Barry, "Hey, how about I come over and we watch an old movie? In the mood for some Bette Davis? Joan?"

"You know I'd love to kid, any other time. But you're not the only one in this town with a social life. This gal has plans tonight. Raincheck?"

"Heading to the Bears' Club? If you have a performance tonight, I'd love to watch." I preferred anything to going home and sulking.

"Derek, I can't," he insisted. "I said I have plans. I have something I need to attend to."

Something, or someone?

■ ■ ■

"Hey, Tommy, what's up?" I called my best friend, hoping he was free.

"Not much," he answered. "Meredith's out with Kit and Bammy. It's Girls' Night. Kit and Shawn found a house they liked. They made an offer and it was accepted, so they're all out celebrating. I'm just crashed on the couch with some bourbon and the remote. You?"

Thank you, I thought. "I'm so happy for Kit! I'll give her a call in the morning. I was thinking I might be up for some night swimming, though. How's that sound?"

"I could do that," he said. "Meet you in the gravel lot at the lake in about thirty minutes?"

I hung up the phone and drove slowly away from the farmhouse. I had about 15 minutes to kill before I needed to head over to the park to meet Tommy, so I decided to swing by Parkville High and take a look. Classes hadn't started yet, so I didn't expect to see anyone there, but sure enough there were several cars parked by the football stadium. Underage students who had no place to go on a hot summer night would sometimes gather under the bright parking lights, toss a football and share a few drinks, creatively borrowed from their parents' liquor cabinets. We did the same thing when we were their age, and I wasn't there to put an end to their fun. It was just a nice trip down memory lane.

Tommy pulled into the parking lot at the lake at the same time I did and he swung his car in the spot next to mine. I had picked up a six pack at the convenience store, and as I held it up to show him he laughed and held up a six pack of his own. There were a few beach towels stashed in the trunk of my car, so I pulled those out and we headed on down towards the dock.

I was pretty sure we wouldn't be the only ones to have the great idea of night swimming, due to the heat, but I didn't expect to hear what sounded like a raging party. As we walked down the grassy hill the voices became clearer and my stomach began to sink with the recognition.

"*Cannonball!*" yelled Fletch as he swung as far out as possible on the rope swing, and then let go to land in the water with a thunderous splash. The dock was littered with bottles and country pop rock was blaring from a portable speaker. Considering there was so much noise traveling up the hill, I had imagined a huge crowd, so I was surprised to find there were only four people there. Luke was sitting shirtless with his legs dangling in the water, Amber Winthrop had her arms around a new guy I hadn't seen before, and Fletch was swimming his way back to the dock, laughing his head off after his thrilling jump.

"Did y'all see that? Was that great or what?" he asked, as he pulled himself up on the dock, the water dripping down his pecs. His wet boxer shorts left little to the imagination, but I'd already seen his junk so many times I could draw it from memory. I was grateful he had for once made an effort to cover up.

"Did you know they'd be here?" Tommy asked, as we quietly made our approach.

"Nope."

"Do you want to stay or go? I'll do whatever you want, man."

Too late. We'd been spotted.

"Well, lookee there, Lukey! Looks like we got us some stalkers! Just couldn't stay away from me, could ya, number two?" Fletch flashed his trademark killer grin my way. Luke looked up and his smile faded, then froze. It was so subtle that I was surely the only one to notice. Amber and her guy were too busy giggling the way that lovers do when they are in on a secret no one else knows. I couldn't believe

Luke was hanging out with her again. Honestly, Fletch was the *worst*.

"Hey, there, bud, I remember you." Fletch approached and reached out his hand to grab Tommy's. "What's your name, again?"

"Tommy."

"What?"

"Tommy."

"What's that?"

"*Tommy.*"

"Oh, yeah. I knew it was somethin'." He grinned at me and raised his eyebrows, then turned and reached down for another beer from the cooler on the dock. What an ass. I couldn't believe I ever thought this guy was golden.

Fletch turned back to his friends. "Hey, y'all got any food? I'm hungry."

"I got a Pink Lady in my purse," offered Amber.

"Ain't that a vibrator?"

"No! It's an apple!" They all laughed, but I wasn't in the mood to join in.

"Hey," I nodded to Luke, over the noise of the crowd.

"Hey," he nodded back, but nothing more. He was blowing me off, and not in a good way.

"I guess you forgot about dinner at Mom's, tonight?"

"Oh, yeah. Sorry. Can we talk about that later?"

Oh you bet we will, Luke. You can count on that, I thought.

"Hey guys, how are y'all doin'?" Amber stood up and walked over to us, pulling her new man behind her. "Have y'all met Todd? Todd Carmichael? He owns that fancy car dealership near the airport. You know the one, with all the Corvettes? He gave me a great deal on Jett's car." She practically cooed as she looked up at him adoringly.

I bet he gave you more than a great deal, Amber. Was he the reason for divorce number three?

"Hey there, guys," said Todd, as he shook our hands. He turned to Amber and said, "Are these the gay guys you were talkin' about? Amber said she knew a gay couple. Y'all are my first."

The idiocy just flourished around here, didn't it?

"Actually, no," I answered, flatly. "I'm gay, Tommy's not. I'm with Luke. *He's* my boyfriend."

"Really?" said Todd. "Well, shit, I coulda sworn he was with…" and his voice trailed off.

"It's cool," I said. "I can see how you'd get confused." I shot Luke a glance, but he didn't bother returning it.

"Enough chit chat," said Luke, standing up. "I'm up next. Grab my phone and make a video, will ya, Amber? You know the passcode." He ran back up the dock past me and Tommy, made his way to the big oak tree by the water, pulled in the rope swing and began preparing for his big move.

"You sure you want to stay?" asked Tommy, once again.

"No, I don't. I think I've seen enough."

We turned and walked back up the hill towards our cars in silence, our untouched six packs and dry towels in tow.

"So… the Firelight?" he asked when we reached the lot, smart enough to avoid the tricky stuff.

"I think I'm done for the night," I said as I leaned on my driver's side door. "I'm sorry to drag you out here with no payoff."

"Hey, at least I can pretend I got some exercise, man." He paused. "Listen, sorry if I'm overstepping here, but I have to ask. Why are you putting up with this shit?"

I shook my head softly. I wasn't even sure I understood, myself.

"It's complicated," I said. "I know that sucks as an answer, but it's true."

"Is it really?" he said. "Because the way I see it, there's nothing complicated about respecting yourself. And I think you're strong enough to realize that without me pointing it out."

I just looked at my friend with a sad expression. I had no words at that moment, so he filled in the silence.

"I love ya man, you know that," he said.

"I do, Tommy. Catch you later?"

"Count on it."

12

THIS FIRE INSIDE

When I got back to our place I decided that I didn't want to pretend to be asleep or act sullen or become an icy cold monster when he finally made it into our bed. Instead, I put on an old Billie Holiday album, poured a bourbon and waited.

Somewhere on side two, between "The Man I Love" and "Love Me or Leave Me," I heard his Jeep pull up in the driveway, and the headlights swept across the living room, rousing me from my self-imposed melancholic reverie on the couch. I'd finished my second bourbon long ago, and I felt a bit wobbly as I stood to carry my glass into the kitchen and fetch some water to bring me back to life. No sense in looking like I was obediently waiting at the door, right? *Oh, the games we play,* I thought.

"I tell you, Amber still has it," said Fletch as they walked in the door, loud enough for the neighbors to hear. Who cares if I was sleeping, which I wasn't? But, still. Damn it, Derek, don't get petty before you've even started. I walked around the corner and back into the living room to see them both sprawled out on the couch, playing on their phones. Did it even matter if I was here or not?

"Did y'all have fun?" I asked. I thought I'd try and be civil before the civil war began.

Luke looked up. "Hey. I thought you'd be sleeping by now."

"I figured we needed to talk, so I stayed up."

"*Ooooh,* Lukey's in trouble with the Mrs.!" said Fletch, laughing at his own joke and clapping his hands together.

"Shut up, Fletch," I said, finally standing up for myself. "I've about had it with your bullshit."

"Well, someone's fired up!" he said, mockingly.

"Derek, come on," said Luke, sternly playing the peacemaker. "That's not fair. Fletch is our guest."

"Oh, he's *your* guest, babe. Not mine. I'm pretty tired of his ass already."

"I've seen the way you look at me," Fletch said, smugly. "You don't mind looking at my ass, at all." He winked suggestively.

"Trust me, I do." My face grew redder as my frustration built. "I'm tired of your ass, your face, your jokes. I'm sick of the way you've been insinuating yourself into every aspect of my boyfriend's life. I'm tired of you trying to take away something from me that is clearly not yours. And for

God's sake, I am *so* tired of the threesomes I hear every morning, afternoon and night coming from the TV screen in that damn room you've camped out in!"

"Now you've crossed a line there, buddy. There ain't nothing wrong with a good threesome, am I right Lukey?" He jokingly ribbed his pal with his elbow, then added, "You and me know a thing or two about having a good time together, am I right?"

Luke grew red, but not the angry red like I had become. He was clearly embarrassed.

"What's that supposed to mean?" I asked, knowing full well that I actually didn't want to know.

"You haven't told him, Luke?" asked Fletch, all shocked and innocent. "Heck, I thought you two lovebirds would've shared everything by now."

"Luke, what's he saying? I swear, you'd better tell me before my imagination gets the better of me."

Luke didn't say a word.

"Oh, I don't think your imagination needs to be *too* active," said Fletch, grinning. "Not much different from that TV screen you were bitching about. Lukey and me used to have a damn good time with the co-eds. We were kings, after all. We were the golden boys! That was before he was gay, of course. But hell, I can't complain. It's not as if I cared too much when we crossed swords every now and then. And I did get me a few *damn* awesome blowjobs."

I froze. "From... the *girls*, right?" I asked, afraid of the answer.

Luke looked up, face red. He moved his head almost imperceptibly from side to side.

"You?" I sputtered. "You... gave him... a *bro job*?"

"And not just once," said Fletch, as he crossed his arms over his head and leaned back, pleased with the chaos he had unleashed. "Hell, back then I didn't care who was down there. He was hella good at it. But I guess you know that part already."

I'd lost this battle. It was time to cut and run. No amount of false bravado could save face in this situation.

"I'm outta here. I don't deserve this."

I lunged for my keys by the door and made my way through before I had even thought about where I was going or what I was doing. I just knew that I had to get out of there, fast. At least one thing was clear in my mind. I wasn't completely wrong about Fletch. He and Luke had indeed fooled around. Maybe it was one-sided, from what Fletch said. But it still stung.

"Derek! Wait!" Luke jumped up from the couch and yelled something at Fletch that I couldn't make out before he slammed the door behind him. Good. He was pissed. He should be.

"Derek, stop! Please! I'm *sorry*. I should have told you."

I was halfway to my car and had half a mind to just keep going. Where? I still didn't know, but the momentum was propelling me away from the sexual frat house I had just left.

"Derek!" Luke sped up and leapt in front of me, then stood there holding his hands up, not daring to touch me. He knew better than that. "Please. Babe?"

There was that word. Babe. Our word. It stopped me dead in my tracks. I was so furious, I couldn't think anymore, couldn't fight anymore. I wanted to give up. I stood there, shaking. My face, like always, betrayed all of my emotions: grief, fear, anger, betrayal, bewilderment. I was completely and utterly lost.

"Derek," he said, softer. "Please, let me explain. Please? I should have told you this weeks ago. There was just never a good time, never the right time. And I kept waiting, and it got worse, and it's not like something happened. *Nothing* happened. You have to believe me. I mean, well, something happened, yeah, but nothing happened *recently*. This was all in the past, okay? When we were in school. When we were younger. All this stuff that he's talking about, it was years ago, okay?"

He placed his hands on my shoulders, gingerly, and then looked me straight in the eyes.

"I have never cheated on you, babe. Never. Once we started dating you were the only guy for me. You know that. Derek, please. Tell me you know that. Tell me you believe me."

My heart was pounding. I was amazed that it still had the energy to beat. In my dramatic mind I felt like I was dying.

"I don't know what to believe."

"Believe *me*," he said, his hands still on my shoulders. "Believe me. I want to tell you everything. Right now. Please, let me. I'm so sorry I waited."

I still had my keys in my hand. I pulled away from him, not forcefully. I was in a dream-like state, and I needed to be somewhere safe. But Luke wanted to talk. My brain wasn't working, but I knew that if I walked away now, all would be lost. And I didn't want that.

At least, I didn't think I did. Nothing made much sense to me right now. I walked over to Willie Nelson and hopped up on the trunk, putting my feet on the shiny chrome bumper. The streetlamp at the corner made fairytale shadows through the leaves of the giant elm that stood nearby. They were comforting, in a way.

He hopped up next to me and then tried to take the keys from my hand, but I resisted and gripped them tighter. If I needed to run away I wanted the freedom to do it my way. He stared into the street, and then began talking softly.

"It started in high school, when we were kids. His parents had a rec room in the basement with wood paneling, a big brick fireplace, a pool table and a bar. His bedroom was down there, too. He had moved from the upstairs in tenth grade to have some privacy. A bunch of us guys would hang out at his house after practice. We'd sneak drinks from his dad's bar, smoke cigarettes. Every now and then someone would score some weed from someone's older brother, or a few pills from one of the moms' medicine cabinets. It just sort of evolved, over time. Stupid stuff, at first. Nothing crazy. One day we found a box of his dad's old girlie magazines in the garage, so we snuck those into his room. I was just hanging with my guys, you know? We'd pull out the centerfolds, compare stories, bullshit. That kind of stuff. Up to that point, I hadn't really done so much, you know? I mean, I'd had girlfriends. Make-out sessions, some over the bra stuff, but not much more than that. Fletch had hooked me up with Amber, though, and he wanted us to be this power couple. She kept pushing me to do more, but I didn't know what to do. I didn't know what was expected of me. You've met my father, Derek. You know Red. I mean, he's not the kind of guy I could go to and ask sex questions. We didn't talk about anything in my house, you know that." He held his fists together, tightly, still staring forward.

"I didn't have anyone I could talk to. I mean, I liked Amber. I did. When we'd make out, I'd get hard, you know? It's not like she didn't turn me on. She did. But I looked up to Fletch. Looking back, I realize that I wanted to please *him* much more than I ever wanted to please *her*. I don't have to explain this to you, because I know you understand. I was gay, Derek, but I didn't have the words for that. That word meant nothing to me. Nothing good at least. In my mind, there was no way I was gay. That just wasn't gonna happen. I thought my parents would never be okay with that. But I knew what I felt around Fletch, and I figured it was the same reason I got hard when I was with Amber, and it all got mixed up in my head and scared me, I guess. But instead of letting it torture me and eat me up inside, like you did, I just didn't think about it, at all. I was hanging with my *boys*, you know? That wasn't gay. I was on a team. This was my *team*. So when we started doing more than just looking at the magazines, I just told myself, *this isn't gay, either.* Guys jerk off. It's a fact of life.

So what if some of us started doing it together? Not all of us, but some of us, yeah. I mean, we were hanging with Fletch Powell. We felt privileged to be there. We went along with it."

"That bastard," I said softly.

"No, Derek. It wasn't like that. I promise. He wasn't some older, creepy molester. He didn't force us to do anything. I've thought back and gone over every detail. He is only two and a half years older than me. We were sexual kids. That's it. I was gay, he wasn't. Who's to know what he understood from that situation. I never really talked about it with him. I mean, we both had fun. I had fun. I'm okay with that. He never forced himself on me, I never did anything I didn't want to do. I was just jerking off with my buddy, and… yeah, I sucked him off a few times. Nothing more. We never kissed. Ever. And you have to believe me on that. Fletch would never kiss another guy. Fletch wasn't gay. He still isn't. It took me years to figure it out, but he just gets off on the adoration. By the time he hit college, he was a football star, you know? He had girls all over him, and yeah, he called me a few times. Amber and I were off and on for a few years, there. I kept hearing rumors that she had cheated on me, but I never cheated on her when we were together, not once. But we were broken up a lot through high school. I'd drive over to UT and hang out in Fletch's dorm. We'd party with these girls, and sometimes things would go pretty far. I was a horny teenager, Derek. I was experiencing this life that I felt was pretty amazing."

"Were you in love?" I asked. Clearer, louder. "Were you in love... with him?"

He inhaled deeply. "That's not... it wasn't." He sighed. "It wasn't love, no. You can't call it that. Infatuation? Maybe. He taught me a lot. I worshipped him. I admit it, I loved being with him, laughing, touching his body, all that. It's like I fed off of him, some crazy sexual energy that I needed. I was lying to myself, Derek. You know that. You understand. I needed to come out, but when I was with Fletch, I *didn't* need to. There was no point. I was just me, and he accepted me for me."

"What changed?"

"The accident," he answered. "When he had that car crash, he just closed up. He was my buddy, and I couldn't help him. He had lost it all. And selfishly, I had lost him. That intimacy we shared. I hadn't realized how much I needed that. Male companionship. That's what I called it, to make myself feel better. *Male companionship*. It was much easier to say that than to admit that I was gay. So, I started looking for it in other places. I drove down to Atlanta once and went to this nightclub called Renegade. It wasn't a gay club, but it was definitely mixed. I felt safe enough to go in alone. I had a few drinks, took off my shirt and danced my ass off. I was free. I got so drunk that I ended up waking up the next morning naked in some guy's bed. I didn't even know his name. I had to gather my clothes and sneak out. I had no idea where I was. I found a taxi number on a bus stop bench and the driver picked me up and drove me back to my car. I was freaked out, totally. I have no idea what I did that night."

"I've seen that guy. That version of Luke. At the Hoze."

"Exactly. But I don't *want* to be him." He turned to face me. "That's the old Luke. That's the Luke who had to get drunk to face who he was, and then went crazy with freedom. When I met you, all of that changed. It took me some time. You know that. But meeting you changed my perspective. I couldn't face it from the beginning, admitting who I was. Who I am. But falling in love with you released this fire inside of me that I had kept down for so long. I found that desire, that strength, to be myself and live my life in the open."

A slow trickle of tears started to fall from my eyes. This was the Luke I knew. Where had he been?

"We need to talk more, you know?" I said. "My mom just reminded me that communication is the key to everything."

"We should. We will. I promise. And I want you to know that I love you. I do. But this thing with Fletch... I have to figure it out."

"What do you mean?" I stopped crying. *What's he saying*, I thought.

"It's not done. There's something there that's not finished. He's my buddy. I love him, but not in the way I love you. And I can't just kick him out. He's hurting. That's why he's puffing out his chest at you. That's why he's being an ass. He's broken, and I need to help him. I couldn't help him after his accident, and I feel like I have the chance now to do some good. I'm asking you, please… give me some time. I just need some time."

I wiped away one final tear. "Fine," I said. "But I can't be here. You have to understand, it's about my self-respect. I need to go. I'll come back tomorrow and get my things. You take your time, but you'd better not take too long. We're not Ross and Rachel. I can't tell the Scooby Gang we're on a break."

"My god, I just wish one day I'd get your pop culture references."

I shook my head. "That's right. You're *Seinfeld* and I'm *Friends*. We shouldn't have even made it this far."

"Can I kiss you goodnight?"

"Do you have to ask?"

■ ■ ■

I left quickly, without looking back. Whatever break or hiatus or hiccup we were experiencing, it had built into one hell of a fight, but the release I felt after that deep conversation was good. I honestly didn't know what he expected to achieve with Fletch, but that was his battle from now on, and not mine.

It was too late to drive to the farmhouse, and honestly, I didn't really want to stay there. Mom and Dad were in the initial throes of their newly ignited domestic bliss, and that wasn't my home anyway. I let Willie find his own way to Barry's, as he always did. I kept my hands on the wheel, but he chose the curvy back roads, our path lit by the strength of the full moon.

I pulled into the gravel driveway and silenced the engine. I could hear music playing so I knew that Barry was still up. I wasn't really in the mood to talk to anybody. Truthfully, I had hoped he would be asleep so I could have just let myself in and crawled into my old bed. He had told me earlier that he had plans, so I guess whatever he needed to do was finished. I tried the side door, but it was locked, which I thought was strange. We never locked that door. I wasn't even sure I had that key. The music was coming from around back, so I walked around the newly landscaped hedges and onto his recently expanded patio.

There, naked in the steaming hot tub, was Tucker Matthews.

"Damn it!" I said. "Doesn't anybody in this whole town ever wear clothes?!"

13

BARRY'S BUNGALOW

"Oh, *shit*!" said Tucker. He dropped his drink by the side of the hot tub, and then submerged himself under the water.

Just then, Uncle Barry opened the sliding glass door in his favorite kimono and said, "Tucker, honey, where'd you put the *ooooh noooo…*"

"*Ooooh yessss…*" I beamed.

His eyes darted to the hot tub, then back to me, then back to the hot tub. "Where'd he go?" he asked.

"In there," I pointed. "I think he's drowning himself."

"Well that just won't do," he said. "Tucker?"

We stared silently as we saw the last few air bubbles make their way to the surface before Tucker finally realized that he hadn't made the best choice and that I wasn't going anywhere. His head surfaced with an audible gasp for air as he wiped his eyes, water dripping from his black mustache.

"Hi, there!" I said, smiling. "I'm Derek. But you already knew that."

"Yes," he said, inhaling deeply. "Hi, I'm Tucker." He looked at Barry sheepishly.

"You were my limo driver the night my boyfriend and I went to the Parkville High prom, right?"

"Guilty as charged."

"And you," I turned to Barry, who seemed to shrink to an impossible size for a man of his dramatic stature, "you knew that all along, didn't you? But you didn't really answer me when I asked."

"Yes? No?" he answered, but it wasn't a question. "I'm confused. What do you want me to say? Can I plead the fifth?"

I shook my head. This was exactly what I needed to lighten the mood of an otherwise horrid night.

"*You*," I pointed to Tucker, "get some clothes on. I was all ready to crash when I came over here, but now I'm wide awake. And *you*," I said to Barry, "you have a story to tell. Family conference in the living room in five." No one moved. "C'mon! Hop to it! Both of you. I have a feeling we're going to need *a lot* of cocktails."

■ ■ ■

Barry scurried about and made a tray of vodka martinis, placed them on the coffee table and began pacing the floor waiting for Tucker to come inside. I was sitting quietly on the new L shaped sofa, enjoying every uncomfortable second. It was nice for someone else to be in the hot seat for a change.

"What's taking him so long?" I asked.

Just then, the sliding glass door opened and Tucker peeked his head in, still shirtless as I could see.

"I don't actually have any clothes out here," he said, shuffling in and holding his hands in the vicinity of his nether regions.

"Dear Lord, Barry, get your man some clothes. He *is* your man, right?"

"I'm not ready to start yet!" he shrieked. He threw his hands up and then ran out of the room, hopefully to retrieve something for Tucker to wear.

Tucker smiled uneasily at me, unsure of what to do or say. I was laughing so hard inside, but I had to feel a bit sorry for the guy. I'm sure this wasn't how he expected to meet Barry's family. Then again, if he really *was* Barry's boyfriend, he had to have some idea of what he was getting into.

"Here, take this," I said, tossing a throw blanket at his feet. I turned my head to give him some privacy as he wrapped the blanket around him. We could hear Barry thrashing about in the other room.

"Thanks," he replied, and then turned his head toward the sound, most likely wishing he had some real clothes on or was anywhere else but here.

I spotted something on the back of his neck. It was your standard Chinese character tattoo, and I shook my head. *When will these kids learn?* I thought. I was hoping there wasn't a ring of barbed wire or a tribal tattoo somewhere else.

"What's your tattoo mean?" I asked. It wasn't my best opening line, but we had to start somewhere.

He reached up and touched the back of his neck. "This one? 'Chicken and broccoli.' All my friends were getting these stupid hipster mustache tattoos on their fingers, so I wanted something ironic. I went to the Chinese place near the dry cleaners and asked the lady to draw it out for me, just to make sure."

Chicken and broccoli? I had to grin. I decided then and there that I liked him.

"How old are you?" I asked.

"Don't answer that!" shrieked Barry, again, practically pole vaulting into the room with a mad bundle of clothes in his arms.

"Here, I didn't know what you wanted. I mean, it's a first impression, after all. There's jeans, chinos, a polo, a button down. Some t-shirts if you want to go casual. The lounge pants we bought online. I even pulled a sarong, but I think that's too advanced for you, at this point."

"Barry," he smiled appealingly, "I think we're already past the first impression. He's seen me naked, remember? But thanks. I'll just be a minute." He then brazenly kissed my uncle on the cheek as he exited, taking the pile of clothes into his arms as he stepped out of the room to change.

"I like him," I said, a minute or two after he was gone, but loud enough that I knew he could hear me.

"Stop! I'm not ready!" Barry's face was turning pink and he kept repeatedly feeling his forehead, as if he had a fever.

"So you keep saying. Martini?" I pointed to the tray.

"Everything's better with a cocktail," said Tucker as he re-entered smoothly. He'd chosen the casual route for his first 'real' appearance, with blue jean cut-offs and a faded grey Queen t-shirt that looked vintage. His body was thin but defined, muscled but not overdone like the steroid pumped fitness models you see on social media these days. In gay parlance, he was an otter, not a twink. His hair was black and full, with a well-groomed mustache that neither looked out of place nor ironic. If anything, it added to this 1970s San Francisco vibe that he pulled off so well. I imagined he'd look great in a pair of white leather roller skates with rainbow laces. All skate in one direction!

"Barry, come sit. You can do this." Tucker reached down and took my uncle's hand and led him to the couch where they both took their places, ready for the inquisition to come.

"So, anything you'd like to tell me?" I asked. Silence and darting eyes. I reached for a martini glass and took a healthy sip. I nearly gagged. "Barry! This is straight vodka. Where's the vermouth?"

"We're out. And besides, who uses the vermouth, anyway? I raised you smarter than that."

He was right. I popped an olive in my mouth to ward off the sting in my throat, and then got back to the business at hand.

"All right guys. Who's up, first? Otherwise, you already know what I'm going to ask."

"I'm twenty-six," said Tucker, firmly. Barry's face tightened.

"Wow." I had to admit I was a bit startled. "So, that's…" I started to mentally subtract the numbers.

"*A lot*," Barry interrupted. "Trust me. We've done the math. Many times. The numbers don't change."

"And we don't care," Tucker said, reassuring him, and me. "Barry's age doesn't mean a thing to me. I just like him for who he is." He held my uncle's hand firmly in his own, and I could sense a genuine bond between them.

"So, how'd you meet?"

"I'll take this," said Tucker, and then turned to face me. "It was me. It was my fault. If you're going to be mad at someone, blame me. I'm the one who chased him."

"I'm not mad," I said, "I'm just… trying to get used to this. When did this happen? How long have you two been dating?"

"Since last year, Dolly," said Barry. "Not long after you and Luke first started dating. I couldn't tell you, of course, because I honestly thought it wasn't going to last. I mean, look at us. Have you ever seen such a mismatched pair? It's *Harold & Maude* for a new generation!"

"I had to Google that, just so you know," said Tucker, to me. "I'm an old movie buff, but sometimes he comes out with these things that I've never even heard of."

"I get ya," I said. "But, I have a feeling you'll catch on quick. I'll loan you my copy of *Auntie Mame* for homework. Most everything you need is in there."

"Oh, we watched that one a few days after our first date," Tucker said with pride. "But I'm getting ahead of myself. I guess we should start from the beginning." He eyed my uncle, and then placed his hand on his knee. "We first met because of Lloyd Barton. As you know, I own my own limo service. What you may not know is that it used to be my grandpa's, but when he passed, my dad had no interest in the business, so it was left to me. I never could have started something like that on my own. Lloyd had hired my grandpa for Secret Sunday for years, so I inherited that route. I never knew a thing about it, of course. Grandpa always said that discretion was the key to keeping customers, and now I know why. When I took over, I kept things pretty much the same. Same limo, same discretion, new driver. The difference was, I was a little more interested in the passengers than my grandpa was. He only had eyes for one person in a dress, and that was my grandma, God rest her soul. Anyway, I was all set to do a pick-up at Lloyd's. It was my first Secret Sunday, and I didn't really understand what I was getting into. I had received a call for a car, and the description was simply 'a handsome gentleman.' Well, when I showed up, Barry was standing out front, and I just assumed he was my client."

"He thought I was handsome," gushed Barry. "This guy. Look at him. Will you just look at him?"

"I see him, I promise," I said, smiling.

"This guy," he repeated, "thought I was his 'handsome' customer. We'd made the call to come pick up Harvey Wilts. He'd had a few too many and we didn't want him to drive, so we called Matthews Limo."

"That's me. Matthews Limo. I kept the same company name," said Tucker. "Anyway, I picked up Mr. Wilts, dropped him off, made sure he was taken care of. Then I circled back. I couldn't get this man out of my mind. I figured, well, everybody likes a limo. Maybe I could just offer him a complimentary ride?"

"Meanwhile, I had gone back inside," Barry said, "and taken my favorite seat at that little cocktail table by the corner of the stage. There were no performers that night, but I didn't feel much like socializing after seeing Tucker. It was as if I'd seen *the* guy, you know? I finally saw *him*, after all these years. My heart was racing and my mind was jumping through hoops and I didn't even have any idea what his name was. I knew I could ask Lloyd, but I didn't want to start any tongues wagging, because trust me, when these girls get going there is no stopping them. And besides, this was all in my mind right? It was all my overactive imagination. I mean, I was planning a wedding, already!"

"Meanwhile, I was out front," Tucker continued. "But I had no good reason to come in. I hadn't received any more car requests. Lloyd just keeps me on call for those nights, but he said that I wouldn't always be needed. So I was parked on the street, waiting for something to happen."

"And then it did." Barry was beaming. "I decided I had had enough fun for the night. I kissed my good-byes to the gang and gathered my things. Normally I leave through the kitchen. It's closer to the parking lot I always use. But something made me decide to use the front door that night. I walked out onto the porch, and I saw him, waiting."

"And I saw him, waiting," said Tucker. "I was standing by the car, and I had already decided that I would leave soon, but I told myself that I felt good things were about to happen, so I had waited."

"Like Cinderella's carriage that had to leave by midnight," Barry added.

"I reached over and held open the back door and I just smiled at him. He looked at me a second and then walked straight down the steps and set himself inside. I said, 'Where to, sir?' And he gave me a funny smile."

"We couldn't come here, to the house," said Barry, "and I couldn't take him to the Bears' Club. I didn't want anyone to see us, but at the same time, I didn't want to embarrass myself. What if I was making this up in my head? So I asked him if we could just go for a drive."

"So we did. I drove him around town for about an hour, and we talked and got to know each other better. I thought he was so interesting. He'd had such a colorful life. I didn't really want the evening to end, but the hour was getting late, so finally I had to ask him where I should drop him off."

"He took me back to Lloyd's, of course. I needed my own car, after all. When he opened the door to let me out, he asked for my number."

"And that was that," said Tucker. "Fireworks."

"And you've been dating in secret, this whole time?" I asked.

"Well, Dolly, to be honest, it just didn't seem real at first." Barry had his hand on Tucker's knee. "I mean look at him. He's gorgeous. I kept waiting for the other shoe to drop, and it never did. It's as if I created my dream man in a science lab, and he was delivered to me in a shiny black limousine. I kept thinking, *surely I'll wake up soon*. Surely, *he'll* wake up soon and wonder what the hell he is doing spending time with me. But suddenly, a month had passed. Then two, then three. Then, *blam*. I had a boyfriend. My first real boyfriend. And I didn't know the first thing to do."

"And it was then that I realized," added Tucker, "that not only did he have things to teach me, but I had things to teach him. He didn't know the first thing about how to be in a gay relationship. Nothing! It's like we had to start from scratch. The age thing was the least of our worries. The age thing never bothered me. Sure, I thought about it, but it was like we somehow evened out. Like, I aged up and he aged down and we met somewhere in the middle. Yeah, every now and then he pops out with these songs or musicians or moments in history that I know nothing about, but in the long run, does that really matter? He makes me laugh, and I feel good when we're together."

I repeated that in my head. *He makes me laugh, and I feel good when we're together.* I understood that. I had that. I still have that. Minus Fletch, of course.

"And every time I look at him," said Barry, "I think, *where have you been all my life?* Then I remember. Oh, yes. You weren't born yet."

And they collapsed in a heap of giggles.

■ ■ ■

"Barry, the hot tub is turned off and I replaced the cover," said Tucker. "Should I turn the outside lights off, too?"

"Oh, no, don't worry. They're on a timer. This old brain can't remember everything it's supposed to. So, you never told us why you came by tonight, nephew." Barry was placing the martini glasses on the counter and I was leaning on the kitchen island where I had pictured Luke kissing David in my fever dream. I shuddered.

"*Ugh.* It's too much of an ordeal to go over right now," I said, exhausted. "In a nutshell, Luke's friend Fletch is causing me all kinds of grief. We just need some time. We'll be fine, but we just need a breather."

"Fletch Powell," he said. "Why can't that golden boy just leave Parkville in the dust?"

"Being a golden boy is overrated," offered Tucker. "I much prefer a man in his prime."

"Prime I've got," said Barry. "Golden will take me a while. I'll be golden in twenty years."

"In twenty years I can do whatever I want with you," said Tucker. "I'll be pushing you in your wheelchair."

"*Oh!*" I gasped. "There's the age joke I needed!"

"Trust me," said Tucker, laughing. "I make them all the time. He just doesn't remember them."

"Careful, Tucker," warned Barry, smiling.

"I really like him, you know?" Tucker said to me, fully aware that Barry was listening. "Your uncle's pretty special. The moment he walks out the door I wish he would turn around and come right back to me."

"I often do," said Barry, chiming in. "I usually forget something. All right, it's bedtime for this old timer. I'm moved down here to the master bedroom, by the way. Your room is just as you left it, Derek. You get that upstairs bathroom all to yourself now."

"And you're sharing a bed?" I teased. "Have fun!"

"No one appreciates your attitude, young man!"

14

LANA LEADS THE WAY

A week passed before I even realized it. I was so busy with the Duke that I didn't have time to worry about my relationship falling apart. I mean, I did, of course. I missed Luke every second of every day, but I had to stay positive and think of ways for everything to right itself, again. Oh, who was I kidding? I was a mess.

I called Kit to congratulate her on being a homeowner. She was so excited she could barely talk. All she could think about was how to decorate and how soon they could have a party. She and Shawn had found a home in an older, established neighborhood near the mall. They were planning a housewarming as soon as they could, and she made sure to invite me and Luke. I didn't want to bring up my continuing troubles when she had such good news, so I just thanked her and said that of course I'd come. I didn't say "we" on purpose, and she didn't seem to notice.

I was still spending my nights at Barry's place. He and Tucker didn't live together, but Tucker was at the house quite often. As a driver, he had irregular shifts, coming and going at all hours. Barry confided in me that he had asked his boyfriend to move in, but the offer had been declined. "I like missing you," Tucker had said. This guy was definitely wise for his age.

I enjoyed watching them together. It was a trip, to be honest. I had spent most of my youth admiring my Aunt Janey and Uncle Barry's perfect marriage that was based on a solid friendship, rather than my own parents' rocky marriage that had ended with a whimper. Barry was a shell of himself after Janey passed, but when they were together, they had so much fun. They were funny and vibrant, and you could really see that they loved each other. But this relationship he had with Tucker was different. Barry was different. Sure, he was the same, fun loving man I'd always known, but everything about him seemed sharper, clearer, more focused. It was a simple belief from inside, of course.

He was free, now. Just like Luke.

For my part, I was staying low. I had gone by the house to pick up some things, and I was just lucky enough to arrive at a moment when they both weren't there. Being back in our house, Luke's house, felt so strange without the man I loved at my side. I felt like an interloper, stealing in and out, removing all traces of myself from the scene of the crime. But I didn't want him to forget me.

That wasn't my goal. If anything, I wanted him to miss me, like I missed him.

People have told me I'm too needy, that I'm too clingy, but I never really cared. I'd rather tell someone forty-two times a day that I love them than regret not saying it when I should have. It's all about communication, right Audrey?

But things with us were trickier. Luke was never one to send text messages, remember, so the only way we did communicate now was by calling each other. Sometimes he answered, sometimes he didn't. I soon realized it depended on his physical distance from Fletch. I was really growing to hate that guy and it was eating me up.

I thought a lot about what Tommy said. Why *was* I putting up with all of this? Why didn't I just quit? Why didn't I just walk away from Luke and Fletch and that whole mess? I had told Tommy that it was all too complicated to explain, but the more I felt like I was swimming through mud, the more I came to see clearly.

The sad truth was, a part of me felt like this great love of mine was my last chance. Sure, I was given plenty of love and support as a kid, and even though my parents divorced, I still knew love. But deep inside, I was afraid I would never know *true* love. Society told me over and over that I wasn't worth it. I should have stayed hidden, lied, covered up who I really was. Why didn't I just get married to a woman like many of the Southern gentlemen I had grown up with? As closeted gay kids, we weren't given many real choices. Or chances. Or moments of truth.

Luke was my grand moment of truth. I had invested everything in him, and even though I knew I deserved to be treated better right now, I had to hope that he would come to that realization, as well. We both deserved better...with each other. And without Fletch.

■ ■ ■

Getting the Duke up and running was certainly taking up most of my time and I was grateful for the distraction from my private life. I had meetings with all my distributors, making sure that our deliveries would run as scheduled. I met the florist, the food vendors and the cleaning company. I had a "liquor guy," now. I loved that! My own direct vodka hook-up. I immediately bragged to Kit and she totally understood where I was coming from.

We had training sessions for the staff, myself included. Lloyd had a certain way of doing things and I didn't really want to rock the boat. Sure, we updated things a bit, but I couldn't scare off the local society matrons. I needed their continued allegiance. The calls had tapered off a bit when Lloyd announced that he sold the company, but I wasn't worried. The back-to-school events, football parties and wedding ceremonies would start soon, and then there would be no stopping us. One couple had already called to ask if we could have a combination wedding reception/ football viewing party. They wanted to know if we could set up a big screen TV so that their guests could watch the big game immediately after the ceremony. I told them that we'd happily oblige. This town loved any reason for a good party, even the ones we didn't talk about openly.

No one had called asking about Secret Sunday, of course. It was simply there on the calendar, listed as "recurring private event," on the last Sunday of every month. The first one was coming up this weekend, and it would be the unofficial first event for Duke Catering and Events. I was a bit nervous, to tell you the truth, but I figured I could handle it. I already knew most of the closeted men in town, anyway, so I wasn't expecting any surprises.

Tucker came by that first week to discuss some limo service business. For a younger guy, he was quite good at separating business from pleasure. We went over his rates and services, and I was impressed with his business acumen. We didn't bring up Barry at all, but his presence hovered around us like the tutu-wearing pink elephant in the room. I knew it was only a matter of time before he'd crack, and sure enough, I heard a knock on the doorframe of my office the next day. I looked up and saw Tucker with an iced coffee in each hand.

"I figured you could use a break," he said. "May I come in?"

"With caffeine at the ready?" I said. "Always!"

He sat down in the leather club chair facing my desk and handed me a cup. The weather had been particularly brutal that week and the plastic container was sweating profusely. Tucker was wearing a striped tank top today with an old pair of men's suit trousers that he had cut off to make into shorts. He made a good effort of balancing hipster and vintage. I admired that.

"I hope you don't mind me dropping by?" he asked.

"Not at all. You're always welcome. What can I help you with?"

He shifted in his chair, and then leaned forward. "It's a social call today. No business. I was hoping we could just get to know each other a bit? Considering, well, you know."

I smiled. In another lifetime, Tucker was the kind of guy I would have dated here in Parkville. Now he was dating my uncle. So did that mean we had the same tastes? I couldn't help but think that genetics were a funny thing.

"I hope I'm not cramping your style by sleeping over at Barry's this week?" I asked. "Luke and I are just taking a little break."

"Like Ross and Rachel? Yeah, I get it. It happens to the best of us. No, it's cool. I like having you around. Barry was a bit uneasy, at first. I could see that. But it's helping him to open up, so that's good. He's been so afraid to tell anyone about us for so long that I think it will take some time for him to adjust to a new reality."

"Do all your friends know?" I asked.

"Most of my friends, yeah. We haven't really gone out in public, but we've hung out at my place or at Barry's. I was kind of afraid, too, at the beginning. The age difference is pretty big. It's funny, but when we met I was actually twenty-five, but my birthday was just a few months away, so I kept saying that I was twenty-six, so our ages would be just a bit closer. Soon enough, I forgot how old I really was!" he laughed. "I kept saying the wrong age when people asked me. But, yeah, my friends are cool with it. The few who have met Barry think he's great. They can see that we're happy together. He's right that it doesn't make sense. It shouldn't work, but it does. I haven't told my parents, yet, though. I just don't know how they'll react. I mean, I guess I do, but I just don't want to deal with it. Barry and I have pretty much forgotten about the difference in our ages, but then when we meet someone new, it all just comes back, pretty hard. We have to explain so much every time. It gets old, but I understand that people are curious. I just wish they'd worry about more important things. *Love all*, right?"

"Exactly," I said. "I don't think most of our straight friends, or our family for that matter, really get it. We get hit with so many whammies. None of them had to announce to the world that they were straight. They didn't have to hide their crushes. They don't have to be worried when they hold their partner's hand. But you're dealing with yet another issue altogether. You're in a multi-generational relationship. Can you handle that? Because people in this town will not be afraid at all to get up in your face and express their opinion when you go public. Trust me. I have firsthand knowledge of that."

"I know," he sighed. "You probably didn't notice, but I came out to support you and Luke during all that crap this past spring. Barry and I came separately, but I told him it was important for me to do something, to try and have my voice heard. I even drove Peaches and all the Chesty Cheese girls to the protests in my limo, for free!"

"Well, I appreciate that. I owe you one."

"You don't owe me anything. It was the least I could do. That's part of why I'm attracted to Barry. He has such strong values and so much history. So many stories. I feel like I learn so much from him every day, but then every now and then I teach him something new as well. It's not one-sided. We're both learning from each other. Did you know your uncle has lived his whole life without glow sticks? We put on some really loud music the other night and started dancing all over the place. I reached into my bag and pulled these glow sticks out and he was like a little kid again. It was amazing! We had so much fun."

I had to laugh picturing Barry jumping about the living room with a glow stick in his hand, dancing his ass off to Donna Summer.

"You guys will really have to go public soon. But I guess you know that," I said.

"Well, you were the first family member, and that went pretty well, so it's just a matter of time, I guess. He hasn't really told anyone else. I hope your mom's cool with it."

"I think she will be. She just wants to see Barry happy, and you seem to have a good effect on him. Do you want me to break it to her or should I leave that to you guys?"

"I think Barry would be happy never dealing with it, but really, it's something he needs to do. He'll figure it out on his own time. I don't want to pressure him."

"Or Mom could just discover you both naked in the new hot tub? I hear that's a great conversation starter."

■ ■ ■

Tucker got a call from a client so he stepped out to carry on with his day. It was just after 5 pm and I was finishing the upcoming employee work schedule when my phone rang. It was a telephone number I knew, but I was surprised nonetheless.

"Go for Cinderella," I answered.

"Funny," she sneered into the phone. "Does that make me the wicked sister? Fair assessment, some would say."

"Sorry, Lana." I felt bad. "I was just kidding. I wasn't expecting to hear from you, that's all."

"Like it or not, you're practically part of the Walcott clan now, so deal with it. I'm trying to, at least."

Luke's sister Lana and I had had our fair share of shaky starts, fights and détentes. We were in a holding pattern as of late, hoping not to crash into one another, yet again. She had begrudgingly accepted me as Luke's boyfriend, but that didn't mean she had to love me. It was more like mutual toleration.

"To what do I owe the pleasure, Lana?" *Be nice*, I reminded myself.

"Seriously, Derek. Like you have to ask? Amber told me that Fletch Powell is back in town."

"And?" I couldn't imagine that Lana would have had anything but love for Fletch. He was everything she wanted her brother to be. Fletch was the standard by which every Parkville High School jock was measured and Luke had come closer than anyone to that level of perfection.

"And?!" she sputtered. I could actually hear her put down her cocktail. I think she even removed an earring. This was serious. "The enemy of my enemy is my friend. Ever heard that one before?"

"I'm confused," I said. "Exactly who's who in that equation?"

"I swear," she said, exasperated. "Sometimes I don't even think you and I are in the same universe. Just get your butt over here, pronto. I'm at the country club. You can't miss me. I'm the one everybody wants to be." And she hung up.

■ ■ ■

The valet parked my car for me and I walked towards the maître de. I didn't even have to say a word.

"Miss Walcott is expecting you," he said, with surprisingly little judgment. "This way, please."

As Lana described herself, she wasn't hard to spot. She had taken over the white leather circular booth by the bar. It was by far the most visible table in the club, and sure enough, all eyes were indeed on her. How could they not be? Lana was wearing a white silk blouse with one more button undone than I would have felt comfortable with. Her long slender legs were wrapped up tight in white designer Capri pants with a very fancy white and gold heel capping her tiny feet. The accessories were gold and pearls, as always, and her blond hair was in the perfect messy chignon.

"All white. Very ice queen," I teased, hoping to crack a smile.

She didn't. "It's not Labor Day yet. Consult Emily Post sometime, will you?"

As I joined her the waiter stopped by to deliver two fresh gin and tonics without even asking. Sure, I could do gin. It never hurt to add to my repertoire of vodka, vodka and vodka.

"Let's cut to the chase," she began. "No need for small talk, right? Not when we have a problem as big as Fletch Powell. Why didn't you call me the moment his nasty head popped back into the picture? I had to hear it from Amber?"

"Newsflash, Lana. You and I aren't that close. And besides, how could I have known that you hate Fletch as much as I do? Care to explain?"

She actually looked flustered, for a change. Usually Lana was the picture of angelic composure, even while flinging the darkest of mud.

"Look, I used to think Fletch was every bit as perfect as everyone else did. When he hand picked Luke to be his shadow, well, I just knew we were made. We'd hit the big time. Amber and Luke, they were set to be the couple of the century and I was on my way to becoming cheer captain. There was no turning back. All good from there, right? Wrong. It wasn't long before I saw what kind of hold

Fletch had on Luke. Go ahead and judge me, but I didn't like the fact that I could see lust in my big brother's eyes. It freaked me out, all right? And it wasn't like I could tell anyone. Mama and Daddy would have never understood, and you know that Rosa and I just weren't close. As far as I was concerned, she belonged in the kitchen and not in our family life. Luke and I were real close, though, and I didn't like the changes I saw in him. It was strange seeing my brother, who I respected, getting googley-eyed over a big lunk like Fletch. We needed him, though, so I figured I could put up with it until he went away to UT. But then that car wreck happened and everything went sour after that. I'm sure you've heard the story about how Fletch crashed his precious Big Orange Mustang into that light pole and his whole football career went kablooey, right? How he spent weeks in rehab, how the whole town mourned his one big mistake? How he decided he had to change his life for the better and leave town? Well trust me, you've only heard part of the story."

■ ■ ■

I was shocked that there were any secrets left in this town that I had not yet discovered, but Lana certainly surprised me with a new one. And it was a doozy. She wanted to take Fletch down badly and she had a plan. We huddled at that table for a good hour, plotting and drinking, scheming and drinking, even giggling and drinking, as if we were friends. We decided exactly how and when we were going to help Luke see Fletch for who he really was, and then, just then, maybe Fletch would loosen his hooks on Luke, once and for all.

"Are you sure about this?" I asked. "I had no idea you cared about me so much."

"My brother has no idea what's best for himself. And though I am loath to admit it, it seems to be you. But don't flatter yourself too much. That's not my only reason for wanting him out of the picture. Isn't it obvious, Derek? Fletch made a fatal mistake. He chose someone else besides me."

And that was it. There was that composure I had seen so much of. I was in awe. Lana was a woman with a mission and no one would stand in her way. Not even...well, I'm getting ahead of myself.

"We have to tell Luke everything in advance, though. It's not fair for him to find out when everyone else does," I said. "He won't take too kindly to that."

"*No*," said Lana firmly. "Look, Derek, if this is going to work, then Luke needs to be just as surprised as everyone else. He's not an actor like you. He wouldn't be able to fake a reaction. It would sound too much like a speech."

"But...he's going to be really angry at us...at *me*. I'm not so sure we shouldn't include him."

"Don't worry about that. I'll take the heat when the time comes. I'm his sister, he'll forgive me."

Yes, but will he forgive me? I thought.

We toasted to the future success of our plan with the last few drops of gin left in our glasses and then she dismissed me in so many gestures. Just because we were working together for a common goal did not mean we were besties. That was fine. I had those in spades.

But I couldn't leave without one final parting jab.

"Thanks for the drinks, Lana. *Oh!* And I've been meaning to tell you, I loved you in *Mean Girls.*"

15

SECRET SUNDAY

The last weekend of the month was upon us and that meant the debut event for the Duke, Secret Sunday.

At Lloyd's suggestion, I had scheduled one bartender and one waiter who knew the crowd well and could be counted on for discretion. The chef had prepared a simple Mediterranean buffet with hummus, crudités, pita bread and spicy meatballs. Everything was waiting for me in the kitchen when I arrived. I unwrapped all the silver serving trays and set everything out on the antique mahogany table underneath the giant gilt-edged mirror in the front room. A lovely bouquet of stargazer lilies stood on the table in the foyer in a hand cut glass vase, ready to greet the guests as they arrived. The large candelabrum behind the bar was lit, as well as a few dozen votive candles, placed here and there. We had done everything we could do to set the proper mood. Now all we had to do was wait.

I still had no real clue who the guests would be or even how many would show up. Lloyd said the attendees could number as low as ten or as high as twenty-five. Since discretion was key, there wasn't even an option to RSVP. I couldn't see how I would ever make any money off this event, but I soon realized it wasn't about the money. This was all about access and knowledge. These men were the secret movers and shakers in town, and it would certainly do me well to find myself in their good graces.

I was dressed in a simple dark blue summer suit, no tie. For one hot minute I almost considered wearing seersucker, but I decided not to take everything from Lloyd. I'd leave him his signature look. It was time to start anew. My bartender, Sam, looked handsome in his starched white tuxedo shirt, black bowtie, cummerbund and black trousers. No jacket, and he was not allowed to roll up his sleeves, just yet. My waiter, Crosby, was dressed identically, and he stood ramrod straight at the door, ready to greet the guests as they arrived.

"Are you ready for this?" Crosby asked me with a wicked smile.

"I'm not sure," I answered. "Is it really that bad?"

"Not if you don't mind getting your ass pinched a few times. It's worth it for the tips."

For a second I thought he was kidding, but then a loud voice brought me to my senses.

"Dolly!" Barry burst through the front door at precisely 6:15 pm, making a scene as he entered. He air kissed Crosby on both cheeks in the European way, paid his entrance fee and glided straight over to me, hastily yelling out a bar command along the way.

"Sam, darling! You know exactly how to make me happy. Set her up!"

Sam dutifully grabbed a highball glass, filled it with ice and began his preparations.

"Look at you, nephew!" Barry said to me, grabbing my hands and holding them high. "I taught you well. I'm loving the suit. Presentation is everything!"

"And you," I said, "have actually surprised me."

"I like to keep people on their toes, after all," he said. "Besides, it's Beret's night off. She comes out for the Bears' Club, but Secret Sundays are just for Barry. Boys will be boys!"

He wasn't kidding. Beret was in the closet tonight, literally. The wig, the makeup, the fancy frocks and heels were all stored away. Tonight, Uncle Barry had pulled off his best Fred Astaire.

"I didn't even know you owned a tuxedo, let alone one with tails. And are those spats?" I asked. "Do they still make those?"

"Special order from Atlanta," whispered Barry. "Tucker found them for me online. I had him order a monocle, too, but I kept winking at the go-go boys too much and losing it in my drink."

"Well, I love it. Welcome to Secret Sunday, Barry."

"*Ooooh, nooooo*, that won't do," he said. "Did Lloyd not tell you?"

"Tell me what?" Have I messed something up already?

"That's just like Lloyd," he clucked. "Absentminded as ever." He grabbed my hand and dragged me back to the bar to fetch his cocktail. "You want to do the honors, Sam?"

Sam smiled and nodded his head as Barry dropped a ten dollar bill in his tip jar. "We refrain from referring to or addressing any of the gentlemen by their proper names while they are enjoying our private event," he recited, as if by heart.

"Exactly!" cried Barry. "Well done, Sam. Sam here knows me as Mr. Blueberry. Lloyd is called Mr. Lingon. And you, Derek, let's see, that's a hard one. You can be Mr. Durian, Mr. Date or… Mr. Dragon, if we really push it."

"These are all fruits, right?"

"Bingo! It's our gay version of *Reservoir Dogs*," he guffawed. "Except nobody here is getting their ear bit off. Well, not unless Mr. Kiwi comes by. Then someone *could* get tied to a chair. Watch out for him, he's a rough one. *Oh*, and look! Mr. Strawberry has just arrived." He turned to greet one of our local prominent bankers as Crosby took the gentleman's coat and placed it in the wardrobe in the foyer.

Mr. Strawberry was soon followed by a whole fruit salad: Mr. Fig, Mr. Lemon, Mr. Melon, and many, many more. As the men arrived I started to feel a bit easier about

the evening. Just like my travel anxiety, I had simply needed the event to start.

It ended up being far less lascivious than I had imagined it would be. It wasn't dirty or naughty or even close to
X-rated. In fact, I'd say the evening just required a touch of
adult supervision, and I assumed that role. The crowd was
distinctly older than your general club crowd, but not ge-
riatric, by any means. These men were here to socialize, to
drink, to gossip, and yes, by the looks of Sam and Crosby's
shared tip jar, they were here to touch the merchandise.

Speaking of, I had wanted to make sure that the men
enjoyed their first of many Secret Sundays under the new
management, so I placed a call to one of the vendors that
Lloyd had suggested in his little envelope, Myrna's Models.
This particular company specialized in adult entertainers;
everything from go-go boys to strippers of both genders.
Lloyd said that the members didn't expect entertainment
every month, but it would be fun to spice up the first event,
so I asked the booking agent if she had any male strippers
available for that evening. Unfortunately, all her regulars
were booked for bachelorette parties, but she informed me
that she had recently hired a new guy who would definitely
be interested. We went ahead and made the deal.

"Mr. Raspberry, I do hope you are enjoying yourself,"
I said to one of our local prominent journalists standing at
the bar. More than anything I was checking on Sam, who
seemed to be getting a lot of attention as the drinks flowed
and the night progressed. He had loosened a few buttons
of his stiff white shirt and let his bowtie dangle down the

side. It wasn't exactly our proper dress code, but he knew what he was doing. That tip jar was damn near overflowing. Crosby was working up a sweat running ice to the bar, filling up the chests. His own chest was wet with sweat, giving the older patrons a nice view of what was behind the buttons. These boys didn't need my help. At all.

Crosby stepped from behind the bar and wiped the perspiration from his brow. "That new guy, Chip, is in the kitchen asking for you," he said. "I told him to wait there. Didn't figure you'd want him to come out here."

"Thanks, Crosby, I'll take care of it." Why was Chip Carter here? He definitely wasn't scheduled for this event.

I left the main salon and passed through the library on my way into the kitchen. Sure enough, Chip was standing there in full motorcycle leathers, helmet and gloves in hand.

"Hey, Chip, what's up? We're having a private event tonight."

"Oh, hey, Mr. Walter. Yeah, I know. I just wanted to come a little early. It's my first gig, and all. I figured you weren't ready for me, yet."

I looked at him, puzzled. "Chip, you're not scheduled tonight. Sam and Crosby have it covered."

"Oh, not that. Yeah, I know they're working the bar and house tonight. That's not why I'm here." He grinned. "I got this gig through Myrna. Myrna's Models?"

"You're the…"

"Stripper! Yeah, that's me."

"This isn't happening," I said, sternly.

"Waddya mean it's not happening? Oh, it's definitely happening. Myrna says this is a great gig and that if you like me I could probably book more. You can't send me home, Mr. Walter. I need these jobs. Listen, I don't want Jett to know all my business, 'cause he's my friend, you know? And he's loaded. But, my parents totally cut me off after that mess this spring. They said I need to focus on football and keeping that scholarship. The catering and Myrna's are the only extra cash I can find right now. I promise you, I won't let you down, Mr. Walter. The crowd'll love me."

I had no doubts about that. We'd all heard the rumors about Chip's endowment, after all. I shook my head. Could I allow this?

"You're eighteen, right?"

"Yes, sir. I'm eighteen. I'll be nineteen in November."

"And you can dance?"

"Oh, I have a lot of sex," he said, very seriously. "Like, a lot."

"You know this is a crowd of gay men, right? Not women."

"Trust me, I'm used to the stares. I know what I'm doing, Mr. Walter."

"Mr. Date," I sighed, already regretting my actions. "Tonight, in here, I'm Mr. Date."

"Whatever you say." He threw his hands up. "As long as I get paid."

■ ■ ■

Twenty minutes later, Chip exited the kitchen and walked around to the front of the building where he entered again as the mysterious, masked rider. Crosby cued the music from the soundboard by the stage and Sam dimmed the lights from the bar. The gentlemen of Secret Sunday clapped their hands with delight as Chip marched to the center of the room and gyrated to a funky, disco beat. He pulled off his motorcycle helmet to reveal a bandana obscuring his identity, but when he began to unzip the leathers, there was no doubt who it was. Chip had indeed been blessed, and if his abs were any indication, he wasn't lying to me. He had definitely had a lot of sex. Like, *a lot*. I don't know if someone tipped him off or if it was just a lucky pick, but when he stripped down to his black thong and chose Mr. Kiwi to sit on the chair in the center of the dance floor and be on the receiving end of the gyrations, that's when I knew I needed some fresh air.

Sam poured me a very stiff vodka and soda and I made my way out through the library and onto the terrace, averting my eyes from Chip's money-stuffed thong as I passed.

The pumping music inside drowned out the sounds of the crickets I had longed to hear. Amazing how we had gone from a simple meet and greet to a room of rowdy, horny old men in a matter of two hours. I was happy that the event was only scheduled for two more. It had been an intense first workweek, and this was just my first event.

"This town," I said to the night air. "This town is crazy times a hundred."

"And don't you love it?" responded a voice to my left.

I jumped, startled that I wasn't alone. The metal gate made a clinging sound as it shut behind him. Tucker had entered the garden terrace from the back, by the kitchen.

"Sorry, I didn't mean to scare you," he said. "I usually hang out back here when I'm waiting on fares. Barry's friends don't know we're together, so sometimes he pops out to say hello, that's all. I hope you don't mind?"

"Not at all." I shook my head. "Can I get you a drink?"

"No, thanks. Driving, remember?"

"Well, that doesn't stop too many people in this town."

"Tell me about it. I took the limo through the Mini-Burger drive-thru the other night. I had booked back-to-back fares and I didn't have time to eat, so I was starving. I ordered half a dozen sliders with some cheese fries and I was trying to wolf them down in between pick-ups. I guess I wasn't doing too good a job of holding on to the steering wheel. I should have just parked, but I was racing to my next call and I figured I could eat and drive. Anyway, next thing I know, the blue lights came on behind me and I had to pull over, after all. The policeman asked me how drunk I was, and I said, 'I'm not drunk, I'm eating my Mini Burgers!' He didn't think that was as funny as I did but he let me off, anyway." He laughed.

"Well, I'll make sure to use your services more often, now that we've met. Or at least I hope to. I guess that depends on Luke. He's a pretty good driver in all situations."

"Barry seems to think y'all will figure it out," said Tucker. "When I drove you two to the prom, I was kind of beaming, myself. I felt like I had two celebs in my car. I'd seen everything you had to go through to get to that point, and I was so proud of you, I really was. And I didn't even really know you, I just knew you through Barry's eyes. He really loves you, you know?"

"Well, I'm pretty sure he loves you, too. I can see that in *his* eyes."

Tucker looked down. "He hasn't said it, yet. I haven't, either. I don't want one of those awful situations you see in the movies where one person says 'I love you' and the other person just freezes. So, we wait. There's no rush to say it. I already know how I feel, and I'm pretty sure he feels the same. I know I'm young, and you probably think it's crazy, but I just feel like I'm supposed to be with him. Like he had this whole life before me, but it was just preparation, just so we could meet and he could make sure my romantic life would be perfect. I look at his face and I can remember things we haven't done yet. He's promised me another thirty-five years, and I'm holding him to it."

Things we haven't done yet. Those words rang in my ears, and I became lost for a moment, thinking of my own romantic entanglements. David had been a disaster, but Luke was truly the only man for me. There were definitely things we had yet to do, moments we had yet to share. And here I had placed my future in the hands of Lana Walcott. What was I thinking?

"And I believe him," he continued. "He says we're going to grow old together. Well, old and older, he says. Did you know he came out for me?"

"Really?" I was surprised. "That was your doing?"

"Well, not directly, but he said it was because of me. Every day he tells me stories of his amazing life, and I'm always in awe of the things he's done, the places he's been, the people he's known. But one day he told me that he envied me and *my* life. He said that he couldn't imagine growing up in a world where it was okay to be gay from an early age. Sure, I got bullied a little, but no more than the black kids or the poor kids or that pretty girl with the lisp in my homeroom. Even middle class white kids got bullied. Bullies didn't discriminate when I was growing up. And I never wanted to get married, never even thought of it. Why would I want to? Marriage equality never even entered my mind. I figured that people just partnered with whoever they wanted, and what did a little piece of paper matter? Who cares, right? But the way Barry tells it, he thinks I never had to struggle for that identity, that I never had to fight to be heard or stand up for who I was, because I never needed to. All the hard work was done before I left high school. Or most of it, anyway. I'd never marched in a pride parade or done anything like that before I went to the Love All protests. It just never seemed like something that would affect me. But when I got caught up in it, when it became personal, then I saw the difference. And that's when Barry said that he and I needed to be on more even terms. He'd been wanting to come out for years, but couldn't find the courage. He said he found that in our relationship. Now it was personal. So he went for it."

"And it was amazing," I said, remembering the moment and picturing Barry's extravagant coming out to a

Diana Ross song at the Love All celebration gala. "Were you there?"

"Yeah, I was. I drove him there that night. He sent your mom ahead without him, and I came over after and helped him get ready and get into the limousine. I figured he deserved a ride in style that night. He was so nervous. I hope you don't mind that I stayed to watch. I figured it was a public celebration, so it was okay."

"Of course!"

"You and Luke had done so much to raise awareness for all of us. I was grateful, and really happy to be there."

"Thank you, Tucker." I smiled. "Well, I wish you'd said hello that night. But I'm just happy you're here, now."

"There you are!" Just then, Barry, er... Mr. Blueberry came running out on the terrace, cocktail in hand, of course. "*Oh*, that was a hoot! You should have seen Mr. Kiwi's face when he realized the tables were turned. This is the best Secret Sunday we've had in months, nephew. Great job!"

"Happy to hear that," I said. "I guess I should go inside and make sure Chip is still in one piece. Thanks for the chat, Tucker." I turned to head back into the building, but felt the need to say one more thing before I walked in. "I think you'd better hold onto this guy, Mr. Blueberry. He's one of the good ones, and they're rare."

"Oh, don't you worry, Mr. Date," he said. "Trust me, I know. That's why I signed him to a thirty-five year contract. I'm just lucky he didn't read the fine print."

16

GET THE PARTY STARTED

"I'm coming downstairs!" I yelled as I exited my room. "Put your clothes on!"

"You think you're so funny," sneered Barry, as he sat in his lounge chair watching a dancing competition on the new big screen TV. Tucker was rummaging about in the kitchen cupboards. Both of them were dressed for a casual night in.

"Well, you never know around here," I giggled. I went into the kitchen to grab the bottle of vodka I had bought to bring to Kit's party. Tucker was just putting the finishing touches on an elaborate snack tray. It looked like they had a full night of movie viewing ahead of them.

"I like your bracelet," I told Tucker. He was wearing a simple string of colorful plastic beads with a dangling tassel that held it all together.

"Oh, thanks," he smiled. "I just found this the other day in a drawer at my parents' house. We made them in kindergarten."

"So…basically yesterday, right?" Barry chimed in from his chair.

"No, yesterday I was in diapers," countered Tucker.

"Oh, that's good," said Barry. "You'll need the practice for taking care of me in the future."

■ ■ ■

Kit called to say that the whole gang would be at her and Shawn's housewarming party tonight, and she wanted me to know that Luke had called to make sure it was still okay for him to swing by. She had reassured him that it was. Everyone knew I was staying at Barry's for the time being, so I appreciated the warning, but truth be told, I was looking forward to seeing him. I missed him so much, missed his arms around me, missed our life together. I hoped that he would leave Fletch behind for a change, but I doubted it. I was really counting on Lana's latest scheme to work. It truly felt surreal that we were both on the same side for once.

I drove Willie Nelson into the rambling old neighborhood behind the mall and followed the directions to Kit and Shawn's new house. It was a split-level ranch with an enormous sloping yard full of massive knotty pines and Douglas fir trees. I parked out on the street, walked up the driveway and heard music coming from over the fenced-in backyard. I pushed open the old wooden gate.

"Baby! You're here!" Kit ran over to me with her arms extended wide and I went in for a deep hug. "*I. Missed. You!* We've barely seen you since you started your new job. I want to hear everything! Does that place have ghosts? Please tell me that place has ghosts. Every time I pass that mansion I think for sure something crazy has happened in there. There must be so many stories in a building like that."

"You don't know the half of it," I laughed, remembering the antics of this last Sunday. "Show me around! This place is fantastic!"

"First, we need to get you a drink," she said with glee. "I'm just not used to seeing your hand without a glass. It's like, *what's wrong with this picture*, you know?"

She rectified the situation with vodka, though she insisted on embellishing my glass with a paper umbrella and a vintage swizzle stick, "just for fun." She then took me on a whirlwind tour. They had three bedrooms upstairs and a man cave down below, with a fourth bedroom that Shawn converted into a rehearsal space for his '80s cover band, Shock the Monkey.

"It's huge!" I said. "What are you going to do with all this space?"

"Well, we can have fabulous parties, of course. And you can stay over whenever you want. It's crazy big, I know, but we got a really good deal and we couldn't pass it up. Since the gallery is doing so well, we just decided we were worth it. But sometimes I can't even find Shawn. We're not used to it. When I'm upstairs he sends me text messages from the man cave."

"Nothing says *I love you* like a text message from the basement," I cracked.

"*I. Know!*" she laughed. "But honestly, if he has his music playing, he can't even hear me if I call for him. We've become that couple that texts from opposite ends of the couch. You just know the millennials would approve!"

"At least he responds to your texts," I sighed. "Luke hates his phone, I swear. 'Why the heck would I want someone to be able to find me at any time of the day?' he says. Like that's a bad thing?"

"So," she nudged, "what's going on? Tommy and Bammy told me a few things, of course, but I don't really get it. *I. Love. You.* And from what it looks like to me, you don't seem to be loving yourself so much lately. And I have too much respect for you to let you go on treating yourself like you deserve anything less than the best."

"Oh, Kit. I love you. How do you hit things on the head so quickly?"

"Sometimes we share the same brain, baby. That's just the way it goes. But even if I get it, I don't really *get* it. Understand?"

"Yeah," I sighed. "But you do. Get it. It's my self-loathing rearing its ugly head again. I thought I had banished that beast years ago after a decade of really finding myself in New York. But coming back here, experiencing all of this with Luke, I think I've reverted, somehow. I've started to believe that I should settle for what I can get, rather than push for what I deserve. And Luke? He's living a lifetime of experiences in a speeded up version of coming out. I tried not to push him, but it was all just inevitable. I mean, he seemed to be fine for a while, but then that damn Fletch appeared. It's like Luke wants to go through his slut phase after coming out, but his relationship with me is holding him back. He loves me. I know he does. And he hasn't been unfaithful. But Fletch is really pulling him in so many directions now that he's free to be himself, to be openly sexual and crave the things that he repressed for so many years."

"Does this Fletch guy really have that much power over him?"

"It's so complicated, Kit. They have this really fucked up history. They definitely shared things that I can't remotely compete with."

"But it shouldn't be a competition, baby," she said, taking my hand in hers. "You've already got him. Look at everything you had to go through. Listen to me for a minute, okay?" We took a seat on the bed in the guest room. "I have a story for you. You know how they say that the dinosaurs were killed by a giant meteor? Well, I think that's partially true, but in my version it was a giant star that came crashing into the Earth. The dinosaurs were wiped out, but all those star particles got mixed up in everything, and millions of years later, we're all walking around with stardust inside of us. Except now we're trying to find the person who is made up of the same stardust as we are. It's a hunt, and it's not easy, but when you find that person with the same crazy particles as you have, well, then it's magic. You and Luke have magic. Don't forget that."

"I love you, Kit," I said, adamant that I wouldn't cry yet again.

"I know that, baby," she smiled. "Now let's get this party started!"

She pulled me from the bed and we went racing down the hall.

■ ■ ■

"I can't believe we used to get away with that," laughed Bammy. Michael was by her side as we sat at the patio table in Kit and Shawn's backyard, sharing crazy stories of our youth over plastic red party cups and chips. Tommy and Meredith had joined us late, but we were all finally back together, minus Luke, of course.

"Did you really pretend to be married?" asked Michael.

"Well, we told them we were engaged," Bammy continued. "I had this massive glass cocktail ring that was my grandmother's, and I used to pretend it was my engagement ring. Derek and I would casually show it to the realtors and say something silly like, 'Daddy says we can only spend two million, but I think I can get him to go higher if we really find a place we love.' Then they'd bend over backwards, driving us around to look at mansions all day long. It was amazing."

"We actually ran into Dolly Parton, one day, remember that?" I said. "We were up in the mountains looking at luxury hilltop cabins, and she was coming out of a viewing as we went in. It took everything I had not to break character and just bow down before her!"

"Oh, I totally would've," said Tommy.

"You don't get much more country royalty than Dolly," Meredith added.

"Did you never get found out?" Michael asked.

"Once we came really close," said Bammy. "We'd made an appointment with a realtor, but she called to say that she had to cancel at the last minute, so she hooked us up with her associate. Turns out, her colleague was Principal Bellman's wife! We had no idea she worked in that office. We hightailed it out of that parking lot before she saw us. We decided right then that we'd had enough fun and we'd better cut it out before we got in any trouble."

"More chips?" said Kit, ever the hostess. "Shawn, baby, can you run around and fill these up, please?" He dutifully jumped up from the table eager to comply.

"Oh, I can't have anymore," said Bammy, waving her hands. "I've already had my share of chips and queso this week, plus three people's share of alcohol!"

"Well, if you get too drunk we can just have a slumber party!" said Kit. "I'm convinced 'slumber' must mean 'drunken gossip and giggling' in some language, anyway."

■ ■ ■

The night was fun, but I had this uneasy feeling in the back of my mind the whole time. I kept looking over my shoulder waiting for Luke to show up. I'd wandered off towards the far corner of the yard while the party raged on close to the house. I heard footsteps behind me and I was relieved when I turned and saw Tommy approaching.

"I didn't scare you, did I?" he asked.

"No, I was just afraid it was Luke. I don't know what I'm going to say when he gets here."

"Just be honest, man," Tommy reasoned. "Tell him that Fletch is a dick and he has to go."

"I tried that. And more. We ended up having a forty-five minute conversation and then I moved out. Problem is, I don't know if I'm really honest, or if I just don't know when to shut my mouth?"

"The second," he nodded. "Definitely the second."

"Thanks, Tommy. I knew I could count on you for your support," I teased, and then we clinked our beer bottles together in solidarity.

"You know I'm just messing with you, man," he said. "Meredith has my brain going in circles right now, so I'm just happy to watch someone else's struggles."

"What's going on?" I asked. "Care to share?"

"It's nothing bad. She's just started to talk about babies."

"Babies?" I said. "As in plural? I didn't even know you'd discussed marriage yet?"

"We haven't," he said. "I'm thinking if I get her a cat that'll work."

"I'm not really a cat person," I said, scrunching my nose.

"Me neither. But at least I can ignore a cat. A dog would be so much more work."

"Oh, yeah," I laughed. "And still way less than a baby. I just don't think I'm ready for that."

"Have you guys talked about kids?" he asked.

"No, not at all. We had that scare with Jett. Thank God that turned out to be false. And right now we have our hands full with Fletch. That's like having the horniest kid in America. Let's get over this hump, then we can talk about other stuff."

"Well, speaking of the horny devil," said Tommy. "Looks like they just walked in."

I glanced over at the wooden gate to see Luke and Fletch entering the back yard. They had brought along a few brown paper bags. Beer, I guessed. That was kind of them, considering how much Fletch drank. I had to admit I was a little bummed that he had brought Fletch along. I was really hoping Luke would have come solo so we could chat in private.

"Luke, baby, we're so glad you could come!" Kit greeted them as if they were all friends, even though she didn't know Fletch all that well. "Put those drinks in the cooler over there and come join us."

Fletch immediately zeroed in on a group of pretty girls standing by the snack table and he started passing out bottles. Luke sat down with Kit, Meredith, Bammy and Michael, giving his half-brother a hug. He hadn't seen me yet, but I could tell from his body language that he didn't feel totally at ease. Was he as nervous as I was?

"You going over to say hi?" asked Tommy.

"In a minute," I said. "Right now I'm just going to enjoy these stars. Something Kit said earlier about stardust. It has me thinking."

"Well, all right," he said. "Just tell us if you need anything." He wandered back to join the gang, stopping at the bar to get another beer first. He gave Fletch a nod of recognition, but he was totally ignored. All Fletch was interested in was boobs tonight. At least that was a step in the right direction.

My phone buzzed and I pulled it out of my pocket to take a look. It was a text from Reggie in New York. *It was great seeing you guys. Hope things are back to normal. Say hi to Luke!*

I wrote back quickly to say how much we appreciated his hospitality. Then I threw in a *Bammy says hi*, just to mess with him. I didn't mention Luke, though. Maybe this was normal for us, now? I hoped not.

"Texting Kit?" I heard his voice as he came up behind me. It was Luke, and thankfully he was alone. "I know how you two love emoji. Sorry, I just can't get on board with that."

"Nah, it was Reggie, actually. He said to say hello."

"Cool."

"Cool," I added. Silence. We tipped our beers back and drank, unsure of what to say next.

"Well, this is awkward," he said, kicking the dirt with the tip of his shoe.

"Sorry," I said. "I don't know what to say. Kit told me this story about dinosaurs and stardust and how you and I are magic together because we're made of the same stars. It made more sense when she said it, I guess."

"I get it," he smiled. "And she's probably right. We are pretty good together."

"So what are we doing?" I said, my voice raising, clearly frustrated. "I mean, this is stupid. I love you, you love me, so why are we fighting? Why are we letting Fletch Powell get between us?"

"It's not just Fletch," he said. "Don't pretend it's that easy. I wish it was, but it's not. I'm the first to admit, Fletch is in the way. And to be honest, I'm pretty ready for him to leave. But once he's gone, will everything just magically pop back into place? I don't think so." He put his beer bottle to his lips and sipped.

At least he was admitting that Fletch was not helping. That was a huge admission that I was grateful to have acknowledged.

"So what's the issue?" I asked.

"It's the same old crap I've been dealing with for years," he said. "Meeting you brought everything to the surface, and fast. But the reality is, I haven't really had time to process all of it. You had your wild years in New York. I never really had those. I mean, I did, in a sense, but I was straight back then. I never had *my* wild, gay years. I never had one night stands, never had my heart broken by a jerk I wanted to be with, never had a health scare. And I'm not saying I wanted to do all those things, but the fact is, I just didn't get to. I didn't experience coming out like you did. Did I miss something? Would I be different now? I'll never know. And then hanging out with Fletch has just reignited all these old emotions and situations I had long buried. Not all of them are good. But still, all that stuff I did, plus all that stuff I wanted to do, well, they're kind of clashing in my head right now. I just feel torn in so many directions. I have my loyalty to Fletch, my loyalties to my family, my love for you. It's all just really complicated, right now. I'm sorry. I just need more time."

"Can I help, in any way?" I asked.

"I just need you to be supportive," he sighed. "I know you are, but it doesn't help this whole situation when I can see you ready to battle Fletch at the drop of a hat. You don't need to be jealous of him, I promise. That guy is a mess, trust me. I think in some way, if I can just try to fix him and send him off, then I'm hoping everything else in my life will get back on track."

"So I'm just supposed to wait patiently while you figure things out?" I asked. "So you get to decide if you're the old, wild Luke, or a new version influenced by your past with Fletch?"

"Or maybe I'm becoming a new Luke, altogether? With the best pieces of all of them. I don't know, just yet. But I can't ask you any other way. I just need some time to figure it out."

My head started reeling. Maybe this plan with Lana was a mistake. Maybe it was all an elaborate scheme of hers to break us up for good. Whatever it was, the balls were already lined up, ready to roll, and I didn't think there was any turning back. Too many people were involved already.

Deep inside I knew Luke would be angry with me for tarnishing Fletch's reputation. But it was well past time that someone took down that golden boy for good. I hadn't even considered the fact that Lana could be lying to me. That simply wasn't an option.

I just couldn't believe that she had convinced me to trust Amber Winthrop, of all people.

17

AMBER ALERT

"So when exactly did you book this party?" my bartender Sam asked. "Because it wasn't on the schedule last week." He, Crosby and a few more cater waiters were gathered in the library at the Duke on a Saturday afternoon, preparing the rooms for this afternoon's event.

"It was very last minute," I answered, not wanting to talk too much about it. "Thanks for being flexible and being available to work. I know things have been a bit slow after I took over the company, but now that we're ready for business, I expect we'll see more bookings." At least I hoped so.

"So who's this party for?" he asked.

"It's for Amber Winthrop. She's the bride-to-be, and she's engaged to Todd Carmichael."

"That Carmichael Motors guy?" asked Crosby as he was polishing silver. "Man, he has some nice cars on his lot. Mustangs, Corvettes, you name it."

"That's the one," I said. "This is their engagement party. The wedding isn't scheduled, yet." And that's all I said. But I wanted to add that Amber used to date Luke in high school and also in college. I wanted to tell them that this past spring she tried to pass off her son Jett as Luke's biological child, until she finally admitted that he wasn't. I wanted to tell them that she'd already gone through three husbands, and that we probably shouldn't try too hard to make sure that she even married number four. I wanted to scream from the rooftops that I didn't trust her at all, but I had no choice. These were the cards I had drawn, the hand I was given, and we were about to play a very interesting game of Liar's Poker.

"Crosby, why don't you finish up that polishing and then go help Sam set up the bar? These people like to drink. Trust me. But first I need one person to set up the cupcake table and I'll tackle these flower arrangements. Oh, and can one of you make sure the hangers are organized in the wardrobe for the guests' coats?"

With their assignments set, the team dispersed from the library towards the bar, outer salon, foyer and terrace. Amber had been very specific in her requirements, and regardless of how I felt about her as a person, I wanted to make sure we hit every note right on the mark. Normally I would say *this is the bride's special day*, but Amber had already had three of these. She kept going after richer and richer men, but I really hoped that this one would stick. If not, well…I owned a catering and event space, and I could use the repeat business.

While Sam started setting up his bar, Crosby wheeled out a round table and placed it in the center of the salon. He draped the table in fresh white tablecloths to the floor, then pinned the edges to make sure nothing would slip. We placed the cupcake tower in the center, added the treats, and then arranged the dessert plates, forks, napkins and votive candles around the tower. We used the large antique mahogany table underneath the giant gilt edged mirror to set up a coffee station, though I was sure no one would drink anything other than bubbles, beer and vodka. Amber had specifically requested orange wine coolers, so Sam had special ordered those and set them up in large metal ice buckets on the terrace. The bride-to-be wanted her guests to have easy access to plenty of drinks, so we obliged.

All of Amber's flowers were varying degrees of red and orange of course. We had arranged a massive bouquet towards the back center of the room, as well as smaller red and orange arrangements throughout the main salon, library and outdoor terrace. I was sure that she'd love it but I couldn't get over the feeling that we were celebrating their engagement in the middle of a fast food restaurant with all these bright colors. Welcome to our McWedding!

A large format poster-sized photograph of the newly engaged couple was prominently placed on an easel by the foyer, ready to welcome the guests. Todd wasn't a bad looking guy, actually. He reminded me a little of Matthew McConaughey, but a touch more hyper than stoned. Todd was from another county so he didn't have any ties to Parkville High, which was a good thing. He hadn't grown up hearing stories of the convoluted history between Amber and Luke, like the rest of us had. Eventually Amber had to look outside of her well-known pool of men in order to find someone untainted by her history, and he just happened to be the latest in a string of fiancés she called *the one*.

It was almost 3 pm and our guests were due to start arriving at any moment. The engagement party was planned as an afternoon cocktail reception, scheduled to end at 5 pm. Amber wanted to save the big celebration for the wedding. There was still no date set for that since Todd had just popped the question last week. Amber swore it was unexpected, but we weren't supposed to believe that, right? She knew exactly what she was doing, at all times.

"Derek! It looks beautiful. I love it!" Amber squealed as she entered the front door of the Duke. She was holding Todd's hand tightly as she marched straight to the center of the room to approve the cupcake tower. "It's just perfect! Look, Mama. Isn't that pretty?"

Mama did indeed find it pretty and I was grateful. Mothers of the bride are always the most vocal of critics, but I figured she had done this three times already so it was old hat by now. She nodded her head and *oohed* and *ahhed* with the rest of Amber's bridesmaids, including Lana

Walcott. Amber's son Jett followed closely behind wearing that special smirk that clearly said *I would love to be anywhere but here.* Trust me kid, I felt the same.

"Hello, Derek," said Lana. "Everything looks beautiful."

"Watch out, Lana," I said, "that almost sounded like you meant it."

She curled her upper lip at me and rolled her eyes. "I was just wondering," she began, "Daddy and Rosa were thinking of having a little gathering..." and her voice trailed off as she pulled me to the side window where no one else could overhear us. "Listen," she said, seriously. "You just play your part and this will all go off without a hitch."

"It had better," I said, smiling through clenched teeth. "Otherwise, we're screwed."

■ ■ ■

The guests began to arrive promptly after Amber and Todd's entrance and they made their way slowly around the room, taking everything in and socializing. Sam had his hands full with guests at the bar while the rest helped themselves to the fizzy orange wine coolers on the terrace. The wait staff passed crab cake appetizers, chicken skewers, and mini quiches on silver trays covered in white doilies and accented with orange flowers. Amber had spared no expense, and I wanted to make a good impression for the Duke, regardless of my feelings for Amber.

The main salon was filling up, so I began directing guests to the outer terrace for some fresh air and cocktails. As I walked outside, Crosby had just offered an appetizer to a gentleman who was double fisting a beer and a wine cooler.

"Well, hell, I ain't got no free hands!" he laughed, and then bent over and sucked a mini quiche into his mouth right off the silver tray. Crosby froze.

"Crosby, why don't we head into the kitchen and refill that tray for our guests?" I said, placing my hand on his shoulder and steering him to the kitchen.

"What the *hell* was that?" he said, slamming his tray down on the stainless steel counter. The chef just stared at him, unsure if he had just insulted her cooking or if there was a different kind of problem.

"Crosby, it's going to be that kind of night," I said. "Why don't you take a ten minute break? And get yourself a drink from the bar. Better yet, get two. Sam already knows what I like."

■ ■ ■

"Derek, what on *Earth* are we doing here?" asked Bammy, after she spotted me from the foyer and waved me down. She and Michael both looked as if they had come to the wrong party. The staff had already taken their coats and placed them in the wardrobe closet off the foyer.

"Bammy, Michael, so great to see you both," I said, ignoring her question and smiling like a man with a secret. "Can I get you a drink?"

"Well, yes," she stammered. "Do you need to ask? But that still doesn't answer my question. Why are we *here*?" she repeated, with emphasis and a sneer.

"Bammy darling, let's get you a cocktail and step outside, okay?" I hinted, strongly.

"Come on to the bar, Bammy," said Michael. "I have a feeling if Amber is involved, then so is Luke, which means fireworks. He's expected too, right?"

"Of course he is," I said. "Now let's introduce you to Sam and his magical cocktail shaker."

Sam set us up quickly with a friendly smile and then moved on to his next guests. I led Bammy and Michael out to the terrace and we huddled by the metal gate in the back, far from the prying eyes and sensitive ears of Amber's friends and relatives who had gathered for this joyous occasion.

"Derek, you know how much I hate secrets," said Bammy.

"Do you? Really?" I said, my head cocking to one side.

"Fine," she said, her eyes narrowed. "I love them. But I loathe not being in on them. You have to tell me what's going on! Why were we invited to this party? Oh, my *god*." She put her hand to her mouth. "Is this another one of those? Like at Red and Rosa's? Oh, my god, Derek. Please tell me Michael doesn't have another secret brother. Or sister! My heart couldn't take it."

"It's nothing like that," I assured her. "You're not involved directly at all this time. There's nothing to worry about."

"Then why are we here? Seriously, Derek. If you don't answer my question, I swear, we will walk out the door right now."

"Bammy, babe. Please. You just have to trust me. You're here to witness a resolution. That's it."

"A resolution? Like a promise? Like New Year's? I don't get it."

"No, not that." I wanted to tell her everything, but I couldn't risk upsetting the universe. All the pieces had to fall just right. "A resolution. An end. Or, at least, I hope so."

■ ■ ■

"Derek, there you are."

I turned to see Lana. She had on that plastic smile that either meant she was pleased, infuriated, or backed into a corner and ready to attack. Knowing her, it meant all three. I'm just glad I wasn't the intended target, this time.

"Will you excuse me, please?" I said to Bammy and Michael, then stepped back and walked away slowly with Lana. She continued to smile and made no sudden moves, her hand in the crook of my arm. We made sure that to any inquisitive eyes it would appear that we were just making small talk.

"They're here," she said, the plastic smile not actually moving. How did she do that?

"Luke and Fletch?" I asked.

"Yes, of course. What did you expect? Code names?" She laughed out loud for the benefit of any onlookers, as if I had just made the wittiest joke of the season.

I touched her arm slightly, then threw my head back in the same staccato laugh and said, still smiling, "Oh, Lana, I cannot wait until you and I can go back to casually ignoring each other, again. You scare the hell out of me, you know that?"

"Of course I do. That's exactly how you should feel. And you do, because you're smart."

"That almost sounded like it wasn't an insult."

"What can I say? You're growing on me." She raised her eyebrow and casually scanned the terrace to make sure no one was listening.

"Where are they? Luke and Fletch," I asked.

"At the bar, of course," she said, "but I expect they'll start wandering soon. You remember what to do next, right?"

"Of course I do, Lana. We've gone over every minute detail like this is the spy mission of the century. At exactly 4:15 pm my staff will start to gather all the guests in the main salon. Amber and Todd will make their special announcement, Fletch will feel the pain, and then we'll pass out the cupcakes while he leaves to make peace with his past and contemplate his future."

"And then he'll run on back to New York to make up with that wife of his who is so pill happy she can't see what's in front of her face," she said. "Fletch isn't the kind of guy who ever put too much effort into caring about anyone else but himself, but if I'm to believe your first-hand account, she doesn't even seem to notice. That's easy enough to fix. They're perfect for each other. Pretty, rich and medicated."

"And you're sure Todd's cool with this?" I asked, again. "He must really love Amber."

"Well, I don't know about that part, but yes, Amber told me she'd tell Todd everything before she made this public scene."

"But did she actually follow through with that?" I asked.

Lana stopped smiling. "She said she would."

"And Amber would never lie to her best friend, right?" I asked, my smile fading, as well. I already knew the answer to that, and so did Lana.

"*Shit,*" she said, all happy pretenses gone. "Where is she? Have you seen her? What time is it?"

"It's five after four," I said, panicking. "In ten minutes the staff is going to start gathering her guests. We have to find her, quick."

"I swear to you, Derek, if this girl pulls another stunt, she's dead to me. No one lies to me twice and gets away with it."

I had no doubts that Lana meant business. There was no way I'd ever cross her, and I didn't even pretend to like her. I admired her strength, though, and that's why I knew better. We had ten minutes to find the bride-to-be and make sure she was still going ahead with our mission as planned.

Please, Amber, do not go off-script, I thought. I wasn't sure we could improvise.

■ ■ ■

Lana and I both quickly scanned the terrace and saw no signs of Amber or Todd. We ran up the steps into the building and peered into the library, eyeing all the booths and tables. Still no happy couple.

"They have to be in the salon. Or the bar?" I said.

"Bathrooms," she said, frantically. "Where are they?"

"Here, down this hall." I grabbed her hand without thinking and it actually seemed like something I would do with a friend. "You take the ladies' and I'll take the men's."

We stuck our heads in and called. Nothing. I stepped inside and looked under the one stall, then opened the door.

"Empty," I said when I met her back in the hallway.

"Mine, too," she answered, the look of anger growing in her eyes.

The main salon was packed, as guests were already making their way in. I spotted Luke standing at the bar with a beer in his hand. He was talking to a man in a suit, his back to me. My view was obstructed so I couldn't see if it was Fletch or Todd.

"Come on, there's Luke." I pulled Lana with me through the crowd, still scanning left and right.

"Hi," I said, and forced a smile. "Sorry for interrupting."

"Hi?" he said, quizzically. "Why are you holding my sister's hand?"

Lana and I both jolted. We looked down, released our hands, and then laughed that eerie staccato laugh from before, hoping it would cover our tracks.

"You two are acting strange," he said. "What's going on?"

"Well, I think it's awesome that your boyfriend and sister are friends," said Todd, standing in his suit, enjoying a beer with Luke.

We didn't have time for this.

"*Todd*!" I practically yelled, then lowered my voice. "Todd, we're so happy to find you. Everyone's gathering for your announcement. Have you seen Amber? Where is she? We need to find her fast, to...uh." I looked to Lana for help.

Just then, a woman's hands appeared from behind Luke's head and covered his eyes.

"Guess who?" she said in a Southern drawl, then popped her head around and kissed him on the cheek. She was a redhead, but the wrong one.

"Brandee!" he smiled and hugged her. "I'm so glad you could make it. Todd, have you met Brandee? This is Fletch's wife. I asked her to come down here from New York. I hope you don't mind that I invited her to crash your party?"

"Not at all, man! You know I got a thing for redheads, after all. I'm about to marry one," Todd said, proudly.

"Brandee, you remember Derek, of course," said Luke. "And this is my sister, Lana."

"Well, doesn't this place look all fancy?" Brandee said, her eyes gazing left and right, up and down. "I cannot wait to take pictures. Y'all are just gonna love my pictures. You remember I'm on Instagram, right? Well y'all just go about your business, but I'm gonna snap away. I'll filter 'em up, tag 'em, the whole deal. I can make amazing collages. My followers love them. I have so many followers. *So* many. You'd be amazed. And they just love everything I post. They'll just be huntin' y'all down after I get through with this. What's your hashtag?"

"Uh…um," I stammered. What the hell had Luke done? *He invited Brandee?* Why?! Where was Amber? Everything was going wrong. Everything. Could it get worse?

"The Duke. One word. Um, hashtag the Duke." Honestly, we didn't even have an Instagram account yet. But I certainly couldn't go into that right now.

"Todd, we need to find Amber." Lana brought us back on track. "Your guests are waiting, and we just want to give her a little pep talk before you start."

She was so focused, even I believed her. Lana quickly glanced behind us, and sure enough, the main salon was filled with partygoers. They had claimed their spots surrounding the cupcake table, as the staff had suggested. But instead of focusing on the sweets, all eyes were on us.

"Well, she's got to be here somewhere," he said, still smiling, then scanned his head left and right, like a gopher popping out of a hole. "'Tell ya what, she's always got her phone on her. That girl loves her phone."

"Oh, I get that," said Brandee. "Me, too!"

We heard the phone ring, the sound coming from just behind us, near the front door. Was she on the front porch socializing? Todd took a few steps between me, Luke and Lana. We followed behind, slowly, as we heard the phone ring again from inside the wardrobe closet.

"Damn," he said. "I guess she must've left her phone in her coat pocket." He placed his hand on the doorknob and pulled it open.

There on a pile of coats on the floor lay Amber, her tongue exploring every square inch of Fletch's mouth, her hands madly pulling his shirttails up from his trousers to get to the prize. For a split second, they hadn't realized the door was no longer closed. When her eyes opened, she frantically pushed Fletch off with a massive flutter of her hands.

"What the *hell*, Amber?" said Fletch, pissed off.

"Oh, *shit*," she said, to no one…and everyone.

18

THE MAN TRAP

Todd lunged at Fletch before anyone even realized what was going on. What happened next was pure chaos, a Tennessee train wreck.

Lana started screaming, out of pure frustration, perhaps? This caused everyone in the main salon to rush towards the bar and the foyer, but especially the wardrobe closet. That was a terrible idea, because as soon as Todd had Fletch in his clutches, he dragged his ass up, out, and slammed him right back into the crowded room, knocking down several guests who couldn't move out of the way quickly enough. That left Amber on the ground by herself, but not for long. Brandee pounced on her like a wildcat and began pulling her hair, slapping and cursing up a storm.

Everything happened so fast, there was no way of telling how or why we chose to go where we did, but we all had to jump in to try and break this up before someone was seriously hurt. The crowd parted around Fletch as he took a fighting stance, eyes wild. I grabbed Todd from behind as he was about to take a swing at the man he just found kissing his fiancée, and Luke curved around me and tackled Fletch to the ground, causing more screams of panic from the guests. Todd immediately threw me off him and I landed back on the bar with a thud. He then body slammed right into Luke and Fletch, and the three of them landed on the floor and flailed about. They made it to their feet just in time for Fletch to hurl Luke into the cupcake tower so he could take Todd on his own. The table collapsed under Luke's weight, the dishes crashed to the floor and the cupcake tower showered red and orange treats across the room.

By now the crowd had flown into a full panic. Guests ran out the front, others made a retreat for the terrace. The orange wine coolers had unfortunately emboldened the men in the crowd, many of whom stayed to watch or throw a few punches of their own. They skidded on cake and frosting as they leapt into the fray. Arms delivered punches, feet kicked whichever bodies were closest, and blows landed everywhere but where they were intended.

Meanwhile, Brandee had dragged Amber out from the wardrobe closet by her hair and was straddling her on the carpet in the foyer, lifting her head up and down, slamming it repeatedly on the black and white tiled floor. Lana grabbed the floral arrangement from the crystal cut vase and began whacking Brandee over the head with the flowers, trying to get her off the bride-to-be, screaming her head off. When that failed to do anything other than add mutilated petals to the already chaotic scene, Lana reached back around, grabbed the vase and dumped the water over Brandee's head. Brandee screamed in rage and let go of Amber just in time for Amber's mother and bridesmaids to knock Brandee to the ground. Lana wasted no time in taking Brandee's place and immediately jumped on top of Amber, herself.

"*What have you done?*" screamed Lana. "What were you thinking?"

"Get off me, you bitch!" Amber yelled.

"*Bitch?!* Just you wait!" Lana and Amber began tumbling across the floor, rolling and screaming, yelling and pulling hair, slapping and cursing.

Surveying the chaos, I was frozen. I felt a tug at my shoulder and turned to see that Jett had hopped up to sit on the bar behind me. He'd poured himself a drink and was watching the nightmare unfold in front of us, smiling as if no other present in the world had ever pleased him this much.

"You sure know how to throw a great party, Mr. Walter," he sneered, then held up his drink, winked and took a sip.

I looked at the mess in the main room and I couldn't even tell who was fighting who anymore. Luke, Fletch and Todd were in a battle royale, with Sam and Crosby trying their best to pull bodies off bodies and hold back the taunting men. Michael had joined in at some point, trying to assist Luke, but there was no helping at this point. Amber, Lana and the bridesmaids had rolled their way precariously close to the same pile. Something had to be done.

I spotted the answer, but I had to get there fast. I made a beeline for the soundboard by the edge of the stage, stepping on a few fingers and tripping over a few bodies along the way. Amber and Todd's engagement song was all cued up, so I raised all the volume levels to maximum and pressed play as quickly as I could. The cloyingly sweet sounds of Céline Dion suddenly filled the air as everyone grabbed their ears, momentarily deafened by the music levels. The mountains of bodies on the floor stopped throwing punches as they sat up, trying to protect themselves from the aural assault. The crowd started yelling, but not for the same reasons as before.

"Stop! Turn it off! Make it stop!" they screamed, not sure where it was coming from or why it was happening.

I pressed pause and yelled, "*No more fighting* or I turn it back on, understand?!"

They grumbled, bitched and moaned, but it seemed the last punches had finally been thrown. Hands started reaching down, lifting those who had fallen in battle. Women were crying, mascara running down their faces. Men had bloody noses, jackets were torn. And every single surface of the Duke was covered in red and orange frosting, the cupcakes smeared across the entire floor, every wall and countless bodies.

"Sam? Crosby? Where are you?" I yelled.

"Over here." I saw a hand raise up from the floor in the middle of the room. Sam had a bloody nose, but he didn't even look as bad off as some of the others.

"Let's get some towels from the linen closet. We need water and ice. Everybody, we're going to need you to help us figure out if anyone's really hurt badly."

I looked down at the pile of people sorting themselves out while my staff picked themselves up and headed to the back to get supplies. There was one pair of eyes locked on me with a pure, focused rage. This was a side of Luke I had never seen, and I knew right then we'd both gone too far to turn back.

■ ■ ■

We helped clean up the injured as best as we could. Amber's mom wanted to call the police, but Amber convinced her otherwise. She didn't want to draw any more attention to this mess than necessary, but who was she kidding? The whole town would know in a matter of hours, if not minutes.

A few people left, but surprisingly many of them opted to stay. They were milling about the floor of the main salon trading war stories and knocking back free drinks. An air of levity had returned for a few. The enemies of moments ago were friends again. Except, of course, for our main combatants.

It was impossible to tell who was on whose side anymore, as they all looked as if they were ready to kill, hide or explode. Luke was outwardly angry with Lana and me. Lana was shooting eye daggers at Amber. Amber and Todd were at odds. Fletch was his arrogant self while poor Brandee just wondered why the hell she was even there to begin with. So did I, for that matter.

We had all calmed down to a point where I thought we could begin to make sense of everything that had just happened and get down to the real matter we had come to discuss. But before I could start our group therapy session, Jett beat me to it and cut through the relative silence.

"That was a lot more fun than your last engagement party, Mama," he started laughing, clearly drunk.

That was the very cue that everybody needed to start yelling again.

"She started it!"

"He punched me first!"

"What the hell was that?"

"I shoulda punched you harder!"

"Get outta my face, man!"

"You're a bitch!"

"I never liked you, anyway!"

"Why am I even here?!"

"ENOUGH!" The voice was loud and authoritative, strong enough to make everyone stop yelling and turn their heads. Only a schoolteacher could command a room like that.

"Since *all y'all* think you know what's going on, but none of the rest of us do, then I think we should probably figure this out, right?" It was Bammy, and she was taking charge. "Now listen up. I don't want to hear another peep out of anyone unless I ask, you got that?" The heads began bobbing slowly, up and down.

"Bammy," I began, but she shut me down, and quick.

"*Not a word!*" she said, threatening me with one authoritative finger. "Unless you wanna lose something you may need, you'll be quiet until you're called on, you got that?"

Jett giggled and she silenced him instantly with her eyes. Bammy had taken the power, and the floor was hers.

"All right then," she began. "Amber, this is your engagement party. I'm gonna start with you." She turned to face her witness directly. "What exactly happened here today?"

Amber looked to Todd and managed a weak smile. I could see in her eyes that she was about to play it coy. "I just don't know," she said sweetly.

"Lying *bitch*!" yelled Lana.

"LANA!" Bammy silenced them both with her voice, yet again. "I've told you all once and I'm not gonna say it again. I have no dog in this fight, and if we're going to get to the bottom of this, y'all need someone impartial. The way I see it, *all y'all* have been in bed with each other in one way or another over the years. We've had enough of the secrets. It's time all your stories came out and that's exactly what we're gonna do. Now, Amber." She stared at her again. "This is your engagement party to Todd, right?"

"Yes, ma'am," she said, seemingly aware of Bammy's now established authority.

"So was it a good idea to make out with Fletch in the wardrobe closet?"

"Probably not."

"Want to tell us how that came to be?"

"How much time have you got?" huffed Amber and folded her arms. A half smile appeared across Fletch's lips.

"Look, Amber, we have all the time in the world," said Bammy, not falling for her delay tactics, "but sooner or later it's all gonna come out. Why don't you take this opportunity to get your version settled before we hear from the others? It's a simple question. Why were you making out with Fletch, and how long has this been going on?"

Amber sighed. There was no way out, she was caught. It was what she came here to do, anyway. And so her tale began.

"First off, let me say to my mama that I'm sorry about all of this. I can explain, but you're not gonna like it. Second, I wanna say to you, Todd, that I *do* love you. I really do, and I hope you'll forgive me, but there's just something about Fletch that still makes me crazy after all these years. Lana," she turned to face her friend, "I'm sorry. I know we had a plan, but I lost my courage. I just couldn't tell Todd before the party like I was supposed to. And then I got here and Fletch was here and, well, something other than my brain took over and *kablooey*, I ended up on that floor in there making out like my life depended on it. But in order to explain all of that, I have to go back pretty far. To you, Luke." She nodded towards him and smiled. "You were my first love, my first real boyfriend. Everything I did, I did for you. When Fletch introduced us as freshmen, he was very clear that he wanted us to be together. And we were everything that everyone wanted to be! I loved it. But by the time we started college at UT, well, my past started to catch up on me. We had broken up and gotten back together so many times, but I figured we'd be good because you knew me so well by then. You'd heard rumors about me cheating, but you stayed, until you couldn't. I guess you were finally fed up with me, but you also had this other stuff, this *gay* stuff to figure out. And I felt really betrayed. And that hurt, Luke," she whimpered. But clearly, he was having none of it. "So I told Lana that Jett was your son, and spent all last spring trying to make your life a living hell. But in the end, none of that mattered. You made me look foolish, again. Which I guess I am. 'Cause here I am again, making a mess of my life, like always." The crocodile tears began to flow, and Bammy snapped her fingers at Sam who ran over with a handful of cocktail napkins from the bar.

"All right, Amber," said Bammy. "We know all this, and I know it's tough, but you're getting closer. That's not the whole story. What else is there?"

Amber dried her fake tears and looked up. "Luke? You know I was cheating on you in college. I admitted that long ago. But what I didn't tell you was, I was cheating on you in high school, too. With Fletch."

Fletch smiled and Luke's glare shifted from me to his best buddy. This part I knew. This was what we had wanted Amber to tell Todd in advance. Well, part of it, at least.

There were definitely more details to come. I just hoped Luke could handle it.

"He didn't love me," said Amber. "I knew he didn't, but that didn't matter. The way I saw it, I had the two hottest guys in school, one of 'em as my boyfriend, and the other one for some extra fun. Everyone wanted at least one of them and I had them both. But it was like we were in a threesome, and I wasn't there half the time. You two kept hanging out with each other and leaving me out, and that pissed me off. It pissed off Lana, too, but for other reasons. She wanted Fletch, of course." Lana grimaced at the memory. "So I figured I needed to do something quick, to make sure I had one of you, for good. So I got pregnant when I was sixteen."

"Amber, we didn't..." said Luke, but Bammy's turn of the head made him stop mid-sentence.

"I know, Luke," Amber said. "We always used condoms. But I never did with Fletch." Eyes began darting about the room. Fletch folded his arms and sank a bit deeper into his chair as Brandee's back stiffened even more. "I was pregnant with Fletch's baby that fall when he started football at UT. He was the hero that semester, winning all his games as a freshman quarterback. I couldn't be prouder. Fletch was already dating Brandee at the time, and I knew I needed to do something. On one hand, I had Luke, but on the other hand, I had a future football star and his baby on the way."

"Amber, you don't need to go there." Fletch spoke up, his apparent irritation growing.

"Yeah I do, Fletch. It's way past time." She reached for a glass of water by her side and took a big gulp before continuing. "Nobody in this room knows what happened next except for me and Fletch. That night he wrecked his Big Orange Mustang and ended his football career? He wasn't alone in his car. I was sitting right beside him."

Everyone's eyes went wide with disbelief. I looked at Lana and her face told me that she didn't know this, either. When we involved Amber, we were just hoping to send Fletch packing. This story went much deeper than either of us could have imagined.

"I had just told Fletch I was pregnant with his baby. I was going to break up with Luke and I wanted Fletch to end it with Brandee. He was furious with me, yelling about his football career and saying we were too young to have a kid. Next thing I know, I'm opening my eyes, staring at a broken windshield. Fletch had wrapped the car around a telephone pole. He was a mess, blood everywhere, but there wasn't a scratch on me. Nothing. He turned to me all dazed and said, 'Get out of here, fast. No one can see you.' And so I did. My door popped right open, and I ran and hid in the woods, crying as I saw the ambulance and police cars surrounding him. I watched it all from the safety of those trees. His career was over, and I was fine, unhurt. Or at least I thought I was. Three days later I lost the baby."

Lana started crying. Even Brandee was unsure of where her loyalties were supposed to lie. Fletch, Todd, Luke and I were all in shock, just staring ahead as the story unfolded.

"Fletch broke up with Brandee and went into rehab. Then they got back together and moved away to New York. I never thought I'd see him again. By then I was back together with Luke, for good, I thought. But I kept cheating, of course. By the time he and I were freshmen at UT ourselves, I was pretty sure Luke and I were a thing of the past, and we broke up for the last time. That same year I took a trip up to New York for spring break with my girls. You went with me, Lana. And when I came home I found out I was pregnant again. A few weeks later I just did the sensible thing and married the first guy who asked me. I thought I could put all of that messy past behind me, for good. The baby wasn't his, of course. That's you, Jett. Mama loves you. I always have and I always will. I married my first husband because I knew he would provide for us in a way that your real daddy never could."

She turned to face Fletch.

"Isn't it about time you acknowledged your son, Fletch? Jett, this is your real daddy. You should say hello."

Every eye in the room turned slowly to Jett.

"Hey there, Daddy!" Jett said, laughing hysterically as he fell from the bar onto the floor.

Amber went on to explain that she had quietly met up with Fletch while on her spring break in New York. He had cheated on Brandee, of course, and Jett was the result. She didn't bother trying to break up his relationship this time, because she knew she'd never have him all to herself. She had what she wanted. She had a piece of him, forever.

"So I married my first husband, and then the second and third. Jett and I haven't had the perfect life, but I can't complain. I never asked Fletch for anything."

"Let me get this straight," said Luke. He turned to Fletch. "You were fooling around with me *and* my girl-friend in high school?"

"Hey, man," said Fletch. "You were gay for *me*, not the other way around. Don't you forget that."

"And you got her pregnant? Twice?" Luke's chest was heaving. He looked like he was about to explode. "And you *knew* about this?"

"Hey, buddy, you're forgetting something," said Fletch, arrogantly. "That whole thing was my set-up. You and Amber? I *made* that happen, am I right? And if I wanted to take some finder's right's every now and then, well, I earned that."

"You sorry son of a bitch." Luke stood up, his chair falling behind him. "You knew Jett was your kid, but you never said anything, even during all that crap I was going through this spring, when my world was falling apart?"

"I've had enough of this," said Brandee, standing up. "Amber? I'm sorry I knocked you on your ass, but you two deserve each other and you can have him if you want him. Luke, thank you for calling me down here to witness this. I know it was your plan for me to make up with Fletch and get him out of your hair, but that's just not gonna happen anymore. Derek? If you cater divorce parties, you let me know. Because I like what you did around here and I'm gonna take my lousy cheatin' ass husband for everything he's worth. I'm outta here." She stormed towards the door, fists balled.

"Brandee!" Fletch called after her. "These people are crazy, am I right? Come on, you know me! You know what I'm like. Hell, you love it!" And he was out the door after her, and not a soul seemed to care that he had left his mess behind, once again.

"Bye, Daddy," said Jett, dissolving into laughter on the floor. "See you in New York!"

19

ALWAYS BE PREPARED

The aftermath was less dramatic, but not by much.

Luke was the next to leave, and he did so without saying a word to anyone, including Lana and me. He was furious and I knew he needed some time alone.

"Well, that didn't quite go as planned, now did it?" I said to Lana, clearly as knocked out as I was. Neither one of us had expected the rollercoaster that Amber had provided. She had only filled us in on Jett's paternity. The rest was news to us, just like the others.

Amber and her mom picked her drunken son up from the floor and made for the nearest exit, crying softly along the way. I couldn't really feel sorry for her, but still, it was an emotional day. Todd didn't say much to her as they left, separately. I had no idea what would become of those two.

My staff worked hard to clean up the physical mess from the day's events. I'd have to compensate them with combat pay and perhaps a therapy session or two to take care of the emotional fallout. This was definitely one party that no one would forget any time soon.

"Thanks for the resolution, Derek," said Bammy with a smirk, as she and Michael came over to hug me good-bye. "Not at all what I expected, but I'm definitely glad I witnessed it firsthand."

"Not quite what I expected, either," I admitted, "and I'm not sure it was worth it, but there was no way I could have retold that story, again. No one would believe me. Can we talk later this week? I'm definitely going to need a friendly shoulder."

"You got it," she said, and kissed me on the cheek. "Come on, Michael. Let's go watch a war movie in 3D or something. We need to calm our nerves a bit after this."

■ ■ ■

I slept in my old bedroom at Barry's place that night. There was no way I could go home to Luke after a day like this, whether Fletch was there or not. I knew he needed time to cool off. I just hoped he'd find his way around to talking to me, soon. I really wanted the chance to explain. Whether or not I deserved that chance, even I wasn't so sure. I was pretty sure I'd crossed one line too many.

I woke up the next morning to the smells of Sunday breakfast. Barry was sitting at the dining room table in his marabou edged peignoir. How he managed anything without those pink fluffy feathers flying into his mouth, I had no idea. His talents lay beyond my comprehension. Tucker was in the kitchen making an egg white scramble and whole grain toast. I liked this scene of domesticity between them. Who cared about the age difference if they were happy?

"Well, you got home late," said Barry as his eyes peered over the paper, then folded it on his lap to take me in from head to toe. "It seems you had a fairly crazy night. Par for the course around here, if you ask me."

"What exactly have you heard?" I asked as I poured a cup of strong, black coffee and walked over to join him at the table. Tucker placed a plate of eggs in the center and sat down, as well.

"Here you go, guys," he said.

"Thank you, Tucker," said Barry, looking over and smiling adoringly.

"My pleasure. I just wanted to make sure Derek had enough energy to regale us with this massive story. They had to have left something out."

"It's not…" I started, eyes widening.

"It is," said Barry, smiling broadly and holding the newspaper out in front of my face.

"Drama at the Duke," read the headline on the *Parkville Post*.

"Oh, *God*," I said. "What's that they say? No press is bad press, right? Damn it. It was bound to happen, I guess. I hope someone got paid, at least."

"Oh, there's no secret about who," Barry assured me. "Amber Winthrop wanted to set the record straight before anyone else spread any 'vicious lies' about her and her family."

"She didn't."

"She most certainly did. Read on, nephew."

I scanned the story quickly, and to my absolute surprise, Amber stuck to the facts fairly well. Sure, she left out the part about leaving the scene of a crime when she survived Fletch's car crash, but she admitted to Jett's paternity, admitted to having made "questionable choices," even admitted to trying to break up Brandee and Fletch years ago. She thanked me and the Duke, specifically, for not pressing charges, and finished by professing her love for her latest fiancé Todd, pleading with him publicly to forgive her. Smart girl, that Amber. I never said she wasn't. I just didn't like her.

"So?" asked Barry. "Do tell!" His elbows were on the table, his face in his hands.

"It's pretty spot on," I answered. "The place was a wreck after that fight. But she's right. We didn't need the police involved. Too many fragile relationships were already in jeopardy. Calling the police wouldn't have solved anything, it would have just created more problems. Besides, I'll just present her with a bill that's double the amount we agreed on. She can afford it. And trust me, she has no room to complain."

Barry rolled his eyes and sipped from his coffee cup. "Well, at least Jett knows who his real dad is now. The truth is always better than a story spun of gold. Speaking of, I heard from Chinois."

"You did? Did she call?"

"Tucker was a doll and set me up with my very own e-mail account. You know how much I hate computers, but hey, what can I say? I teach him things and he teaches me things. I'm learning for the sake of others." He smiled at Tucker. "Anyway, it took me about an hour to type the damn thing, but I sent off a mail to New York, congratulating her on her continued success and telling her how happy I was that you found her for me."

I grimaced. I had a feeling another one of my stories was about to have its legs pulled out from underneath. Oh, Barry, Chinois *asked* me to lie about her life. Here we go, again.

"Barry, I…" I started.

"*Oh, no,* nephew." He waved his finger in front of me. "No need to backpedal. She beat you to it. Chinois told me everything, including her HIV status. I guess she wanted to come clean if we were going to rekindle our friendship. It's much easier to keep your story straight, so to speak, when you're not adding layers of untruths."

No more layers of untruths. That's definitely a lesson I should have learned years ago.

■ ■ ■

A few days later I stopped by Parkville High on my way to the Duke. School hadn't started yet, but the teaching staff had already reported for duty, preparing their lessons and classrooms for the new wave of students. I peeked in through the glass windows of the office and saw Miss Mabel peering over her eyeglasses, dutifully typing away at her desk. I sometimes wondered if she was really working at anything remotely school related. Her fingers rarely left that keyboard, except to fetch a shot of bourbon from the secret flask buried in the back of her desk. Maybe she was really working on her own life story?

"Writing the Great American Novel, Miss Mabel?" I asked as I entered the high school office.

"Some of y'all should be damn scared if I do, one day," she said, not looking up. "Did you bring me my coffee, Derek Walter?"

"Now you know I did, Miss Mabel. Do you really have to ask?" I placed the to-go cup on her desk and she promptly removed the plastic lid, quickly fishing her flask out to add a nip. I knew she could move fast when she really wanted to. I had seen that firsthand.

"I take it you've missed me?" I asked, smiling.

"Now just why'd that be the case?" she said, finally looking up, peering over the edge of her eyeglasses. "I don't need you here to hear all about your goings on. Y'all boys done got the whole town talking. Again. My sister Addy May done filled me in on all the fun." She pursed her lips together, and I swear I could see a smile start to form in her eyes. Addy May was Amber's housemaid and Miss Mabel always loved a good story.

"You know we like to keep things exciting around here," I said.

"Excitin's one thing. Baby daddy drama's another. I think it's 'bout time y'all played it safe for a while. Pressin' your luck, you ask me."

"I couldn't agree with you more, Miss Mabel. I'm shutting down the drama train. From here on out it's just business and healthy living."

She stared up at me, eyes questioning. "Who you think you foolin', boy? I wasn't born yesterday. Now get on up out of here before I give you the whoopin' you deserve. And make up with that man of yours. I don't think he can do this all alone. You may be a drama queen, but you're *his* drama queen. Don't you forget that."

"Yes, ma'am. I'll try."

"You better do more than try. You can only fix things so many times before they're unfixable." She looked back at her computer. Our conversation was over. "Bammy's back there. Now git."

■ ■ ■

"Happy to be back at work?" I asked Bammy. We were having our coffee in the two leather chairs by the window in her office.

"Lord, I had to come to work today before my liver fell out. Michael and I have been having a little too much fun, lately. I needed a day off from drinking, so this was as good an excuse as any." She shifted in her chair, getting to the real gossip. "So is Fletch really gone?"

"Apparently so," I said. "Luke isn't talking to me, but Lana said that's what she had heard. Luke's not speaking to her, either, I understand."

"Who would have thought that at the end of this you'd be friends with Lana?"

"I wouldn't say we're friends, exactly, but familial intrigue makes strange bedfellows."

"Fletch really went back to New York?"

"That's what she overheard at the country club. She's still not talking to Amber, either. I have a feeling they'll find their way back to each other, but she's insisting for now that their friendship is burnt. Anyway, Fletch has agreed to Brandee's petition for divorce. I guess he figured that chapter was over for good. Besides, he always preferred his buddies to his women, though I can't say he's treated either group any better. She's put herself up in a fancy hotel at Fletch's expense, of course. They're ironing out the property and alimony details. That's going to be a profitable day for the lawyers. Lots of billable hours."

"And how do you feel, now that he's gone?"

"Relieved," I admitted. "Part of me wishes we had never made that trip to New York. But then I realize we would have eventually had all these troubles, anyway. All that stuff in Luke's past was just hanging there, unresolved. Now it's cleared out, I think. But I don't blame him for being angry with me. In every relationship I've had I've always pushed people too much, tried to make them bend to my will instead of seeing things on their own."

"You do that with me, but I just ignore you," she said, smiling.

"That's the thing. You can. You and I aren't living together. If you get pissed off at me, we can just go our separate ways for a few days and then bond all over again over a few drinks or some romanticized stories of the indiscretions of our youth. But with Luke, it's different. I didn't just interfere. I *really* interfered. He wanted to deal with Fletch on his own. He had a plan with Brandee. He knew it was important to get Fletch settled back in New York, again. But I got all caught up with Lana, with Amber. He must feel that we conspired against him, that he couldn't handle it on his own. And on top of that, he was dealing with his own mixed emotions about Fletch's return."

I hadn't shared with Bammy any specifics of Luke's past dalliances with Fletch, though he himself had alluded to them at Amber's engagement party. Sometimes the things we barely said gave more details than the stories we actually told.

"Every time I think Amber's pulled out her last trick, she finds another," said Bammy. "Give credit where credit's due. She knows how to keep her brand current."

"We could all learn things from her. At least she name checked the Duke in that newspaper article. The phones have been ringing off the hook ever since. At this rate, I'll get my investment back sooner than I thought."

"What about Todd Carmichael? Surely he knows a lemon when he sees one. He's a used car salesman!"

"Apparently not," I chuckled. "Lana told me that Todd is considering taking her back. He said that she can't possibly have any secrets worse than the ones she has already confessed."

"Are you kidding me?" She was stunned.

"I swear." I held my hand up. "What can I say? Love is blind."

"Well, his love needs corrective eye surgery."

■ ■ ■

I walked out to the parking lot and saw Luke down on the football field supervising the grounds crew. They were refreshing the lines and giving the stadium the once over before the season began. I was sure he'd be super busy with after school practices soon and I'd barely see him. Who was I kidding? I wasn't seeing him at all. Old habits are hard to break. I left without even trying to say hello. What was the point? He'd speak to me when it was the right time for him. I'd pushed him enough in our time together. But this time I'd pushed him so far that I was pretty sure he wasn't coming back.

I drove Willie over to the Duke to start my workday. The cleaning crew was there, still working diligently to expunge the last remaining smears of orange and red frosting from the place. They kept finding crusty, colorful smudges in the oddest locations. I hung my coat in the wardrobe closet and I couldn't help but relive that image of Amber and Fletch rolling around on the floor. I shuddered.

As I told Bammy, the newspaper article and the ensuing publicity were a windfall that I could ill afford to lose. We needed the business, and Amber's story was driving us in the right direction. I couldn't be so angry with her, after all. The society women loved nothing more than a scandalous tale. We booked birthday parties, engagements, weddings, and even a divorce party. Our December calendar was filling up very quickly with office and family Christmas events. I just made sure that the last Sunday of every month was saved for our recurring private gathering, Secret Sundays. I didn't schedule any go-go boys or strippers for the next one, though. I was pretty sure we had had enough excitement for the time being.

My day went quickly and I was happily surprised to see a friendly face looking down at me from the doorway to my office as the clock approached 5pm.

"You up for a quick drink before you head home?" said Tommy.

"Hey! What are you doing here?"

"I just figured I'd drop by and give you something other than yourself to talk about," he laughed.

"Please! I need the distraction."

"Clock out then. You're the boss, remember?" he said. "Meet me at the Tater Tot."

■ ■ ■

He beat me there by a few minutes and scored a sweet table on the back terrace.

"Two Bloody Bachelors," he said to the waitress as I took my seat. "I figured you could use a good meal," he said, laughing. The Bloody Bachelor was the Tater Tot's version of a Bloody Mary, spiced up and filled to overflowing with a piece of crispy bacon, a cheesy crouton, pickled okra and a stuffed pimiento cheese-filled, deep fried pepper. They even added an extra shot of vodka and a biscuit, served on the side. It was a drink and a feast, all at once.

"What are we celebrating?" I asked.

"Meredith and I have some news." He cocked his eyebrow.

I froze. "You're not?! Tell me you're not pregnant!"

"I'm not," he teased. "And neither is she."

"Then, what?"

"We're getting a cat," he laughed. "She agreed we're not quite ready for a kid, yet. Honestly, I'm relieved. I'd pop the question, but y'all have scared the shit out of both of us."

"It's a circus, isn't it?"

"I didn't think there was any possible way to make this town any crazier, but you and Luke keep finding new ways to stir it up."

"I thought we weren't going to talk about me?"

"Since when did we ever *not* talk about you? Admit it, Derek. Your life is not boring."

No, my friend. My life was indeed not boring. And cheers to that.

20

THE LAKE HOUSE

Later in the week I received an unexpected invitation when I answered the phone at work.

"Duke Catering and Events, this is Derek."

"Derek, it's me, Lana. You're coming over for lunch on Saturday."

Actually, it was less of an invitation and more along the lines of an order. I just didn't feel like complying.

"Lana, why did you call me at work and not on my cell?"

"You wouldn't answer, of course," she said matter-of-factly.

She had me there.

"Listen, Lana, I appreciate the effort, but you don't have to keep this up. Thanks for the lunch invite, but you can't be that hard up for social events that you have to resort to eating with me. I know you don't like me very much, and you must have other friends besides Amber.

"Derek, honestly. When will you learn? Sometimes we have choices in this world, and sometimes we don't. This is one of those times."

"A time when I have a choice, right?" I hedged.

"Saturday at noon at the lake house," she repeated firmly. "And don't bring anything. I just don't have the energy to pretend I appreciate whatever silly thing you think is appropriate."

And with that, she hung up.

■ ■ ■

I went out Friday evening with the Scooby Gang. We met at the Firelight and took over our regular booth. Everyone was there but Luke, of course. The night felt empty without him, but I tried to fill the void with vodka. Nobody mentioned him, not even Michael. It became so awkward that I had to say something.

"Luke's not dead, you know?" I said, when the conversation had lulled. Meredith and Tommy had just returned from getting more pitchers of beer and cocktails from the bar. Kit and Shawn looked over at me quietly, while Michael and Bammy shifted uncomfortably in their seats.

"No one thinks that, baby," said Kit. "It's just a stupid little argument. It'll be fine."

"It's a bit more than a little argument," added Michael, barely looking up.

"Michael, we don't need to get involved," said Bammy.

"C'mon, Bammy," he answered. "Who are we kidding? He's my brother. It's not like I *can't* be involved."

"Michael," she started, "I think…"

I had to cut her off. "Bammy, it's okay. Really. I'm not asking anyone to take sides. It is what it is. I dug my own hole and now I'm stuck in it, yet again. My story is an endless lesson in how not to lead a life."

"Well that's just bullshit," said Kit, taking a drink from her martini glass. Shawn suppressed a laugh and tightened his arm around her shoulder.

"Kit, I love you," I said, "but even I know when I've gone too far. He wanted to handle Fletch on his own, and Lana and I thought we could do it our way. It didn't work."

"I don't see Fletch around, though, do you?" asked Bammy, testing the waters.

"No," answered Michael. "But I don't see Luke, either."

■ ■ ■

I woke up Saturday morning feeling a little thicker in the head than I normally do after a night of drinking. Mixing vodka and teachable moments never did work out very well for me. I skipped the Barry and Tucker breakfast show and escaped for an early morning run by the lake to clear my thoughts.

The two of them were working in the yard when I had finished my run. I showered upstairs, and then snuck back out the side door. I didn't feel like explaining to them where I was going. It was weird enough that Lana and I were on friendly terms, but even weirder to imagine sharing a meal with her, alone. We had only ever dined together at the Walcott mansion, with Luke, Red and Rosa present. I wasn't even sure I had enough conversation topics ready for a one-on-one. I hoped that she enjoyed talking about pop culture and eighties music, because those were the only things I felt safe discussing with her. I was sure that anything else would expose a hidden land mine.

I pulled into her driveway and walked up to the door and rang. Hers was definitely not a home that I would have felt comfortable just walking into.

The door swung open quickly, but just wide enough for her face to appear. "Can you pull that thing around back, please? I don't want anyone to think I have anything to do with that junker." She let the door go and it slammed in my face. No *hello, how are you?* Nothing.

Why exactly was I here again? I trudged back down the steps, drove Willie Nelson around and parked behind the house, as instructed. This was not going to be fun, and I already regretted saying yes.

"Get in here, quick," she said from the back porch, then let yet another door quickly close in my face.

This time I didn't bother to ring or even knock and I walked right in. What's the worst she could do to me? Out me in front of the entire town and try to get me blackballed from my job? Too late. I already survived that the last time.

"Lana, why am I here if you're just going to continue to treat me like garbage?" I said as I walked in and tossed my keys on her kitchen counter. I was over it and we hadn't even started.

"Oh, don't start a hissy fit," she said. "Here. Vodka." And she shoved a tall, cool drink in my hand.

"Well, normally I wouldn't stay after the way you've treated me, but this is a decent first step to making up." It was good vodka, after all. Lana never went for the cheap stuff. "What's for lunch?"

"You're holding it."

"I drove all the way out here for a cocktail hour?"

Just then the front doorbell rang.

"Of course not," she said, irritated. "You drove out here to fix things. Now drink your drink and stand over there and get ready. He doesn't know you're here."

"You didn't." My heart rate began to increase and I could feel the sweat collecting down my back.

"I'll do whatever I need to do. You know me well enough by now. My needs always come first. And right now I need my brother to like me, again, and for you two to make up. So check your face in that mirror over there, and quick. You look like you had a rough night."

She turned and made a beeline for the door. Damn it, Lana. I wish I'd had a full night's sleep. I wasn't prepared for this.

"What's going on, Lana? What's so damn important that I had to drive out here?" It was Luke.

"Hey there, big brother!" She was trying the sweet voice routine.

Even I knew he wouldn't fall for that. I downed my vodka and pinched my cheeks, trying to bring my face back to life. He spotted me in the mirror and I turned quickly to face him.

"Hi," I said, sheepishly. "I didn't plan this. I swear."

He stopped dead in his tracks. "Lana," he said sternly, "I'm not in the mood for your games today."

"Now, come on, Luke," she started, thick as molasses. "Let's just get this little 'ole thing over with, shall we? We all know it's all just gonna blow on over, so why don't we just race to that finish line, all right?"

He stared at me, nostrils flaring slightly, not saying a word.

"Luke, I..." I hesitated. His eyes were practically piercing right through me.

"No," he said, and cut me off tersely.

"No?" I answered. "No, what?"

"No, I'm not doing this," he said. "Not today, not tomorrow. You and Lana think you have it all figured out? You two can keep trying, without me." He turned to face Lana. "I told you I wasn't ready. You'd better start listening to me, Lana. One day you'll stop fucking with your friends and family and you'll realize how much you need them in your life. You'd just better hope we're still around to give a shit."

He kept walking without looking back and the door slammed behind him. We heard his car pull out of the driveway before either of us dared to speak.

"What were you thinking, Lana?" I said, quietly.

Her arms were folded, her forlorn gaze still directed down the hallway her brother had just stormed down. "You know your way out." It wasn't said with spite, but rather the sad, last breaths of a woman who felt she had lost her way.

I picked up my keys and left through the back, alone.

■ ■ ■

When I got back to Barry's, my uncle was sitting on his newly expanded outdoor terrace and typing away on Tucker's laptop.

"This thing is amazing," he said, barely looking up. "I've been chatting with Chinois all morning. That lady is a hoot. She was in a pretty tough state, but I think I've been able to cheer her up. She's giving me weekly updates on her health and she's brought me up to date on the drag scene in New York. The Chelsea Hotel isn't home for her, anymore. She moved out to Brooklyn in the early '90s to escape the hustle and bustle and the skyrocketing rents, but now it seems the kids all followed her out there. It's a good thing she's got a great deal with her landlord, otherwise she'd be off to Jersey. And nobody wants that! Oh, I'm so happy that we found each other again. Thank you, Derek."

"No worries, Barry," I said. "Just doing my part to make other people's lives better than my own."

"Okay, sad sack. What gives?" He typed a quick sentence, swiftly closed the laptop and then set it down on the table by the chaise lounge. "What's with the puffy face?

We have some fresh cucumbers in the fridge if you need 'em. Joan Crawford used to swear by them, but honestly I didn't see the difference when I tried it. I just got hungry."

"Thanks. The only vegetable I want right now, though, is potato in a bottle."

"I know you'll find this shocking," he said, one eyebrow raised, "but maybe you've had enough. I could use a little of your advice, actually, and I'd rather we take this one sober. You up for it?"

"Who *are* you and what have you done with my uncle?"

"Oh, I have my moments. They are rare, I will admit that. But lately I don't need as much liquid fortitude as I used to." He smiled, and it was easy to understand why.

"Boy, has Cupid's arrow done a number on you," I ventured.

"And how." He was smiling like a teenager in love.

"Speaking of, where's Tucker?" I asked.

"He's gone out for the day. He has a few clients, and then he needs to swing by his place to pick up some clothes. He's spending a few more nights here a week than we planned."

"Look at you," I said, smiling. "I'm impressed. You're really making this work."

"Are you so shocked? Don't answer that, I'll beat you to it. Because I don't understand how we pulled it off, either. I guess you could say we really like each other. A lot."

"Is there any doubt?"

"Not really," he began, and then shifted in place to relax for story time. "Oh, sure, at the beginning it was all just for a laugh. A lark. I mean, we're not exactly ready for the cover of a magazine. But who *is* without all that retouching? Certainly not this old beauty queen. But seriously, I never thought we'd get this far. When we first met, I thought he was playing with me, just being kind to the old guy in the back seat. But he was so damn charming. And smart and funny and cute. I just got all caught up in how good I felt when I was with him. *Normal.* I never thought it would last, of course, so I just didn't try so hard. I didn't worry about it. Maybe that was the secret with Janey all those years? We never really had to try. She was my best friend and we just clicked. I feel very much the same with Tucker. He's my best friend, too, but we clicked in a different way. We started spending more time together, more dates, more secret dinners. Suddenly he was making back stage visits at the Bears' Club a few times a week. Then when Audrey moved out he began spending the night, just once or twice, here and there. He used to park his car down the street, just in case anyone came by. We were both so nervous. Cautious. Then we started easing up. Before I knew it, he was here four or five nights. He's barely at his own place anymore and I love it. It's nice to come home to him, and I love when he shows up after a day's work. We've figured out our habits together, and I gotta tell ya, Dolly, I really miss him when he's not here."

"That's sweet. I get that," I said, but I thought I knew where he was really going with this. "No one wants to deny you love, Barry. I hope you know that."

"Oh, I do, kid. I don't doubt that. My family is everything to me, and I feel that love, I do. But I'm still scared. I'm not sure if scared's the right word," he winced, "but I think you know what I mean. This past year has had so much upheaval already. You moving back, your breakup with David, you and Luke, the Love All protests, your dad showing up. I even came out of the closet dressed in a Diana Ross wig with strippers in a can-can line and disco balls overhead. It was a dream come true! And now, Tucker."

"And now, *Mom*, right? Isn't that what you really mean?" I knew where he was going with all this, even if he hadn't quite caught up with his own feelings.

He smiled, and then collected his hands in his lap. He inhaled deeply, and then released the pressure within.

"Your mom and I have always been so close. But we lived our lives in different circles that only met on certain days in just the right climate. We never fought, ever. But every interaction was planned, nothing was spontaneous, and it just became second nature. The casual white lies, the moments unspoken, the emotional highs and lows of our lives that were never mentioned. We just fell into a relationship where we didn't tell each other anything that delved too far beneath the surface. I knew she was having problems with your dad when you were a kid, but we never said a word about it. I don't know if she kept other secrets from me, but I certainly kept secrets from her. She knew everything, of course, but we didn't talk about it. Nothing was said, so it was all okay. That's just how it worked between us and we never saw the need to change it, until recently. Coming out to her this past spring opened a floodgate of emotions that I still haven't properly dealt with. We just skipped over it, like we always did. We talk about shopping and cooking and what's on the television. We bond over you and our friends, this house and this crazy town. But we don't dwell on the hard stuff too much, and I'm not sure I can continue like that."

"So just tell her. That's all you have to do, you know? Just tell her. She won't be upset. Like you said, she already knew you were gay, so maybe she already knows about Tucker?"

He rolled his eyes and suppressed a small laugh. "Well, I wouldn't doubt that. Your mom has instincts that even science hasn't figured out."

"Trust me, I can second that. She was ready to kick David to the curb much earlier than I was, but she would have never interfered. That's just not her thing. She's too Southern. It's not real until we say it out loud, but once we do, you'd better have a plan to deal with it."

"So," he said, sitting up and finding his courage, "I guess I'd better come up with a plan? You in?"

"Well, event planning *is* my new career."

"Then let's get started," he said, excitedly. "But you got another thing coming if you think I'm paying you."

21

FAMILY MATTERS

"I must have done something really horrible in a former life," I said to the heavens as Jett entered my office on Monday.

"I hope you don't mind, but nobody was tending the bar downstairs so I helped myself," he said, a cold long-neck beer in his hands. He ignored my comment and took a seat opposite my desk. "You should really be more careful about leaving alcohol unattended like that. Especially in this town."

"You're seventeen years old, Jett. And it's 11:30 in the morning."

"Exactly. In New York they call that brunch, right?" He smiled his best wicked smile. "Don't worry, I left a tip in the jar, at least."

"That was kind of you," I laughed. Jett was an ass, but I had to admit he was a charming one. "Real money, or an IOU?"

"Now, Mr. Walter. I'm shocked. I know you and I have had our fair share of tussles, but you know I'm good for it. Especially now, considering my latest and greatest daddy."

"Well, Jett, normally I'd say 'I hope this one sticks around,' but truthfully, I don't know if he's the best role model for you in the long run. I'd steer clear of that one."

"Ain't that sweet of you to care," he grinned. "But yeah, I get ya. Fletch wasn't my first choice, either. Mama and I may have tricked you guys into thinking that Luke was the one, but we both know how that ended up. And I gotta tell ya, it coulda been fun. I wouldn't admit that to everyone, you know, but it's the truth. You and Luke aren't bad people."

This was a side of Jett I had never expected to meet, and it made me even warier. There had to be a reason he was being nice and I had a feeling I was about to find out.

"Exactly how many beers have you had today, Jett? Are you feeling all right?"

He laughed out loud. "Oh, man. Yeah, I know I can be a handful. But I can see things from both sides, sometimes. I guess you can say I'm maturing."

"Maturing? Or figuring out how to manipulate more people to get what you want?"

There was a gleam in his eye as he took another swig from his bottle and then answered. "Fletch may not be the daddy I wanted, but he's all I got, so I may as well make the best of it."

"And while you're making the best of it, you may as well benefit, right?"

"You learn fast," he said.

"Let's just say that I'm pretty good at reading people, by now. And I've known my fair share of bullshitters. And you, Jett, have a bright future as a real sonofa…"

"Now," he cut me off before I could continue, "no need to knock me down while you're complimenting me. I'll just take the good stuff, please."

"I would expect no less of you." I leaned back in my chair and took in the sight. This kid had balls, for sure, and I had no doubt he would succeed in life. A part of me did like him, but I knew better than to trust his motives. Jett would always look out for Jett, first. Of that I was certain.

"What are you doing here, Jett?" I asked, narrowing my eyes. "Can we just skip this little dance?"

He threw back the final drops of beer and jauntily balanced the empty bottle on the corner of my desk.

"I just figured I'd come say good-bye. You can tell yourself all you want how much you don't like me, Mr. Walter, but I know better. And if I don't get back here for a few years, well, at least I'd like to leave on friendly terms. You do throw one hell of a party, and I wanna make sure I get an invite on my next visit. I'll just skip those Sunday get-togethers, though. Not my kinda crowd." He winked.

How the hell did he know about Secret Sundays? Chip, of course. So much for a secret. But something else was in the air.

"What's going on? Is Amber shipping you off to some boarding school? God help those kids if she does."

"Funny. Nope. This time it's my choice. I'm heading to New York and I was wondering if you wanted to give me any pointers. I heard through the grapevine you had a DJ friend. Maybe I could get a club hook up?"

"You're not serious. Fletch?"

"Like I said, I'm maturing. And I take my offers where I can get 'em. It doesn't hurt, of course, that Mama sued Fletch for seventeen years of back child support. He settled before they ended up in court. I guess being a big pharma salesman has paid off over the years. You know how my mama operates. As long as Amber has her money, I can do whatever I want. And right now I want outta this town. Now that Brandee's left Fletch he says there's plenty of room in that penthouse for me. I'm transferring schools and I'll do my senior year up in New York City. Yeah, I'll miss my friends, but Chip will be busy with football, anyway. He can come visit over Christmas break. I'll be sitting pretty in the Big Apple by then, and we'll have a blast."

"Jett, you have no idea what you are getting into. Fletch is a train wreck, and New York is like nothing and nobody you've ever messed with."

"Trust me," he said, "I can handle myself. I think you've seen that in action. Besides, Fletch'll be easier to handle than Mama, and she was cake. As long as I get my own key, I'm golden."

The golden football god and his golden son living the life in Manhattan. I had to admit it, Jett was right. Fletch would supply a steady stream of booze, babes and ballers. Anything to win over the son he always knew he had, but never acknowledged. And it would piss off Amber, as an added bonus. Jett could definitely handle himself. In fact, maybe I needed to reassess my initial reaction and transfer my worries to Fletch. Could *he* withstand Hurricane Jett?

"I take it back, Jett. New York *and* Fletch have no idea what they're in store for. What you lack in age, you more than make up for in brashness."

"Aww, Mr. Walter, you can say 'balls' around me. I won't think nothin' of it." He grinned and narrowed his eyes. "Why, if I didn't know any better, I'd say I have your blessing."

"I wouldn't go that far. But I'm definitely going to follow your social media feeds. Something tells me that you'll be taking advantage of every hidden corner of that city. And that's something I can get behind."

"I hope you don't mind if I don't picture you behind *anything*?" With that, he stood up and thrust his hand forward, unable to carry through without one final smirk. "Truce?"

I stood as well and offered my hand. "Truce. But promise me one thing before you go?"

"Shoot."

"If you're gonna do this, you tough it out, no matter what. I've seen so many strong people just get swallowed up by that city. I once said that New York was like the coolest girl in school and you just want to be her friend. But she likes to go it alone, and she prefers people who can stand on their own two feet, without any help. Use Fletch for what he is, but don't count on him. You have to make your own way. You can be anything you want when you get there. Think about that. New York was designed for people who need a reinvention and I don't want to hear that you've become just another finance guy who wastes his life chasing a cliché, all right?"

He took a beat, then answered. "It's a deal. But you have to promise me something in return."

"What's that?"

"Go get your boyfriend back. Y'all fucked up. Both of you. Now get over it. You may think we all don't give a shit, but you're wrong. Parkville ain't against you. You two *are* Parkville."

■ ■ ■

I thought about what Jett said all week. It was all I could think of, really.

This argument felt different from any other situation we had been in, and we had experienced some doozies. I wasn't even sure we could still call it an argument. What was it exactly? A misunderstanding of epic proportions? Somewhere along the way I had undervalued what Luke had gone through in his journey to get to where he was. That was so typical of me, to only see how the world affected my situation and to expect everyone else to just hop on the ride with me. Now I was paying for it. It took me too many years to understand that it didn't matter who you were, what your social standing was or how much outward happiness you projected, we could never truly understand what was lurking inside someone else. Mom was right. Communication was indeed everything.

Speaking of Mom, she gave me a call during the week to ask me over for dinner. She wanted to know if she could invite Luke.

"Mom, that's kind of weird," I said. "I know you mean well, but…"

"But what?" she said, clearly annoyed. "But don't interfere?"

"It's not that, it's just…"

"Just that you both are too stubborn to face reality? Get over it. Life's too short, Derek. I don't have time to hold grudges."

I sighed. "Fine. Whatever. You do you."

"Then I will. See you Friday. Barry's coming, too."

"What's for dinner?"

"Honestly, son, you know I hate that. Have I ever poisoned you?"

"Well, there was that one time."

"Oh, how the hell was I supposed to know that wasn't pre-cooked? Those letters on the package were so tiny. And how long are you going to hold that against me, anyway?

What did I just tell you about grudges? Dinner's on Friday at 6 pm. Don't be late."

Click.

■ ■ ■

"Barry, what the hell?" I had stepped out of my car to find my uncle standing on Mom and Dad's front porch. He was wearing a dark navy suit with a crisp white dress shirt and a deep burgundy tie. His hand was frozen in midair, seemingly unsure, as if he was going to either twist that doorknob or flee.

"What?" he answered in a daze, turning to look at me, slack-jawed.

"Barry, what's going on? I mean, you look dashing as all get out, but this is a version of you I haven't seen in years. The tuxedo was one thing, but what's with the suit? I didn't even know you still *had* suits."

"They were in the attic, behind the pageant gowns that are too big for my bedroom closet," he said matter-of-factly, as if everyone favors their couture to the detriment of their business attire.

"Of course," I said, stifling a laugh. But he didn't look like he was enjoying anything. In fact, he looked a bit green. "Barry? Are we going in, or not?"

"I haven't decided, yet," he said. There was a look of pure terror on his face.

"Barry. *Beret.* She's your sister. She loves you, no matter what. You know that."

"I know that," he repeated, but it sounded less like a statement and more like a question.

"Come on." I reached up and put my arm around his shoulder. "I got your back. Let's go."

"Let's do this." He breathed in heavily, then reached forward, turned the handle and pushed the door open.

"Oh! You're both here!" said Mom, flustered, as she placed a final tray of hors d'oevres on the coffee table in front of the couch. Her hair had been done and she was wearing a flirty blue cocktail dress. The lighting was un-characteristically subdued and the room was filled with lit candles. "Johnny! They're here! Come quick!"

Dad came running out of the kitchen, wiping his hands with a small towel, which he then quickly threw be-hind him into the empty room in a panic. He, too, looked exceptionally groomed and well put together in his best linen suit. What was going on here? He sped to Mom's side and grabbed her hand, the two of them standing nervously in front of the couch.

"Did someone forget to tell me that it's dress up night?" I asked, trying to break the tension. Barry stood paralyzed by my side.

"No, honey, not at all," Mom cooed. "It's just such a special night, that's all. We wanted to do this right."

"But, how did you...?" Barry stuttered, then turned to me. "Derek?"

"I didn't do anything," I said, lifting my hands up in the air.

"Oh, Barry," said Mom, not understanding our confusion. "We love you. Of course we wanted you to be here for the announcement."

"Announcement?" he sputtered. "But I haven't... I haven't said anything, yet? Have I?" He turned to me, again.

"You haven't done anything, Barry," said Johnny. "There's a reason why we asked you both to be here tonight." He nodded to me, then my uncle. "Audrey and I, well, we..."

"Your dad asked me to marry him, again!" Mom was practically bursting with joy. "We're getting *married*! Did you hear that? *We're getting married!*"

The reflection of the diamond ring that she waved far outshone the forced smile that lit Barry's face for the benefit of his beloved sister.

■ ■ ■

Glasses of champagne were passed around before I could truly catch Barry's eye. He was grinning wide, but I felt so bad for him. Sure, I was happy for Mom and Dad, but I knew the pressure that my uncle was feeling inside. I understood the courage that he had built up, and now there was no outlet. That had to change. But for now, Mom was talking wedding plans.

"Every bride wants a beautiful wedding, regardless of her age," she said. "And I know you just recently opened, Derek, but we were hoping, of course, that we could have the ceremony and the reception at the Duke?"

"I'd be honored, Mom," I said, smiling.

"And we'll pay, of course," said Dad. "I'm not asking for any freebies."

"No freebies," I assured him. "I have bills to pay! But I'll make sure it's all perfect. I know the bride pretty well, after all. I think she'll give me free reign on this one."

Barry still hadn't spoken. He had a death grip on his champagne flute, but he hadn't lifted the glass to the frozen smile on his lips once.

"We want to do it soon," Mom continued. "We don't want to wait any longer. We wasted enough years, and now we have a chance to put everything back together. We were thinking Sunday, in two weeks?"

I quickly found the date in my head. Of course Mom would pick the same date as a Secret Sunday. "A day ceremony, or evening?" I asked.

"Daytime," my dad answered. "I get up at 4:30 in the morning. There's no way I can stay up for a party, even if it is my own."

"Great," I said, relieved. "We have a private event that same night anyway, so as long as everything is cleared out by 5 pm we should be good to go." I looked to Barry to gauge his reaction, but there was none.

"We don't want it too fancy," Mom said, her hand resting in my dad's. "Just a simple ceremony, then a cocktail reception. I don't want to do a sit-down. We were thinking a buffet. Is that all right?"

"Sure," I said. "If the weather's nice you can get married out on the terrace. We can set up the chairs out there and start with a welcome cocktail. We'll arrange the buffet inside in the main salon, and then follow that with the cake cutting. Do you want a band or a DJ? And what kind of flowers do you want? Why don't you two come by my office this week and we can decide everything together?"

"I think your mother should probably handle all that," Dad said.

"Tell you what," I offered. "You just go to yoga and Mom and I will take care of everything."

"I like the sound of that," he said.

"And a dress!" Mom exclaimed, excitedly. "Oh, I'd forgotten about that. I don't even know what I want. I was thinking a pearl grey. Or is that too matronly? How about silver? Barry, you'll have to help me. You know I can't figure those things out without you. Where should we go? Do we need to take a road trip down to Atlanta?"

Barry was staring ahead, still lost in thought. He hadn't moved an inch since we sat down on the couch to talk about the wedding and I was getting increasingly worried.

"What was the name of the place where we bought that dress I wore for Derek's graduation? It wasn't Irma's, was it? Or was that in Chattanooga? My memory!" She laughed. "Oh, Barry, we'll have so much fun!"

I placed my hand on my uncle's knee and tried to revive him. I watched his jaw clench as a small bead of sweat dropped from his temple and landed on the sleeve of his suit. This wasn't good.

My dad spoke up next. "Derek, I wanted to ask you something, too. I'd like you to be my best man." I could see the start of a tear in his eye.

I turned quickly to face him, my hand still on Barry's knee. "That would be an honor, Dad. Of course I will."

"And Barry," said Mom. "I wanted to ask you, too. It would mean the world to me. But I want it to be on your terms. It's up to you, really. Will you stand beside me as my brother, or as Beret? I never thought about it, but we could wear matching dresses even!" Her smile was infectious; she was so caught up in her dream. But she hadn't noticed how quiet her brother had been all evening, until that very moment.

"Barry?" she asked. "Barry, what's wrong? You're not saying anything."

There was a full five seconds of complete silence. My uncle's eyes locked with those of his sister, and suddenly all the tension he had bottled up for the last hour came flooding out in an endless, rapid fire stream of words.

"*I'm in love. I'm in love, I'm in love, I'm in love.* I'm seeing someone and his name is Tucker and I love him. He's everything. He's my everything. I never thought it would happen, never thought it could happen, but it did. I met him and he likes me and I like him and he's mine. We're together. Tucker. He's with me. Tucker and I. We're together. And I'm happy. *Happy, happy, happy.* I haven't felt like this in years. I didn't think I could feel like this, again. Happy. Together. With him. With Tucker. And I don't care how old he is. I don't care. *I don't, I don't.* And you can say whatever you want about it, but *I don't care.* I'm not breaking up with him. Ever. He loves me, and I love him. And I'm coming to your wedding and I'm happy for you and of course I want to stand beside you and you'd damn well better let me help you buy the dress, but there's no way in hell I'm gonna do matching, and whatever I wear will look fabulous because Tucker will be there with me because *I love him.*"

We all froze, unsure of what to do next. Barry's hands were shaking and the champagne was tipping from the top of his glass, threatening to spill over. I reached for it calmly, loosened the grip of his fingers and placed it on the table in front of him.

"What are you doing?" he turned to me and shrieked. "Are you crazy? I need that now more than ever!" He grabbed the champagne flute and downed the entire thing in one shot, bubbles and all.

"Johnny, honey," my mom said calmly, never taking her eyes off Barry. "Can you go grab the vodka bottle from the freezer? We're gonna need that right now."

22

DOWN THE AISLE

Mom, Barry and I refocused a bit after a quick shot of vodka. The family that drinks together comes back from the brink together, right?

Barry was clearly frustrated that his big announcement had been overshadowed by Mom and Dad's upcoming wedding, but in the end he was able to share in their joy. After his emotional tirade, and a few more fingers of vodka, he was able to start from the beginning and tell them everything he had already told me. Mom didn't even flinch when he finally revealed Tucker's age. She assured him that she only cared if he was happy and he promised her that he was. My dad even offered a congratulatory high five for scoring a "trophy boyfriend." I had to admit that it made me laugh to see them all so emotionally available to each other. We had come a very long way as a family and we were about to complete the circle again.

"Home is a fire of emotions," Mom reminded us.

But we had the courage to take care of one another in our times of need. We were truly lucky to have each other. All that was missing for me was Luke. Mom had invited him for the evening, as she said she would, however he had politely declined, and she didn't push the matter any further.

I was so busy the next few days that I didn't have time to remember that I was horribly depressed. I just pushed through the haze. By some miracle, Mom and I were able to plan an entire wedding in less than the two-week window we had. She and Barry came by the Duke on Monday as planned and we went over every detail. The chef had prepared a sample lunch for us featuring our signature buffet items and Mom quickly chose her favorites. After our meal, Barry gave Sam instructions for specialty cocktails while Mom and I went to the flower market to look over roses, peonies and lilies. We were going for a feminine yet elegant look and she was pleased with the results.

"This is fun! What's next?" she asked.

"Cakes. We'll need to special order, of course, but unless you're going to ask for some crazy recipe, they should have a sample of pretty much everything at the bakeshop downtown. I made an appointment for tomorrow."

At the bakery she chose a red velvet with buttercream frosting for the bride's cake and a German chocolate extravaganza for the groom. We made arrangements for delivery the morning of the ceremony, and then headed over to Irma's Bridal to meet Barry. He had a few hours before he had to be at the Bears' Club for their mid-week cabaret. The back of his car was filled with wigs and dresses to bring to his dressing room. Every few weeks he cleared out the old and brought in the new. He liked to keep his regular fans guessing as to what he could pull off next. His rekindled friendship with Chinois had reignited his passion to go big or go home, as we said in the South. And now that he was out, he had even decided to donate some of his older, gently worn gowns to Irma's. The store maintained a section in the back for women who were unable to find the funds they needed to make a memorable entrance on those special occasions, and Barry's hand-me-downs were special, indeed.

"You make sure someone *grand* gets that one, you hear me, Irma? It's hand beaded. I just can't fit my ass into it, anymore."

Mom stifled a giggle as he made his way back to us in the center of the store. We'd taken a seat in the bridal gallery and Irma's best girls were taking care of us. Mom had tried on a few gowns, but we hadn't found just the right one, yet.

"Sorry I was late," he said, kissing the air around us. "I got stuck behind a tractor. And I only *wish* that was a euphemism for something more fun than it was. What'd I miss? Oh, *God*. Irma! *Irma!* What were you *thinking*? Get this rack out of here! My sister deserves better than this. Hell, half the town does. What were you trying to do? Pawn off the shit that no one else wants? Save that for the girls from Burlington, Irma! We Parkville broads know better than to wear second-rate goods." He then stage whispered to no one in particular. "If you want something done you have to do it yourself these days, right?" And with that he disappeared into the back room as if he owned the place.

"This is fun," I said, laughing.

"Seriously," Mom said. "Who needs mood enhancers when you've got Barry around?"

"As long as he's on your side!" I said, and then we cackled like only blood relatives can.

"What are you two laughing about?" said Barry, his head popping out of the swinging stockroom door. "This is serious business. Audrey, get your clothes off. *Now!* I'm not kidding. Jump behind that curtain. I'll be back in a jiffy."

It took all of ten minutes before the three of us knew we had a winner.

"Mom…*wow*. That's it."

"It is, isn't it?" she said softly, staring at herself in the full-length mirror. She was twirling lightly on the circular white pedestal in the center of the gallery. Barry was standing by her side, casually fussing about the edges of the dress, smoothing the imaginary wrinkles in the fabric.

"It's beautiful," he said, then stopped fidgeting. "*You're* beautiful. You're perfect."

And the tears began to flow, but at least this time, we all had happy tears.

■ ■ ■

The other errands worked themselves out in no time. Before we knew it, it was Friday, just two days before the wedding. I messaged Bammy that morning and asked her if she wanted to meet me for lunch. We hadn't been to Cochon's BBQ in forever and today seemed like just as good a time as any. I told her I would pick her up since I was on her side of town anyway, which wasn't quite the truth. In reality I was hoping I would run into Luke. We'd barely spoken since that ill-planned meeting at Lana's and he hadn't come to Mom and Dad's the other night. There was nothing I loved more than faking an accidental meeting, and sure enough, my plan worked like a charm.

Luke walked out of the school just as I was locking up Willie Nelson in the Parkville High parking lot. I couldn't have timed it any better. I turned to face him and put on my best *I hope you can't see that I'm dying inside?* smile.

"Hey," I offered. I was well known for my eloquence, after all. Sheesh.

"Hey," he said. Well at least he stopped. I had been afraid he would just walk on by.

"Off for a run?"

"Yeah, I thought I'd head to the park. The kids are running circles around me. Don't want to get coach gut, you know?"

"I doubt that's in your future," I said, lightly kicking the path with my foot. I was nervous and knew it was obvious.

"Your mom called. She invited me to her wedding. I'm happy for her. For your dad, too."

I looked up. The pause was excruciating.

"But you're not coming…" I said, filling the empty space that surrounded us.

He inhaled deeply, and then took his own turn looking down.

"It's okay," I mumbled. "I get it. Listen, enjoy your run. I'm taking Bammy to Cochon's for lunch. We can do this another day, okay."

"Yeah, sure," he said, noncommittally, then picked up his pace and headed straight for his Jeep, not looking back at me as I stood there watching him walk away, for good.

"I'm not giving up, you know?" I called after him. "I'm a greyhound."

He stopped, but didn't turn. "I never doubted that."

I turned to fetch my lunch date, a fresh tear forming in my eye.

■ ■ ■

"I don't know what you were thinking inviting company over on the night before your mom's wedding," said Barry, exasperated as he scurried about the house fluffing pillows and hiding away piles of newspapers and junk mail.

"And I don't know why you're freaking out," I said. "It's just Bammy and Kit. They're like family."

"They may be *like* family, but they haven't met the *whole* family, yet," he huffed.

"That's why you're freaking out? Tucker?"

"Yep," said the man in question as he relaxed casually on the couch and plucked another potato chip from the bag. Tucker had purposely not scheduled any rides for the evening as he and Barry had planned on watching a few movies in the living room.

"Must you parade those carbs in front of me?" said Barry in a tizzy. "All I have to do is smell them and I'll be off my game tomorrow. You and that damn twenty-something metabolism. It defies logic."

"What can I say?" said Tucker. "I prefer fries with my reality."

"You two have become quite the show," I said, bemused.

"He's wigging out over this wedding tomorrow. But really it's about me meeting your mom and dad. I'm cool with it, but he's having a fit." He leaned over the couch and yelled after Barry, who was still frantically opening cabinets and shoving things inside. "Your sister's going to love me, Barry. We have nothing to worry about."

"He's right, you know?" I added, but Barry was having none of it.

Just then the girls knocked on the sliding glass door from the terrace.

"*We. Are. Here!*" said Kit, peaking inside the house. "And we brought wine coolers! There's nothing more fun than a redneck drink in a hot tub, right?"

"I'm kind of fond of *rednecks* in hot tubs," said Tucker. "They always look like lobsters in a boiling pot."

"*Ooooh*, this must be Tucker!" said Bammy, inviting herself in and extending her hand. "We've heard so much about you!"

Tucker put the chip bag down, stood up and grabbed her hand. "Well I hope I can live up to the hype."

Kit eyed him up and down and said, "The view's pretty damn good from where I'm standing."

"Okay, y'all," I laughed, "that's enough. No more flirting with my uncle's handsome *trophy boyfriend*."

"That was your dad who called me that, right?" asked Tucker.

"Yes," interjected Barry. "But you've already got an older man, so get back in here and pay some attention to *me*. Derek? You and your friends play outside. Love you. Now, *scram*!"

■ ■ ■

"So first the washing machine died, and then the dryer. After that the freezer decided to conk out, and this was right before we found out that there was a swamp in the backyard on heavy rain days. Now we have a mosquito infestation on top of everything. And did I mention the flood in the basement?"

Kit was telling us about the pleasures of being a new homeowner. Apparently it wasn't at all like she imagined it would be.

"Poor Shawn has been to the home repair store so many times that people have started to think he works there. I told him he may as well. We need the discount!"

Kit, Bammy and I were in the hot tub enjoying the last few hours of the evening. Barry and Tucker had retired to their bedroom hours ago, but thankfully they left the exterior lights on for us. I half expected Barry to kick us out and tell us we needed our beauty sleep.

"Shawn's so excited about tomorrow, though," said Kit. "He can barely contain himself."

Mom and Dad couldn't decide between a preacher, a rabbi or a Buddhist monk, so I suggested they ask one of their friends to get ordained online and perform the ceremony instead. They asked Barry to do it, but he had his heart set on his place in the wedding party. That's when Kit suggested Shawn.

"He's been wanting to do this forever, so he was just happy to have an excuse. He can't wait to start marrying people," she giggled. "Like he suddenly has new powers or something."

"Men are such children," added Bammy. "They all want to be superheroes."

"And then they come home to mommy because they're hungry," said Kit. "If only they'd fix the damn freezer so I wouldn't have to go to the store every day. Seriously, it would *kill* him to go grocery shopping."

"Speaking of food," I said, "I'll go get us some more drinks. Bammy you haven't even touched your wine cooler."

"I don't feel so hot," she said and placed the warm bottle on the deck. "I've had an upset tummy since Cochon's. I tell ya, if I'm getting a stomach flu, it had better be a good one. I could stand to lose a few pounds. Those Walcott boys are in shape. They make us look bad, right Derek?"

She said it before she even realized it. The bubbles were rolling in the hot tub, but even I could see Kit deliver a swift kick beneath the water.

"*Oh, Derek*. Honey, I…" Bammy started.

"It's okay. *Stop*," I said. "It is what it is and there's not much I can do about it. I've tried to talk to him and he knows how I feel. I just have to be patient, I guess."

The air around us was eerily still. Even the grasshoppers had chosen to shut up and listen.

"Wow," said Kit, finally. "You're really trying to be an adult. I'm impressed."

"I know," I admitted. "Scary, right?"

■ ■ ■

We woke up to a beautiful sunny day, and it looked like we would be enjoying an outdoor wedding on the terrace of the Duke, after all. Barry, Tucker and I had breakfast at the house early in the morning, then Barry shooed us off so he could prepare for the day. The wedding was set to begin at noon, but I had asked Mom and Dad to be there and ready by 11:00 am so we could start on time. In order to make that happen we had a lot of people to coordinate. Tucker had reserved his car for a full day of Walter family driving, and he and I started the day by heading over to Dad's place to pick him up first.

"Thanks for doing this, Tucker," I said on the way. "I hope you know how much we appreciate it."

"Hey, it's my job," he said. "I love to drive. But really, I'm just happy to be invited. It means a lot to Barry and me."

"You're more than just invited," I said. "You're definitely one of us now. And by the end of the day you'll have met everyone. It's well past time."

We pulled into the driveway and Dad was already waiting for us on the side porch. I rolled down the side window as we approached.

"Your mom already kicked me out," he yelled out as we parked. "She didn't want me to see her before she gets ready. She's being all mysterious. I have to admit, I kind of like it."

"It's a big day," I said after I exited the car and gave him a hug. "Are you nervous?"

"Not at all. It is my second time, after all. I know what the hell I'm doing now. I hope," he said, winking. He then turned to face our driver and extended his hand. "And you must be Tucker!"

"Yes, sir, that's me. It's a pleasure to meet you."

"Well, he's definitely polite," Dad said to me and smiled. "It's very nice to meet you as well, Tucker. I'd say if Barry likes you then we're all set. It took him a bit to come around to me, but you're already in the winner's circle, so that bodes well for you. Now let's go! I understand you boys have lots to do."

Tucker dropped Dad and me at the Duke before heading back to get Mom and Barry. I set my dad up with a nice cup of tea in my office so he'd be out of the way as I directed the last minute efforts with the staff. He had his wardrobe bag with him to change, but I'd already put on my suit. Sam and Crosby were there to set up the bar and coordinate the tables and chairs. They had signed for the delivery from the florist and the cake was getting a few last minute additions in the kitchen. I felt like I was running in circles, but truthfully, it was all for show. My team had it all covered and I decided that I would rather enjoy my time as a guest for the rest of the night.

"Sam, you're in charge," I said. "I don't want to do anything else today. Can you handle Secret Sunday tonight, too?"

"You got it," he said. "Just enjoy yourself. I'll make sure everything's locked up after." He walked out to the terrace to supervise as the others were placing chairs out for the ceremony.

I double-checked that we had curtained off the library for Mom to use as a private dressing area before the wedding began. Tucker picked up her and Barry at 10:30 and they were scheduled to arrive right on time. It was important for her to be out of sight before the first guests arrived.

"The bride's here!" I heard someone shout from the front room.

I turned to see my uncle in full regalia as the entire staff stopped what they were doing, put down their dishes and chairs and began applauding.

"Oh, please," said Beret. "This old thing?" She then stepped aside and did her best game show hostess hands to present Mom, who appeared right behind her.

"Who are you calling old?" Mom teased, and they both began laughing.

"You look amazing," I gushed. "Yes, *both* of you. Before you even ask!"

They had chosen dresses in a subtle shade of shimmering grey satin, but the styles could not have been more different. Mom was the picture of elegant, Southern grace. She looked demure and gorgeous. Beret, on the other hand, went for more pageantry, but somehow pulled it off with panache. She wasn't trying to outshine Audrey, just complement her, and it worked perfectly.

"Quick," I said. "Let's get you stashed in the library before any of the guests see you."

"I don't care where you stash me, just bring me a cocktail," said Barry.

"I heard that!" said Sam, from the bar. "I've got you covered, Beret."

"Thank you, darling boy," she cooed. "But don't get too flirty. I'm taken, after all."

■ ■ ■

With Mom and Beret stashed safely in the library, and Dad having his moment of Zen up in my office, I decided to enjoy a cocktail of my own before the guests arrived. Sam poured me a bourbon, neat, and I stood by the bar, ready to fulfill my role as a greeter. Kit and Shawn were the first to walk through the door.

"You ready to do this?" I asked as I gave Shawn a hug on his way in.

"Definitely!" he said, clearly excited. "Your parents are awesome, man. We had a lot of fun writing their vows."

"Well, I can't wait to hear what you guys have planned for us," I said. "They've pretty much kept me in the dark regarding the ceremony."

"There are a few zingers in there," he said, laughing. "Now I know where you get it from."

Tommy, Meredith, Bammy and Michael were the next to arrive. The front room started filling up quickly as Sam and Crosby began to pass out welcoming glasses of champagne and white wine.

"Sam, can I get a few drinks over here?" I asked. My bourbon had run dry and I wanted to have a toast with my Scooby Gang. He carried over a silver tray full of glasses and we passed the champagne flutes around as we stood in a circle.

"A toast," I said, "to all of you. Bammy and Michael, Tommy and Meredith, Kit and Shawn. When I moved back home just over a year ago, I had no idea what to expect. I was running away from things more than I was running to anything, but all of you made my homecoming something that I couldn't have imagined. I'm home again, and I'm actually happy here. I knew I needed to leave Parkville so many years ago when I did, but now I can't imagine living anywhere else. Thank you for your love, your support, and your friendship. *To us!*"

The glasses clinked and we all enjoyed our first sip of bubbly for the day. Well, not everyone, I noticed.

"What's up, Bammy?" I asked. "Is your stomach still off from the barbecue?"

She nodded and smiled. "Yes, and no. It's definitely off, but not from Friday's lunch. I took a little test this morning. It seems I passed."

Michael was barely containing himself he was beaming so much.

We all began yelling and crying and laughing so hard that any bystander would have thought we were all absolutely crazy. Our amazing Bammy was pregnant, and the day just simply couldn't get any better.

"*Baby!* You're having a baby!" Kit yelled.

Just then, Crosby appeared at my side and gave me the nod.

"All right, everyone," I cried out. "It's time! If you could please make your way out to the terrace. The ceremony will begin in ten minutes."

I gave Bammy a massive hug, then ushered my friends out through the double glass doors. I knew Mom was okay in Barry's hands, but I hadn't checked on Dad since I deposited him in my office over an hour ago. I climbed the stairs, and then tapped on the door.

"You ready to go?" I asked as I turned the knob.

"Ready as I'll ever be," he said, but I could see he was visibly nervous. He had practically paced a new path in the carpet.

"Dad, I know you don't drink anymore, but maybe a little bourbon would take the edge off?"

He nodded vigorously. "Good idea. I think that's a good idea, son."

"I'll be back in a jiffy. Then we have to get out there, okay?"

He nodded in agreement. I turned to bound down the steps and into the main salon, suddenly deserted and quiet. The staff and guests had all moved out to the terrace, awaiting the bride and groom. As I walked towards the bar I noticed that someone had left the front door ajar. Momentarily forgetting my bourbon mission, I walked over to the foyer and tugged on the handle, but I met some unexpected resistance. I was surprised when the door pulled itself back to reveal someone standing outside on the porch looking in straight at me. He was wearing a perfectly tailored grey suit with a blue tie and a crisp white pocket square. If I hadn't known any better I would have said he either stepped out of an ad for a menswear store or he was created directly from my dreams. We both stood there for a moment taking each other in, unsure of what to do. I knew I was supposed to go get my dad, but suddenly nothing and no one else in the whole world mattered to me. Time simply stood still.

"Hi," I said, looking him directly in the eyes. "My name is Derek."

"Hi. I'm Luke."

ACKNOWLEDGEMENTS

After the success of *Home is a Fire* and *The Fire Went Wild*, I knew that the story of Derek and Luke was not yet finished. The colorful inhabitants of Parkville, TN practically insisted that I bring them to life at least once more. I hope you are happy with the result.

Once again, many friends stepped in to help me complete this next novel in the *Home is a Fire* series. I would like to thank Karyn Adams, Eunice Chang, Cynthia Tady and Angie Vicars for taking the time from their busy lives to help out a friend. From small word choices to larger storytelling suggestions, they offered edits and critiques that only succeeded in improving the work. I take full responsibility for any typographical errors that remain.

I could not ask for a better cover artist than Patrik Nerséus. Thank you, again. Sandy Haggart took a fantastic author picture, and I am grateful to him. To my large network of friends around the globe who continually pushed me to keep writing, I thank you for the heartfelt words of encouragement.

To Jeff Adams, Will Knauss, Kim Smith and Mark Willis, your online marketing efforts, websites and podcasts are supporting an entire army of independent writers, and for that we all thank you.

It's not every day a first time novelist from Tennessee is featured in the *New York Times* and the *Advocate*. To say that I am extremely grateful for all of the kind reviews and support is an understatement.

And finally, thank you, Jan, for putting up with the mood swings of a writer.

ABOUT THE AUTHOR

 A graduate of the University of Tennessee, Jordan Nasser was raised in the South before moving to New York City. His well-reviewed debut novel, *Home Is a Fire*, draws from many of his own life experiences. *The Fire Went Wild* is the second novel in the series, and both were featured in an article in the *New York Times*.

Mr. Nasser currently lives in Stockholm, Sweden. *This Fire Inside* is the third novel in the Home Is a Fire series.

jordannasser.com

www.ingramcontent.com/pod-product-compliance
Lightning Source LLC
Chambersburg PA
CBHW030420180626
46812CB00005B/2104